アメリカ文学と「語り」

―― 白鯨からポストモダン文学へ ――

野口健司　著

開文社出版

目次

まえがき ………………………………………… v

Ⅰ 「私」の世界
  1. アメリカの小説と「私」 ………………………… 3
  2. Poe の "The Cask of Amontillado" ……………… 23
    ― Montresor は復讐に成功したのか―
  3. Drabble の *The Millstone* ……………………… 37

Ⅱ 白鯨を求めて
  1. What Is Moby Dick? ……………………………… 51
  2. The Resurrection of Ishmael …………………… 73
  3. Pierre in Contrast to Ahab ……………………… 89
  4. "Benito Cereno" における恐怖 ………………… 103

Ⅲ ポストモダン管見
  1. エドワード・オールビー ……………………… 119
    ―幻想の破壊と生の再生―
  2. Vonnegut's Desperado Humor in *Slaughterhouse-Five* …… 149
  3. *Cat's Cradle* を読む …………………………… 167
  4. Raymond Carver ………………………………… 183
  5. *Beginners* を読む ……………………………… 199

Ⅳ 研究余滴
  1. Kawabata's *Snow Country* ……………………… 213
  2. 漱石の見た耳納連山 …………………………… 221

初出一覧 ………………………………………… 239
あとがき ………………………………………… 241

まえがき

　子供の頃から絵を画くのが好きで、戦後の学制改革の時期に当たる中学・高校の時代は美術部で絵を画いていた。しかし画家として身を立てる程の覚悟ができていた訳ではなく、将来の目標が定まらない芸術家気取りの文学青年であった。幸いに、京都大学文学部へ進学することができた。

　文学部では英語英文学を専攻した。指導教授が中西信太郎というシェイクスピア学者であったことと、文学研究の基本を学ぶにはやはりシェイクスピアだという考えから、学士論文（1957）ではシェイクスピアの『リヤ王』を選んだ。当時のシェイクスピア研究では、ブラッドレーに代表される性格批評の伝統が根強く残っていたが、それに批判的な歴史主義的批評やニュークリティシズム的批評も華やかであった。

　修士論文（1960）でアメリカ文学の最高傑作の一つといわれるメルヴィルの『白鯨』を選んだ。これが私のアメリカ文学研究の出発点となった。『リヤ王』のイメージ分析で体得したニュークリティシズム的手法で書いたこの論文は、翌年刊行の大阪府立大学紀要に "What Is Moby Dick?" と題して発表したが、1971年版のノートン社の *Eight American Authors* のなかで、ナサリア・ライトによって "Moby Dick is…the symbol of what men are living for to Kenji Noguchi." と紹介された。

　私のアメリカ文学研究は、大きく、メルヴィルに関するもの、不条理文学に関するもの、一人称の語りに関するもの、の三つの分野に分けることができる。

メルヴィルでは『白鯨』の次に『ピェール』を論じた（1965）。『マーディ』、『白鯨』『ピェール』を神の探求を主題とする三部作として捉え、その視点から『ピェール』を論じた。まず、『マーディ』では風刺という形で神への接近が試みられ、次に『白鯨』では狂的探求者エイハブが創造されるが、『ピェール』では神無き世界に神を求める人間の崩壊過程が描かれるとした。

　1967年、「ベニト・セレノ」における恐怖の主題を論じた。この中編小説の題材は黒人奴隷の暴動であるが、その主題は暴動を描くことではなく、暴動によって引き起こされる恐怖を描くことにあるとし、その恐怖が描き出されてゆく技法と構成を分析した。この論文は『英語青年』（1968）の新英学時評で斎藤光の評価を得た。

　その後1971年から1972年にかけて、文部省在外研究員として一年間留学した。最初の八ヶ月余りをイェール大学で、残りの期間をロンドン大学で研究した。イェール大学でピアソン教授の演習を聴講し、その時初めてヴォネガットの『屠殺場5号』を読んだ。この小説はトラルファマドール星人という架空の視点によって、ドレスデン空襲を戯画化したものであるが、読みながら、この作品の語り手と『白鯨』の語り手イシュメイルとの間に共通するものを感じた。帰国後、"*Slaughterhouse-Five* and Vonnegut's 'Genial, Desperado Philosophy'"（1975）を発表し、その共通するものを明らかにした。この陽気なならず者の哲学は、イシュメイルが危険極まりない捕鯨船上で、死の恐怖から逃れるために身に付ける哲学である。

　ヴォネガットにメルヴィルを重ね合わせることは当然の帰結として、メルヴィルを不条理文学の視点から読み直すことになった。その結果が "The Ambiguity of *Pierre* in Relation to *Moby-Dick*"（1980）である。この論文ではピェールとエイハブがいずれも捕捉できないものを捕捉することを運命的に強いられる探求者として措定されて

いることに着目し、『白鯨』ではその捕捉すべき対象として白鯨という虚構が導入されるために、エイハブという英雄像の形成が可能となるが、『ピエール』では捕捉可能という幻想性が物語の進行と共にはぎとられてゆくために、探求者としてのピエール像は崩壊せざるを得なくなるとした。

　メルヴィル論としては他に「メルヴィルにおける自然像の変貌」(1990) がある。作者によって描き出される自然像がタイピーの谷の理想郷から、ガラパゴス諸島を魔の島と観る『ピアザ物語』の暗部へと推移する過程を、メルヴィルの世界観の反映として跡付けた。

　次に不条理文学に付いて述べる。ベケットの『ゴドーを待ちながら』がパリで初演されたのは1953年である。すぐに日本でも評判になった。フランスの不条理演劇についてはその頃から惚れ込んでいた。そのなかでも特に好きなのがイヨネスコであった。その関連でオールビーには早くから関心があり、英文学会九州支部大会で、『ヴァージニア・ウルフなんか怖くない』について発表したのは、初演から5年後の1967年であった。

　1984年に山口書店から刊行された『アメリカ文学の新展開・詩・劇・批評等』で、オールビーの章を担当し、イヨネスコと対比させながら、幻想は破壊されなければならないというオールビー劇の命題が、初期の作品から後期の作品に至るまでどのように展開されているかを概観し、前期の悲劇的作品から後期の挽歌的作品への転回を明らかにした。

　私が不条理文学の分野に入れているヴォネガットを初めて読んだ経緯については既に述べた。昔から落語や駄洒落が好きであった私には、ヴォネガットのスラップスティック的語りにはまり込む素地は元々あったようだ。ヴォネガットについては、在外研究から帰国して一年半後の1974年の九州アメリカ文学会の例会で紹介的発

表を行い、その後は講読用教科書として三点の短編選を編注した。(1976、1982、1987)。わが国おけるヴォネガットの紹介では草分け的な役割を果たしたのではないかと自負している。

　しかし、論文らしいものにまとめたのは、九州大学での最後の年の1995年であった。一つは "Vonnegut's Desperado Humor in *Slaughterhouse-Five*" で、もう一つは「Vonnegut の *Cat's Cradle* について」である。前者では「屠殺場5号」の笑いの特質について述べた。この小説は既に述べたように、宇宙人という虚構の視点を導入することによってドレスデン空襲の恐怖を矮小化し戯画化したものであるが、たとえ虚構の上に築かれたものであっても、このような笑い無しには人類は生きる意欲を失ってしまう程、現代の状況は暗いという現実認識が、ヴォネガットの笑いの根幹にはあることを説いた。後者では、この小説は自嘲的な笑いと駄洒落に満ちた物語であるが、その笑いには人間の愚かさに対するヴォネガットの鋭い警告があると指摘した。

　一人称の語りのテーマは、『白鯨』の一人称の語り手イシュメイルからの自然な成り行きである。ヴォネガットの他に、文部省在外研究員として初めて読んだ作家に、マーガレット・ドラブルがあった。ドラブルはイギリスの現代作家であるが、1976年にその作品『碾臼』を、一人称の語り手「私」の告白体小説として論じ、その技法と主題を分析することにより、緻密な生のリアリティの構築過程を明らかにした。

　アメリカ文学の分野では、1983年に九州大学出版会から刊行された『現代の文学』で、「アメリカの小説と『私』」の章を執筆し、イシュメイルとハックを典型的なタイプとする一人称の語り手の「私」が、『グレイト・ギャッツビー』と『ライ麦畑の捕手』の場合にどのように展開しているかを、特にその機能的な面から論述した。

以上見てきたように、私のアメリカ文学研究はメルヴィルを主軸とし、他の分野の研究はそれから派生したものといえる。審美的批評を基本とし、それに伝記的批評、歴史的批評による修正を加えて、作品を一個の完成した芸術作品として読むところに、私の研究方法の特色があるかと思う。極めて個人的で趣味的な読み方である。ただその場合に、個人的な読み方に必然的に伴う偏見を、アカデミックな研究で是正し、できるだけ正しい読み方を目指すということを心掛けた。文学研究とは文学を読むための補助手段と考えている。

　ではなぜ文学を読むのか。それは生きていることの体験の拡大化、欲を云えば普遍化のためである。生きていることの体験の場としては日常の生活がある。それは時間的にも空間的にも、ごく限られた狭いものである。若い頃結核で延べ三年余りの療養生活を強いられ、主治医に「あなたはひびの入った茶碗だ。大事に使えば長持ちするが、乱暴に使えばすぐに壊れる」と言われた私は、特にそのことを痛感した。人間とは何か。知的にも、感覚的にも、人生というものをもっともっと掴みたいという欲求を痛切に感じた。それが私の文学を読むことの原点であった。

　以上私のアメリカ文学研究の航跡を辿らせて頂いたが、「語り」を主題とする本書では適宜選択をし、更に最近書いたものを追加して編集した。すなわち、一人称の語りに関するものを第一章「『私』の世界」とし、メルヴィルに関するものを第二章「白鯨を求めて」としてくくり、不条理文学に関するものにレイモンド・カーヴァーを加えて、第三章「ポストモダン管見」としてまとめた。なお、マーガレット・ドラブルの『碾臼』はアメリカ文学ではないが、現代における一人称の語りの代表的な小説として、敢えて「『私』の世界」に加えた。最後に、日本文学の海外への紹介を兼ねて英文で発表した川端康成の『雪国』と「漱石の見た耳納連山」を、「研究余滴」

として第四章に収めた。

I 「私」の世界

アメリカの小説と「私」

I

　小説を語りとしてみますと、散文で語られた架空の物語といえます。しかも人生の真実を語るものといわれます。なぜ架空の物語が真実を語ることになるのか、この疑問に答えることは、今の私には手に余ることで、迷路に踏み込んでしまいそうに思われますので、ここでは、架空の物語の方が真実を語り易いからですとだけ、お答えしておくことにします。

　そこで小説には語り手が必要になります。その場合、作者自らが直接語り手になる場合と、物語のなかの架空の人物の一人に、語り手の役割が委託される場合とがあります。ここで取り上げるのは後者の場合であります。つまり、作中人物の一人が「私」として自らの体験や見聞したことを語る場合であります。まずこのような「私」に語らせることには、作者にとって、どのような利害得失があるのか、そのようなところから話してみたいと思います。

　小説がフィクション、つまり架空の物語であることは今述べましたが、小説はまたノヴェルともいわれます。すなわち、目新しい珍しい話ということであります。聞いたこともない珍しい話だからこそ、小説は多くの読者を魅きつけることができます。しかしそれだけに、読者の不信感を招きやすいということにもなります。そんな話なんてあるはずがないという不信感であります。この不信感を中

断させるには、体験者あるいは目撃者に、いや本当ですよ、私が体験者ですからといった調子で語らせるのが一番手っ取り早い方法です。このようにまず聞き手（読者）の不信感を中断させるという利点があります。

　それからこの語り手は、たえず「私」として聞き手の前に存在し、告白体で語りかけます。個人的に自己の内面をさらけ出す形で語りかけるのです。語り手と聞き手との間には親密なコミュニケーションの場が形成されることになります。このようなコミュニケーションの場の成立によって、作者はより生々しい物語を語ることが容易となり、読者は、直接的な臨場感を味わいながら物語を読むことになります。さらに読者の心には、作中人物である「私」の人柄が触覚的な鮮明さをもって感じられることになります。

　このように、「私」を語り手として設定することにはいろいろな利点がありますが、これまでおびただしく書かれてきた小説のなかで、「私」を語り手とする小説は、数の上では、明らかに少数派に属します。その理由はこの形式をとることによって、作家には大きな制約が課せられるからであります。

　近代的小説の特色のひとつは、作者が登場人物を批判的に描き出してゆくところにあります。その批判的自由が大幅に制限されます。「私」を語り手とすれば、作者はその「私」を通してしか語れなくなるのです。ある事件が語られる場合、その実況報告者としては「私」は極めて効果的な力を発揮しますが、その事件についての背景的あるいは解説的情報の提供者としては、限られた役割しか果たすことができません。すなわち、「私」という限定された人物が使える情報や判断力しか使えないからです。作者は自ら創造した「私」という語り手によって、まるで手枷足枷をかけられたような拘束を受けることになります。

語りの自由の束縛が作者にとってマイナスとなるのは自明のことです。しかし、それはあくまでも一般的な場合であります。その束縛が、作者にとってかえってプラスとなる場合があるのです。ある芸術的な効果を目的として、作者が作為的に限定された情報を、その作為性を感じさせることなく、自然な形で、読者に伝えたいと意図する場合であります。その場合には「私」という語り手の枷が有効になるのです。つまり作者は、「私」という窓口を設定してそれに適当な偏向性を与え、読者にはその窓口からしかのぞかせないようにすればよいのです。

II

　アメリカのみならず世界でも、もっとも偉大な小説のひとつに『白鯨』があります。1851年、ハーマン・メルヴィルによって完成されたものです。物語は、白鯨に片足をかみ切られたエイハブ船長がその復讐を企て、まる一年の歳月をかけた追跡のあげく、白鯨の逆襲を受けて船もろとも破滅してしまうというものです。そしてこの物語がただ一人の生還者であるイシュメイルという「私」によって語られます。

　小さなボートで獲物に接近し、銛(もり)を打ちこんで仕留めるという当時の捕鯨技術では、暴れ回る鯨によって乗組員が不具になったり、殺されたりすることは、何も珍しいことではありません。また、大きな鯨が捕鯨ボートを破砕したり、捕鯨船を沈没させた話は当時の記録にでてまいります。メルヴィルはこれらの記録を参考にしたといわれています。当時の捕鯨方法の危険性を考えるとき、片足をかみ切られたエイハブの事件は、むしろ日常的な事故として処理され

るのが自然のように思われます。ところがエイハブは、巨大とはいえ鯨にすぎない、この「事故」の加害者に対して、「アダム以来の怨念」をもって復讐を企てるのであります。エイハブの部下の一等航海士スターバックの言葉をまつまでもなく、異常な「瀆神的行為」といわなければなりません。

　しかし、物語に耳を傾けるにつれ不思議なことに、このまともな航海士が憶病者に思われ、気違いの船長が英雄にみえてまいります。一介の鯨にすぎないものが、永遠の謎をひめた白鯨に変貌してゆきます。この不思議な変貌の魔術をつかさどるのが語り手イシュメイルであります。

　イシュメイルは鯨にとりつかれた男であります。この偏執狂的視点から、エイハブの白鯨追跡は語られ、その意味が追求されます。根源的な問いは、鯨とは何かということであります。ところがこの問いは、問えば問う程ますます謎を深めるといった類のパズルであります。常識的意味の世界は消失し、それに代わって、底知れない謎の世界がその存在を露わにします。そしてこの謎の焦点に白鯨の像が浮かび上がってまいります。鯨の謎を解くことを宿命的課題とするイシュメイルにとって、エイハブの追跡は、まさにその謎の根源への肉迫であり、理性的存在としての人類の生存を賭けた闘いであります。狂的エイハブは必然的に英雄的エイハブへと変貌するのであります。

　聞き手である読者は、このような特異な視点からみることを強制されるわけですが、その際、きわめて自然に語り手の視点に誘いこまれます。この誘導において、先程述べた「私」という一人称の語り手の利点が発揮されるのです。ただ一人の生還者の体験的告白に接して、不信感を中断させられる読者は巧みな語り口にのせられ、いつのまにかイシュメイルの世界に誘いこまれてしまうのです。

イシュメイルの巧みな語り口については、お話しすべきことが多いのですが、ここでは、予告の手法についてだけ触れておきます。これは何かあるものを聞き手の前に提示する場合に、そのものについての予告をつみ重ね、聞き手の期待と予感が充分に高まった段階で初めて実際に提示し、そのものの持つ意味を深めるという手法であります。この手法の最大の成功が白鯨の提示であります。この小説は、モダン・ライブラリー版で566頁に及ぶ厖大な作品ですが、その殆んどすべての頁が白鯨についての予告といえます。白鯨が実際に姿をみせるのは、536頁目であります。

ところで、「私」という語り手には、イシュメイルのように、主として目撃したものを語るタイプと、主として自己自身について語るタイプとがあります。後者の典型的な例を、私達は『ハックルベリ・フィンの冒険』にみることができます。

III

『ハックルベリ・フィン』を読まれていない方でも、『トム・ソーヤの冒険』は御存知と思います。この作品のなかに、天衣無縫の自然児ハックがトムの親友として登場します。ミシシッピー河畔の田舎町セント・ピーターズバーグのお上品さがいやでたまらないのは、トムもハックと同じですが、トムは読書によって親しんだ騎士や盗賊のロマンスの世界にとらわれています。それに対して、ハックには自然のままに感じ、考え、行動するといった趣きがあります。

作者の遍在的視点で語られている『トム・ソーヤ』と違い、『ハックルベリ・フィン』は、このような自然児ハックの一人称の視点によって語られています。すべては文明に背を向けた自然児によって

語られるのですから、それがそのまま文明批評となるのは理の当然であります。しかし、これは作者マーク・トウェインの意図ではあっても、語り手ハックの意図ではありません。ハックは自己の体験について、見たまま、感じたまま、考えたままをできるだけ忠実に再現してゆくことだけで、精一杯であります。

　ここで、「私」という一人称の語りの構造をもう少し検討しておく必要があります。この語りには明らかに二つの視点があります。行為者の視点と語り手の視点であります。『白鯨』の場合でいえば、平水夫イシュメイルの視点と、回想記を語る生還者イシュメイルの視点であります。そして両者の関係には、行為者の視点という限定された角度から写し出されたものが、語り手の視点という限定された角度から照明を与えられ、その意味を深化するというような構造がみられます。実際には、これら二つの視点は動的にからみ合い、立体的な語りとなります。しかし、この構造が特徴的にみられるのは、イシュメイルのタイプの語り手の場合で、ハックのようなタイプの場合には、二つの視点がより密着したものになり、両者の識別はより難しくなります。

　イシュメイルのタイプの語り手を設定することが、何か異常なものの表現に適していることは、このような二つの視点の構造から判断しても、おわかりになると思います。ではハックのタイプの語り手は、どのような領域において、もっとも効力を発揮するのでしょうか。二つの視点が密着していることは、語りが全体として実況中継的なものになることを意味します。すなわち、もっとも有効な領域は、迫真的臨場感の醸成であります。

　『ハックルベリ・フィン』の物語は三つの部分に分けることができます。第一部は、ハックがセント・ピーターズバーグを脱出し、ジムと出会うまでの導入部であります。第二部はハックとジムの逃

避行であります。第三部はハックがトムと再会し、ジムが自由の身になるまでの結末部であります。物語の中心は第二部で、第一部と第三部はいわばその額縁を構成する部分とみなすことができます。

　この物語の中心的主題は一般にハックのイニシエイションといわれます。イニシエイションとは、一人前の大人として社会に受け入れられるための通過儀礼を意味し、小説では、世間知らずの主人公がさまざまな体験を経て、真の自我に目覚めてゆく過程をいいます。

　ハックにとって最も重要な体験は、逃亡奴隷ジムとの出会いであります。奴隷制社会で奴隷の逃亡を助けることは極刑に値する罪であります。ハックの社会的良心はジムの逃亡の密告を命じます。しかし自然な感情は、それが人間として許されざる行為であると戒めます。この社会的良心と人間的良心との二律背反的命題に悩みながらも、ハックはジムとの友情を深め、最後にはジムを救うことを決意し、たとえ地獄に堕ちても構わないと心に誓います。ハックはジムに導かれる形で、人間としての自己の真価に目覚めてゆきます。

　ハックはこのような心の成長を、さまざまなエピソードを交えながら、俗語的口語体で親しく語りかけます。告白的語りに特有の親密なコミュニケーションの場が形成されます。ハックの体験を、行動と心理の両面にわたって追体験する読者の心にはハックの生気にあふれる人間像が形成されることになるのです。

　アメリカ小説における語り手「私」の二つの典型として、イシュメイルとハックをみてまいりましたが、両者に共通する特質について、すこし補足しておきます。それは社会のアウトサイダーであるという特質であります。ジムが自由の身となり、万事めでたく解決したあとも、ハックは文明社会への復帰を拒否し、ひとり辺境の地へ旅立つことを決意します。この自然児ハックの疎外者的性格については、これ以上述べるまでもないと思われます。

一方イシュメイルですが、実は、素性はおろか名前さえ定かではない人物であります。『白鯨』は "Call me Ishmael" という言葉で始まっています。名前はイシュメイルとでもしておきましょうか、ぐらいの意味です。語り手は勝手にイシュメイルと自己規定しているのであります。イシュメイルとは、すべての人にそむき、世界を放浪するという宿命を背負った聖書の中の人物です。自らを世界からはぐれた放浪者と規定しているのです。そして、エイハブ船長のピークオッド号には、ふさぎの虫を封じるピストルの「代用品」として乗り組みます。そのピークオッド号上で無二の親友が生まれるのは確かです。しかしそれは、文明社会とは無縁の、南海の蛮族の長クィークェッグであります。

　以上で語り手「私」の大体の輪郭はおわかりいただけたと思います。ではこのような「私」の角度から、『グレート・ギャツビー』と『ライ麦畑の捕手』をみてゆきたいと思います。いずれも 20 世紀アメリカ小説の代表作であります。

IV

　『グレート・ギャツビー』は第一次大戦後の、失われた世代といわれる作家の一人、フィッツジェラルドによって、1925 年に書かれました。戦後景気にわき立つニューヨークが物語の舞台であります。そして、暗黒街のボス達が酒の密売によって巨万の富を築いた禁酒法の時代が、その背景を成しています。

　主人公は名をジェイムズ・ギャツといい、ジェイ・ギャツビーと自称する若者であります。ノース・ダコタの貧農の家に生まれ、子供の頃から夢想的野心に燃える男であります。その夢は 17 歳のと

き、ゴールド・ラッシュと投機で富豪となったダン・コウディの知遇を得て、実現への第一歩を踏み出します。コウディの信頼を得て莫大な遺産の相続人となります。結局その遺産は一文もギャツビーのものになりませんが、成功の夢は彼の心に確固とした根をおろします。その後陸軍に入隊し、中尉としてケンタッキーのルイヴィル駐屯中にデイジーを知り、成功の夢はデイジーとの恋として具象化されます。しかし大戦終結後、デイジーはギャツビーの帰国を待たないで、トム・ブキャナンと結婚します。傷心の心をいだいて復員したギャツビーは、無一文で街を放浪中に、暗黒街のボスと知り合い、酒の密売等で巨富を得ます。そして、デイジーの住むロング・アイランドのイースト・エッグと、湾を隔てて相対するウエスト・エッグに豪壮な邸宅を購入し、週末ごとに盛大なパーティーを催します。周辺の人達はもとより、ニューヨークの中心部からも大勢の人達が押しかけます。それらのパーティー参加者の一人として、偶然に訪れるであろうデイジーとの再会が期待されているのです。結局、二人の再会は、デイジーのまたいとこで、ギャツビーの隣に住むニック・キャラウェイの世話によって実現します。二人の間に愛が再燃します。しかし、再会までの4年以上もの歳月の間に、いよいよ高まりをみせたギャツビーの思いは、デイジーに対して無理な要求をすることになります。二人の愛の完全な成就を願うあまりに、トムとの間の愛の存在を、過去にまでさかのぼって否定させようとするのです。トムも同席したホテルの一室で、決着のつくはずもないこのようなことが、険悪な空気のなかで話し合われた直後、デイジーの運転するギャツビーの車は、トムの愛人マートルを誤ってひき、そのまま逃げてしまいます。マートルは即死です。マートルの夫ウイルソンは、トムにそそのかされて、ギャツビーを加害者と思いこんで射殺したあと、自殺します。ギャツビーの埋葬は、生前の

華やかなパーティーとは対照的に、郷里から駆けつけたギャツビーの父とニック以外には、ほとんど参列する者もないという淋しさのなかで行われます。ギャツビーの死に責任を感じるべきデイジーは、電話連絡ひとつよこさない冷淡さをみせます。

　主人公ギャツビーの身の上には大体このような出来事が生じます。そして私達読者はこの出来事を、語り手ニックの目を通してみることになります。ニックが「出来事」のなかにみたものを、みることになるのです。ニックはイシュメイルのタイプの語り手です。イシュメイルが独得な視点によって、エイハブと白鯨を驚異的な映像に転化させたように、ニックはその偏った視点によって、ギャツビーの恋を特異な詩的映像に転化させます。

　この小説がはじめて世に出たとき、すばらしい作品ですわ、でも、ギャツビーの背景は説明不足ではないかしら、という趣旨の批評が著者のもとに寄せられたそうです。これに対して、ロバート・エメット・ロングという評者は、そのような背景、特に暗黒街の顔役とのかかわり合いなどを書けば、ギャツビーの人物像はその神秘性と大きさを失うことになると反論しています。また、ロング氏は更に、ギャツビーとデイジーの恋愛心理が書かれていないという別の不満に対しても、そんなことをすればギャツビーの恋の偉大さは損なわれてしまうと述べています。[1]

　まさにその通りです。そんなことをくだくだしく書けば、ギャツビーは恋にのぼせた愚かな成り上がり者にすぎなくなり、作品の芸術性は著しく低下します。そんなマイナスになることを述べなくてもよいように、作者はニックという語り手を創造したのです。

　語り手ニック・キャラウェイは中西部の都市の裕福な家庭に生まれます。東部の名門大学イエールで教育を受け、第一次大戦に従軍します。復員後、「宇宙の果て」とも思える中西部をあとにし、ニュー

ヨークのある証券会社に就職します。たまたまギャツビーの邸宅の隣に住むことになります。しかし、東部での生活に幻滅して帰郷します。1922年の晩春から初秋へかけての短い期間のことですが、その幻滅感は人間不信に陥るほど深いものです。ただ、ギャツビーにだけは激しい嫌悪感と同時に強く魅かれるものを感じ、結局、ギャツビーのことを語ることになります。

　ニックは自ら認めるように、若い頃から寛容な性質で、人に信頼され、よく知らない者からも秘密を打ち明けられるような人柄を持っています。他人のことをいろいろと穿鑿（せんさく）することなどとは、およそ縁のない人物です。語り手に必要な情報の入手者としては、受け身的な情報収集者といえます。最後には行きがかり上、葬儀に立ち合うなど関わり合いを持ちますが、所詮、ギャツビーはニックにとって行きずりの人であります。このような語り手の人柄から考えても、ギャツビーの金の出所やデイジーとの恋に、穿鑿的興味が示されないのは当然のことです。

　また、金の出所を探るには、暗黒街という壁があり、デイジーとの恋愛心理を探索するには、プライバシーという壁があります。穿鑿趣味のないニックは言うまでもなく、もともと、一人称の語り手、つまり登場人物達と同じ次元で一市民として生活している人物には、無理な課題であります。

　ニックという「私」を語り手とする限り、ギャツビーの正体は神秘のヴェールにつつまれざるを得ないのです。明らかに、作者の意図はギャツビーの客観的映像を描き出すことではなく、ニックという語り手の主観的視野にとらえられたギャツビーの映像を表現することであります。

　先程もふれたことですが、ニックはギャツビーに反発しながらも魅かれています。ギャツビーのなかに彼がみたものに魅かれている

のです。彼がみたもの、それは一言でいえば「希望に生きる非凡な才能」であります。

　中西部の「宇宙の果て」から出て来たニックは東部の華麗な都会生活に幻惑されます。しかし同時に、その華麗さが虚飾と堕落に彩られたものであることを見抜く覚めた目を持っています。この時、ニックはちょうど30歳であります。青年から壮年への人生の分岐点に立っているわけであります。この30という年齢の持つ意味は、本人にも意識されていて、ニックはそのことに二度言及しています。

　ギャツビーがデイジーに対して、トムとの間には愛がなかったと言明させようとしたホテルでの出来事のすぐあと、ニックは次のように語ります。

　　　　私は30だった。私の前途には新しい10年が不気味に、脅かすようにのびていた……独身者である友人は数が少なくなり、熱意はさめてゆき、頭髪はまばらになってゆく孤独の10年間が待ち受ける30歳であった。[2]

　二度目は、デイジーに紹介されて交際したジョーダンとの最後の別れのときですが、「僕はもう30だ。自己を偽って、それを名誉とするには5歳は老けすぎているね」[3]と語ります。

　これらの言葉には、青春との別れを強いられ、現実との妥協を余儀なくされる年齢に達した者の悲哀がにじみ出ています。ニックがニューヨークへ出たのは、恋を求めてではありません。郷里での恋を清算し、証券業という実務につくためであります。恐らく、永遠に失われてゆく青春というものを強く意識していたに違いありません。まさにこのような時機に、ギャツビーと出会い、そこに永遠の青春をみるのです。

ルイヴィル時代のデイジーとの恋を語るギャツビーの話に耳を傾けながら、ニックはある思い出に駆られます。

> 　途方もない感傷性にみちた話ではあったが、彼が話している間ずっと、私は何かを思い出そうとしていた。遠い昔どこかで聞いた捕捉し難いリズム、失われた言葉の断片といったようなものを。[4]

　ニックがどのような思いに駆られたのか、それは誰にも分かりません。それは明確な形象をとらないまま、永久に人に伝えることが出来ないものとなった、とニックはこの時の言葉を結んでいます。しかし、それがニックの消えた夢、すなわち過去の青春と何か関わり合いのあるものであろうことは容易に推測されます。ニックはギャツビーの話を聞きながら、そこに自己の失われた青春の幻影をみたのではないでしょうか。
　このような角度から捉えられたギャツビー像の典型を、われわれは第一章の終わりにみることができます。ウエスト・エッグに住まいを定めて間もなく、トムとデイジーに夕食に招かれて帰宅した夜、ニックはじめてギャツビーの姿を目にします。その時のギャツビーの姿は次のように表現されているのです。

> 　彼は暗い海に向かって異様な恰好で両手をさし伸ばしていた。かなり離れた位置の私にも、彼が身を震わしているのは確かであった。ふと私も海の方角をみた。桟橋の突端と思われる遥かかなたに緑の灯が微かに認められる以外は、何ひとつ見えなかった。[5]

　この緑の灯はデイジーの住む対岸の灯であります。決してつかまえることのできない灯をつかまえようと両手をさし伸べるギャツ

ビーの姿に、失われゆく青春への郷愁を重ねながら、ニックはギャツビーの偉大さと虚しさを哀感をこめて語るのであります。

V

『ライ麦畑の捕手』は、1951年に、ジェローム・デイヴィッド・サリンジャーによって書かれました。1960年代にアメリカ全土に広がり、伝統的価値感を根底から揺るがすことになった若者の反乱の先駆けをなす小説といわれます。語り手は、ホールデン・コールフィールドといい、ハックのタイプの「私」です。この物語の主人公でもあります。ハックは浮浪児でしたが、ホールデンは学校の落第生です。

　語り手としてのホールデンは、カリフォルニアで療養中の17歳の少年です。前の年のクリスマスの頃からノイローゼになり、病床の身ですが、今ではまもなく退院できるまでに回復しています。クリスマス休暇の前の三日間、正確にいえば、退学が決定したペンシー・プレップ・スクールを飛び出す土曜日から、家に帰る月曜日までの出来事が語られます。

　物語は別れの挨拶のためにスペンサー先生を訪問する場面から始まり、真夜中に寮を出るまでのいきさつ、ホテルやナイト・クラブでのこと、ガール・フレンドとのデイトといさかいのこと、幼くして死んだ弟のアリや妹フィービーのこと、旧師アントリーニのことなどが、そのときの思考や感情をまじえて、語られます。ハックの場合と同様に「私」の身の上に起きた物理的心理的出来事が、ほぼその実際の継起に従い、実況中継的な生々しさで語られるのです。俗語的口語体の語りもハックの場合と同じです。

ホールデンは落第常習者であります。ペンシー校の前にも、少なくとも二つのプレップ・スクールから落ちこぼれています。英語は得意ですが、それ以外の学科には身を入れて勉強する気がありません。そして、自分の怠惰を、学校は「いんちき」だといって正当化しています。学校だけではありません。勝手につくり上げた自分の世界以外は、すべて「いんちき」であります。妹のフィービーによれば、ホールデンは非現実的なことだけが好きで、現実的なことになれば、大人になって自分のしたいことでさえ、何ひとつ具体的に考えることのできない少年であります。また、旧師アントリーニによれば、現実には与えられない何かを求めて、破滅の淵に向かって進んでいる少年であります。

ニックが理想を求める青年期から覚めた壮年期への転回点に立っているとすれば、ホールデンも同様に、子供から大人への転回点に立っています。ただ、ニックが永遠に失われゆく青春という現実をはっきりと意識しているのに対して、ホールデンは大人になるという現実から目をそむけ、子供の世界への復帰を願っています。大人になることを怖れ、子供のままでありたいと願っています。いつも同じ位置に静止している博物館のインディアンやエスキモーの像に象徴されるような、時間の流れのなかでの永遠の静止を願っているのです。このようなホールデンにとって、「いんちき」でない世界が、弟のアリや妹のフィービーに象徴される子供の世界だけであるのは言うまでもないことです。

物語の最後に、回転木馬でぐるぐると回るフィービーを見守りながら幸福感にひたる場面があります。この場面にホールデンの救いをみる批評家も多いのですが、それが真の幸福ではなく、大人になることを拒み、子供の世界へ帰りたいと願う心に訪れる束の間の幻想にすぎないことは、その後まもなく、神経症として療養の身とな

ることからみても、明らかであります。

　『ハックルベリー・フィン』をハックのイニシエイション物語と申しましたが、この物語もホールデンのイニシエイション物語といわれます。しかし、ハックとホールデンの体験に対する態度には対照的な違いがみられます。ハックは新しい体験をみずみずしい感覚でとらえる開かれた心を持っています。それに対して、現実との対決を回避するホールデンの心は閉ざされています。ハックは未来志向であるのに対して、ホールデンは過去志向であります。ハックと同じようにホールデンも「西部」にあこがれます。しかし、それはろうあ者を装うて世間から孤立した生活を送りたいという、いわば隠者としての人生を夢想するものであります。

　このような閉ざされた心に成長がおきるとすれば、それは三日間の出来事の過程におきるのではなく、精神的衝撃から立ち直って「出来事」を包み隠すことなく率直に語るという行為によっておきるのです。語ることによって、ホールデンの心は開かれるのです。言い換えれば、語ることによってホールデンは「出来事」を真の意味で体験し、真の自己に目覚めてゆくのです。語り終えたホールデンは、おしゃべりって不思議なものだ、いやな奴でもそいつのことをしゃべると懐かしく思えてくるんだから、と補足的に述懐していますが、ここには開かれた心がうかがわれます。そして、そこに、読者はホールデンの将来を予感し、「救い」を感じることができるのです。

　しかし、この小説の目的は、そのような「救い」の過程を分析し、それを明らかにすることではありません。ホールデンにそのような自己分析を要求することは無理というものです。大人になりつつある現実を拒否し、大人の世界に反発するホールデンに、思う存分しゃべらせることが、この作品の目的であります。

　以上のようなホールデンを一人称の語り手とするこの物語におい

て、読者に伝えられる主なものが、個々の出来事の鮮明な映像ではなく、それらの出来事に対するホールデンの生々しい反応であることは言うまでもないことであります。読者の心を圧倒するのは、ホールデンの心の動き、すなわち、その怒りや苛立ち、そしてあざけりの笑いであります。

　ホールデンの感情を伝達する手段として、一人称の語りの形式と共に注目しなければならないのが、その特有の俗語的口語体であります。まず最も目立つのが罵り言葉の多用であります。この作品全体がまるで罵り言葉の博覧会場であるかのような観を呈しています。罵り言葉が何を意味するかは、「クソッ」、「チクショウ」といった言葉を二、三頭に浮かべていただければ、それで結構かと思います。日本語は幸か不幸か、罵り言葉が貧弱ですから、この小説の翻訳者は大変お困りになっただろうと思われます。それから、「マア」、「………ナド」、「………ナンカ」など緩意表現といわれるものも目立ちます。これは対象を明確化しようとする態度からではなく、対象に対する情緒的な反応を優先させようとする態度から生まれる場合が多い表現であります。

　白髪三千丈式の数字の誇張も、特徴的な話し方です。しかしホールデンの場合は、中国風の大まかで悠然としたユーモアではなくて、話題についての苛立ちや嫌悪感を滑稽化によって紛らわせようとする表現のように思われます。誇張された数字が明らかにでたらめで、しかも具体的なところが特色です。例えば、しょっちゅうホールデンの部屋にやってくる隣室の男、アックリーは「一日85回ぐらいはやってきやがるんだ」となります。

　その他、安藤貞雄氏も指摘するように、[6] 比喩、反復、省略、感情の this などの強意的表現が盛んに用いられます。感情の this というのは、例えば、単に「クルマヲカッタ」というべきところを、すなわち、

実際には、近くに指し示すべき車はないのに、「コ ノ クルマ ヲ カッタ」というような語法で、聞き手には、コノが何を指すのかは分からなくても、話し手がクルマに特別な感情をこめてしゃべっているということは分かる、といった表現方法です。

　以上の大ざっぱな説明からも、ホールデンの言葉が分析的表現よりは、情緒的表現に適していることが、おわかりになっていただけたと思います。

　このような語り手を設定することにより、サリンジャーはホールデンという人物の創造に成功するのであります。この作品には、確かに、大人の「いんちき」に対する若者からの告発という性格もありますが、それは読者が感じとるホールデンの、触知可能なほどの実体感に比べれば、第二義的な副産物にすぎないように思われます。

　以上、イシュメイルとハックを典型的なタイプとするアメリカ小説の「私」が、『グレート・ギャツビー』と『ライ麦畑の捕手』の場合に、どのように展開されているかを、特にその機能的な面からみてまいりました。この「私」がアメリカ文化の特質とどのような関わりを持つのかなど、まだお話しすべきことは残っていますが、時間も終わりに近づきましたので、今日のところはここで終わらせていただきます。

注
1. Long, 159–60.
2. *Gatsby*, 142.
3. *Gatsby*, 185.
4. *Gatsby*, 118.

5. *Gatsby*, 27-28.
6. 安藤, 28-36; 135–73.

引用文献

Fitzgerald, F. Scott. *The Great Gatsby*. Harmondworth, Middlesex : Penguin Books, 1958.

Long, Robert Emmet. *The Achieving of* The Great Gatsby. Lewisburg, Pa.: Bucknell UP, 1979.

安藤貞雄『英語語法研究』東京：研究社, 1969.

Poe の "The Cask of Amontillado"
―― Montresor は復讐に成功したのか――

　この短編は 1846 年 11 月に刊行された *Godey's Magazine and Lady's Book* に発表された。主人公の Montresor は 50 年前に成し遂げた復讐を「彼のことをよく知っている聞き手」(415) に、一人称の語りとして話して聞かせる。死期を悟った Montresor の神父に対するざんげの告白と解したいが、その語りの調子にはそのような趣きはなく、自らの復讐劇に酔った自慢話としか思われない。Montresor は自らに課した復讐成立の二つの要件をいかにクリアしたかを語り、復讐劇の成功を浮き彫りにして見せる。しかし、その成功は Montresor の主観的判断にすぎないのではないか。二つの要件は果して満たされているのか。この課題を検証する。[1]

I

　まず復讐劇の舞台であるが、事件はいつ、どこで起きたのか。Montresor が語ったのを 1846 年とすれば、事件が起きたのはその 50 年前であるから、18 世紀末と考えられる。場所については諸説があり、確証はないが、フランス革命後フランスに支配されたイタリア北部と考えるのが妥当ではないかと思う。フランス革命によるルイ王朝の崩壊が 1792 年であり、ナポレオンのイタリア遠征が、ちょ

うど 50 年前の 1796 年である。

　フランス革命によって旧体制が倒れ、商工業者を中心とするブルジョアが新しい支配階級としてのし上がる。啓蒙思想を信奉するフリーメイソンはその指導者的存在であり、旧体制側のカトリック教会はフリーメイソンを敵視する。このような両者の対立は、この復讐劇の背景として、抑えておく必要がある。

　Montresor は没落したフランス系貴族のカトリック教徒であり、Fortunato はフリーメイソンに所属するイタリア系市民である。次の Montresor の語りは Montresor が没落貴族であり、Fortunato がそれに代る新興階級であることを示している。

　　　"Come," I said, with decision, "we will go back; your health is precious. You are rich, respected, admired, beloved; you are happy, as once I was. You are a man to be missed. For me it is no matter. (417)

二人は友人関係にあり、Fortunato はその二人の関係にいささかの疑念を抱いている様子もないが、Montresor は表面的には友人関係を装いながらも、内心では明らかに Fortunato を憎んでいる。その憎しみには、フリーメイソンに対するカトリック教徒の怨念も込められているようだ。

II

　Fortunato は自他共に認めるワイン通である。その長所を逆手に取り、Montresor は Amontillado を餌にして Fortunato を酒蔵となってい

るカタコンベの最深部へ誘い込み、そこで生き埋めにする。これが物語の粗筋である。

冒頭部は次のように語られる。

> The thousand injuries of Fortunato I had borne as I best could, but when he ventured upon insult I vowed revenge. You, who so well know the nature of my soul, will not suppose, however, that I gave utterance to a threat. *At length* I would be avenged; this was a point definitively settled—but the very definitiveness with which it was resolved precluded the idea of risk. I must not only punish but punish with impunity. A wrong is unredressed when retribution overtakes its redresser. It is equally unredressed when the avenger fails to make himself felt as such to him who has done the wrong. (415)

ここに Montresor は簡潔に、復讐の理由と決意、そして二つの復讐成立の要件を述べている。

第一の要件は「復讐者は処罰されてはならない。もし復讐者が報復を受けるようなことがあれば、復讐によって悪が正されたことにはならない」であり、第二の要件は「復讐者は己に害をなしたる相手に、己がその悪を正すための復讐者であることを分からせなければならない」というものである。

まず、第二の要件の方から検討を始める。次の引用に見るように、この事件以前には、Montresor は Fortunato に対して自分が悪意を持っているなどということは毛頭示していない。

> It must be understood that neither by word nor deed had I given Fortunato cause to doubt my good will. I continued, as was my

wont, to smile in his face, and he did not perceive that my smile *now* was at the thought of his immolation. (415)

　先にも述べたように Fortunato は Montresor を親友であると信じている。Montresor に不愉快な思いをさせたことがあるなどという意識はなく、まして侮辱したことがあるなどということは彼の頭には全くないようだ。それに重要なことは、彼はしたたかに酔っている。この二つのことは、だまし討ちを意図する Montresor にとっては極めて好都合だが、第二の要件を満たすためには厄介な障害となる。
　復讐の決意を固め、Fortunato 処罰の準備を万端怠りなく整えた Montresor は、カーニバルの夕方酔ってすっかり上機嫌になった Fortunato に偶然出会い、絶好のチャンス到来と喜ぶ。

It was about dusk, one evening during the supreme madness of the carnival season, that I encountered my friend. He accosted me with excessive warmth, for he had been drinking much. The man wore motley. He had on a tight-fitting parti-striped dress, and his head was surmounted by the conical cap and bells. I was so pleased to see him that I thought I should never have done wringing his hand.[2] (415–16)

　その場で早速 Amontillado の鑑定を頼まれた Fortunato は、「君は風邪のようだから」とためらいの素振りを見せる Montresor を促し、Montresor 家のカタコンベへと急ぐ。しかし、カタコンベに着いてからも Fortunato は依然として酩酊状態である。

The gait of my friend was unsteady, and the bells upon his cap jingled as he strode.... He turned towards me, and looked into my eyes with two filmy orbs that distilled the rheum of intoxication. (417)

　更に、Fortunato の咳を鎮めるためにと称し、Montresor は Medoc ワインを奨める。Medoc を飲んだあと、二人は地底の奥深くへ進んで行く。二人の話題は Montresor 家の広大なカタコンベのことから紋章のことに及ぶ。

"These vaults," he said, "are extensive."
"The Montresors," I replied, "were a great and numerous family."
"I forget your arms."
"A huge human foot d'or, in a field azure; the foot crushed a serpent rampant whose fangs are imbedded in the heel."
"And the motto!"
"*Nemo me impune lacessit.*"
"Good!" he said.
The wine sparkled in his eyes and the bells jingled (418)

紋章は、濃紺の地に描かれた黄金の巨大な人間の足が鎌首をもたげてかかとに喰いついている蛇を踏みつぶしている絵柄であり、そのモットーは「われを害するものは必ず報復を受ける」というものだ。Fortunato に加害者意識があり、彼が酩酊していなければ、実に美事な復讐の大義の呈示と言える。しかし, Medoc で更に酔いが廻った Fortunato はただ Good! と答えるだけで、その時の彼の様子は、引用に見るように、酔いの深まりが描写されているのみである。
　更にカタコンベの奥へ進んだところで Fortunato は Medoc をもう一杯と求める。それに対して Montresor は De Grâve ワインを与える。明らかに英語の Grave が連想されるワインで、これから殺害しよう

とする相手に渡すワインとしては痛烈な皮肉が込められている。しかし、Medoc を求めて De Grâve が渡されたことに、Fortunato はいかなる疑念をさし挟むこともなく一気に飲み干す。

> He emptied it at a breath. His eyes flashed with a fierce light. (418)

Medoc と De Grâve の見分けもつかないというのはそれ程に酔っている証拠といえる。[3]

　De Grâve を一気に飲み干した Fortunato は笑い声を挙げ、空にした瓶を奇妙なジェスチャーで宙にほうり上げる。Montresor にはその動作が一体何のことやら分からない。

> I looked at him in surprise. He repeated the movement—a grotesque one.
> "You do not comprehend!" he said.
> "Not I," I replied.
> "Then you are not of the brotherhood."
> "How!"
> "You are not of the masons."
> "Yes, yes," I said; "yes, yes."
> "You? Impossible! A mason!"
> "A mason," I replied.
> "A sign," he said, "a sign." (418–19)

とサインを求められた Montresor は「これだよ」とマントの下から石工のコテを取り出す。そのコテで生き埋めにしようというのであるから、実に巧妙且つ皮肉な復讐方法の呈示である。余りにも意外なサインの呈示に Fortunato は数歩下がりながら「冗談はやめてく

れよ」と叫ぶ。ぐったりと Montresor に寄り掛からなければ歩けないほど酔った Fortunato に、それが自分を生き埋めにしようとする道具であるなど分る筈がない。このような酩酊状態で、ただひたすら Amontillado を求めて進む Fortunato は、誘導されるがままに、遂に Montresor の仕掛けた罠にかかり鎖に縛られてしまう。

　Montresor の石とモルタルによる生き埋めの作業が始まる。一段目の石積みが終りかけた頃には、Fortunato の酔いもかなり醒めている。そして石の壁が Montresor の胸の辺りに達した時、二人の間に大きなどなり声の応酬が始まる。

> A succession of loud and shrill screams, bursting suddenly from the throat of the chained form, seemed to thrust me violently back. For a brief moment I hesitated, I trembled. Unsheathing my rapier, I began to grope with it about the recess; but the thought of an instant reassured me. I placed my hand upon the solid fabric of the catacombs, and felt satisfied. I reapproached the wall. I replied to the yells of him who clamoured. I re-echoed, I aided, I surpassed them in volume and in strength. I did this, and the clamourer grew still. (420)

Monsresor が Fortunato の非を責め、その罪のあがないとして Fortunato は死ななければならないのだということを彼に分らせるには、Fortunato の酔いも醒めたこの時点が又とない機会である。しかし、Fortunato のかん高い叫び声の先制攻撃に慌てたせいか、Montresor は相手の叫び声に対してそれをオウム返しに叫び返すのみで、最後には音量と勢いで相手を黙らせてしまう。この場面の二人の間に、コミュニケーションの成立は見られない。

　石とモルタルの壁で Fortunato を封じ込めてしまうという作業も、

あとはただ最後の石をはめ込むだけという最終段階にはいった時、突然 Fortunato の低い笑い声が聞こえ、Montresor はそうけだつ恐怖に打たれる。

> But now there came from out the niche a low laugh that erected the hairs upon my head. It was succeeded by a sad voice, which I had difficultly in recognizing as that of the noble Fortunato. The voice said—
> "Ha! ha! ha!—he! he! he!—a very good joke, indeed—an excellent jest. We will have many a rich laugh about it at the palazzo—he! he! he"—over our wine—he! he! he!" (420)

日頃の高貴な態度をかなぐり捨て、おい！冗談はよせと自分を生き埋めにしている相手に懇願する Fortunato の苦悶はまさに悲痛そのものである。

ところで、Fortunato が Montresor の行為を悪ふざけと見るのは、懇願のための擬装であろうか。それとも本当にそう思っているのか。もし、後者、すなわち悪ふざけだと思っているのだとすれば、Fortunato は Montresor の行為を自分に対する復讐とは感じ取っていないことになる。

この笑いの懇願は更に次のように続く。

> "He! he! he!…. But is it not getting late? Will not they be awaiting us at the palazzo—the Lady Fortunato and the rest? Let us be gone."
> "Yes," I said, "let us be gone."
> "*For the love of God, Montresor!*" (420–21)

既に真夜中である。鎖につながれた Fortunato は、最後に次第に衰

えてゆく全身の力を絞るようにして Montresor に訴えるのであるが、それに対して Montresor は相変わらずオウム返しに "Yes...for the love of God!" (421) と相手の言葉を繰り返すのみで、このあと Fortunato は一言も発しない。ただ彼の帽子の鈴の音が聞こえるばかりである。

　このように見てくると復讐成立の第二の要件がみたされたとは到底考えられない。Montresor の方は、自己の行為が復讐であることを、相手にはっきりと伝えたと思っていても、それはあくまでも彼の主観であって、相手にそれが伝わったとは思われない。

III

　では、第一の要件はどうか。Montresor は何らの処罰を受けることもなく、殺人という報復を成し遂げたのであろうか。この「告白」までは確かにその通りである。しかし、この「告白」によって事件は白日の下に晒され、Montresor が社会的な制裁を受けることは自明の理となる。

　では何故、自らに課した禁を破ることになる告白を敢えてしたのか。これまでに見てきたように、少なくとも主観的には Montresor は自らに課した復讐成立の要件という二つの難問を見事に解決し、復讐を成し遂げる。相手に自らが復讐者であることを知らせ、何らの報復を受けることもなく、復讐を見事に成功させたと思っている。世間の人に自慢したくなるのは当然ではないか。しかし、問題はそれがカタコンベという地底の密室で行なわれなければならなかったことである。

　自慢したくなる気持を抑えに抑え、事件のあと 50 年を経た今、遂に我慢の限界に達したとき、堰を切ってあふれ出す水の如く、

Montresorは嬉々として真相を語り始める。その語りの調子には、見事な技を披露する曲芸師の晴れやかさはあっても、前述したように、殺人という大罪を犯しながらその罪に対するざんげの趣は見られない。

　一般に作中人物は作者の分身と言われ、多かれ少なかれ作者の性格を受け継いでいる。特にPoeではその傾向が濃厚である。Poeは自分の性格について、次のように述べている。

> "It is the curse of a certain order of mind," he [Poe] once wrote, "that it can never rest satisfied with the consciousness of its ability to do a thing. Still less is it content with doing it. It must both know and show how it was done." (Fagin 207)

この気質は役者の子として生まれたPoeの天性ともいうべきショーマンシップである。

　そして、Montresorはこの気質をそっくり受け継いでいる。折角演じた復讐という見事な演技が、地底の密室という闇の中に埋もれてしまうことには到底我慢できなかった。世間という晴れの舞台で再演せざるを得なかった。言い換えれば、敢えて自らに課した禁を犯しても、世間の拍手喝采を浴びたかった。その再演がこの物語である。[4]

　しかし演目は殺人、それもだまし討ちという卑劣な方法による殺人である。拍手喝采は「お縄頂戴」とならざるを得ない。まさに自縄自縛である。散々得意の皮肉でFortunatoをからかい、見事に復讐を遂げた筈のMontresorがこのような自縄自縛に陥るとは、まことに皮肉なことである。そしてこの最後の皮肉に、Poeの倫理感の貫徹を見ることができる。すなわち、PoeはMontresorの完全犯罪

を見逃すことなく、その皮肉な結果を示唆することによって、彼の罪を厳しく弾劾しているのである。

　この物語のような一人称の語りでは、聞き手である読者は語り手の色眼鏡を通してしか物語を聞くことができない。その結果読者は、物語の内容について客観的な判断を下すことが極めて難しい立場に置かれる。従って若干のあいまいさは残るが、これまで見てきたことでお分かりのように、Montresor は復讐には成功しなかった。これが筆者の結論である。

注
1. テキストには Thompson 版を用い、適宜 Mabbott 版を参照した。Thompson 版の引用には頁数のみを記す。
2. 引用の最後の文の "I should never have done wringing his hand" の部分について現在市販されている邦訳ではいずれも、「握った相手の手は二度と離してなるものか（と思った）」と解釈している。しかし、Amnotillado を餌とする自分の仕掛けた罠に絶対の自信を持つ Montresor が、相手の手を掴まえていなければ絶好の機会を失うかもしれないという不安に駆られているとは思えない。この文についての筆者の解釈は次の通りである。

　　そのような彼と出会った私はすっかり嬉しくなり、その喜びは握った彼の手はいつまでも固く握り締めておきたいとおもったほどであった。

"wringing his hand" は 'shaking hands with him' と解す。最高のタイミングと条件で相手が罠に掛かって来たと判断した Montresor は、この上なく無邪気に喜んでいるのである。
3. Fortunato が Luchresi を評して言う言葉 "Luchresi cannot tell Amontillado from Sherry" (416) を根拠として、Fortunato は Amontillado が Sherry 酒

であることも知らないのだから、実はワイン通ではないという説がある（Thompson 416, 注8）。しかし、この文は Mabbott も指摘するように、「ルクレジーにはアモンティラードとただのシェリーの区別もつかんぞ」（八木 345）と解釈すべきである。この文に付した Mabbott の注は次の通りである。

> The difficulty of telling Amontillado from (ordinary) Sherry is mentioned in the 1845 versions of "Lionizing." (Mabbott 1264)

4. Poe の作品のなかで、自己の巧みな芸を自慢したくなる誘惑に負け、そのために犯した罪が露見する最も有名な例が "The Black Cat" の「私」の次の場面である。

> "Gentlemen," I said at last, as the party ascended the steps, "I delight to have allayed your suspicions. I wish you all health, and a little more courtesy. By the bye, gentlemen, this—this is a very well constructed house." [In the rabid desire to say something easily, I scarcely knew what I uttered at all.]—"I may say an *excellently* well constructed house. These walls—are you going, gentlemen?—these walls are solidly put together"; and here, through the mere phrenzy of bravado, I rapped heavily, with a cane which I held in my hand, upon that very portion of the brick-work behind which stood the corpse of the wife of my bosom. (Thompson 355)

作品

Mabbott, Thomas Ollive, ed. *Collected Works of Edgar Allan Poe*. 3 vols. Cambridge: Belknap Press of Harvard University Press, 1969–78.

Thompson, G. R., ed. *The Selected Writings of Edgar Allan Poe*. New York: Norton, 2004.

田中西二郎訳「アモンティリャアドの酒樽」『ポオ全集』佐伯彰一・福永武彦・吉田健一編, 東京創元新社, 1969, 第 2 巻 513–22.

八木敏雄訳「アモンティラードの酒樽」『黄金虫・アッシャー家の崩壊

他九篇』八木敏雄訳, 岩波書店, 2006, 341–56.

参照文献

Fagin, N. Bryllion. *The Histrionic Mr. Poe*. Baltimore: Johns Hopkins Press, 1949.

Gargano, James W. "The Question of Poe's Narrators." *College English* 25 (1963). Repr. in Thompson 823–29.

Kozikowski, Stanley J. "A Reconsideration of Poe's 'The Cask of Amontillado.'" *American Transcendental Quarterly* 39 (1978): 269–80.

Moldenhauer, Joseph J. "Murder as a Fine Art: Basic Connections between Poe's Aesthetics, Psychology, and Moral Vision." *PMLA* 83 (1968). Repr. in Thompson 829–44.

Stepp, Walter. "The Ironic Double in Poe's 'The Cask of Amontillado.'" *Studies in Short Fiction* 13 (1976). Repr. in *The Tales of Poe*. Ed. Harold Bloom. New York: Chelsea House, 1987. 55–61.

Vintanza, Victor J. "'The Question of Poe's Narrators': Perverseness Considered Once Again." *American Transcendental Quarterly* 38 (1978): 137–49.

Drabble の *The Millstone*

　私が始めて Margaret Drabble の小説を読んだのは、1972 年の夏、アメリカからイギリスへ渡って、ロンドン大学夏期セミナーに参加した折のことです。アメリカで、Vonnegut や Burroughs を読まされ、その新奇さにいささかとまどいを禁じ得なかった私は、Drabble に、その古典的手法にもかかわらず、かえって新鮮な魅力を覚えたのを思い出します。それは単に私の保守的体質のせいだったかも知れません。或いは単に目先が変ったためだったかも知れません。だがどうもそれだけではないようです。それ以上の何かがあったように思われます。

　確かに、人間を戯画化し、危機的状況を笑いとばしてくれる Vonnegut は面白いものです。ふさぎの虫を追っぱらい、生きる活力を与えてくれます。しかし平和な毎日の生活感覚からはどこかかけ離れたものがあります。平凡な生活に明け暮れる私達は、やはりその平凡な感覚で、生きていることを確かめたいという強い欲求を持っています。云いかえれば、日々の暮しのなかに、生きていることの確かさを見たいのです。そのような欲求をそっくりかなえてくれないまでも、そのような願望をもつ人の心に直接訴えるのが、Drabble の小説なのです。Drabble を読む人は、特に女性の読者は、思わず『これが私だ』と叫ばずにはいられないのではないでしょうか。[1] 人間をいわばネガの画像として描き出す Vonnegut と違って、そこには、人間の日常的生活がずっしりとした重量感をもってくっ

きりと描かれているのです。恐らく、この手に触れることのできるような生の実在感に私は新鮮さを覚えたのだろうと思います。

　1939 年、工業都市 Sheffield の中産階級の家庭に生れた Drabble は、Cambridge の Newnham College で英文学を学び、優秀な成績を収めて卒業、20 代前半の若さで、処女作 *A Summer Bird-Cage*（1963）を発表しています。以来矢つぎ早に発表された作品は、*The Garrick Year*（1964）、*The Millstone*（1965）、*Jerusalem the Golden*（1967）、*The Waterfall*（1969）、*The Needle's Eye*（1972）です。[2] その何れもが、時を待たずして、Penguin Books で刊行されていることにも、現代の George Eliot とたたえられて文壇に登場した彼女の人気のほどがうかがわれます。以上の作品のうち、*Jerusalem the Golden* と *The Needle's Eye* をのぞけば、いずれも、一人称の女性を主人公とし、物語はその限られた「私」の視点から語られています。*Jerusalem the Golden* は、三人称の形式をとっていますが、その殆どの部分が主人公 Clara の単一視点から語られ、基本的には一人称小説と云えます。*The Needle's Eye* は、Rose と Simon の二人の主人公を持ち、その二つの視点から語られ、他とやや性格を異にしています。しかし、共通して云えることは、物語の世界がきわめて限られたせまい舞台の上に組みたてられていることです。時間的には、一・二年ですし、空間的には、主婦の、或いは未婚の女性の身辺に限られています。実験的作風をきらい、『私は新しいいやな伝統の創始者となるよりは滅びゆく美しい伝統の終りを飾りたい』[3] と云う Drabble が、古典的リアリズムの手法を用いて、混沌とした現代を描こうとすれば、小さな世界に退くことを余儀なくされるのは当然と云えます。だがその退却を甘受することによって、彼女は、偉大なとはいえないまでも、密度の高いすぐれた作品を生み出すことに成功したのです。[4] Drabble のこれまでの作品のなかでもっとも高い完成度をもつ

と思われる *The Millstone* をたどりながら、その成功の秘密を探ってみたいと思います。

　The Millstone は母としての存在に生の確かさを見出す女性の物語ですが、この主題はすでに前作 *The Garrick Year* にみられます。 *The Garrick Year* の Emma は、Wyndham との浮気な関係を清算したあと、母として生きることの自信を、俳優としての将来に希望を失い川に飛び込んで自殺をとげた若い Julian に託し、次のように語っています。

> I used to be like Julian myself, but now l have two children, and you will not find me at the bottom of any river. I have grown into the earth, I am terrestrial. (170)

この大地にしっかりと根をおろした母としての存在を、浮気などとの関係ではなく、ただその一点に焦点を絞って刻明に描き出すのが *The Millstone* なのです。

　主人公は、中産階級出身の社会主義者である両親に、独立心と強い倫理感をしつけられて育った聡明な女性、Rosamund です。経済学者である父の仕事の関係で、両親ともアフリカへ出かけて留守の今は、自由な独り暮しを楽しみながら、British Museum に通い、博士論文を書いています。しかし、その生き方にはどこか欺瞞的なところがあります。親の偽善には厳しい批判の眼をむけながら、自分の偽悪ぶりには寛容です。その端的な例は異性関係にみられます。Joe と Roger の二人のボーイフレンドを持ち、Joe と逢うときには Roger と関係ができているように思わせ、Roger と逢うときにはその逆に思いこませるという巧妙な仕組みで、性的関係を楽しんでいるようにみせかけながら、実は、憶病に純潔を守っているのです。そ

んな彼女が、Joe に同性愛的感情を懐いているらしい George と、全く偶然のはずみで性的関係をもち、そのはじめての経験で妊娠するという皮肉な結果となります。

　"emancipated woman" を気取り、自由な世界に羽ばたいていたつもりの Rosamund は、この妊娠・出産という現実に直面することによって、今までの生き方が観念的虚構にすぎなかったことを知らされます。すなわち、次のように述懐せざるを得ないのです。

> I felt threatened. I felt my independence threatened: I did not see how I was going to get by on my own. (39)…. I was trapped in a human limit for the first time in my life, and I was going to have to learn how to live inside it. (58)

　三文小説の知識を頼りに試みた堕胎の失敗のあと、産むことを決意し、更にひとりで育てることを決意する Rosamund を待ち受けているのは、国民保険医の診断、入院の予約、若いインターンに囲まれての内診、定期的通院、出産・育児の準備等、彼女にとっては未知の経験の連続です。おとぎの国から突然現実の世界へほうり出されたに等しく、異邦人としての自己を見出す彼女は、孤独と不安のなかで、そのような困難のひとつひとつに耐えてゆかなければならないのです。

　しかし、半ば居直りにも似た気持で、憶病になりがちな自分を、自信と勇気でふるいたたせながらじっと耐えてゆくとき、はじめは偶然の所産にすぎなかった胎内の「物体」がある意味をもってきます。

> It seemed to have meaning. It seemed to be the kind of event to

which, however accidental its cause, one could not say No…. The more I thought about it, the more convinced I became that my state must have some meaning, that it must, however haphazard and unexpected and unasked, be connected to some sequence, to some significant development of my life. (66-7)

そして彼女には、それまで馬鹿にしてきた或る超自然的なものの力が感じられてくるのです。やがて友人のLydiaが彼女のフラットの一室を借りて同居することになり、このことは、個人教授をやめJoeやRogerとも別れたあとの孤独をやわらげるとともに、育児と研究の両立を保証することになります。

　Rosamundにとって、Octaviaの誕生は、殆ど啓示的に、生の證しとなります。はじめて赤ん坊を胸に抱くときの喜びは、次のような描写で始まります。

> …I sat there looking at her, and her great wide blue eyes looked at me with seeming recognition, and what I felt it is pointless to try to describe. Love, I suppose one might call it, and the first of my life. (102)

母としての存在に、愛をはじめて自分のものとする彼女は無上の幸福感と充足感に酔うのです。ところが、この喜びを、あるとき見舞いに来たJoeに聞かせると、彼の言葉は、"What you're talking about …is one of the most boring commonplaces of the female experience." (103) とにべもないものです。二人の世界は全く隔ってしまったのです。

　10日目に退院すると、はじめての育児で心配や不安なことばかりが多いのですが、幸せな母子の生活がLydiaをまじえて始まります。

Octaviaの可愛いらしさに心をとられながらも、エリザベス朝詩人の研究は順調に進み、学者としての将来を約束する博士論文も完成します。幸福なひとときです。しかし、まもなく、再度の試練が訪れます。Octaviaが、ある生れつきの疾患のため、大手術をうけなければならなくなるのです。極度の心配と懊悩は、手術直後の面会を病院の規則をたてに断られたとき、半狂乱のヒステリーとなって爆発します。幸いに、術後の経過も良好で、ヒステリーのおかげで病室での付添看護を許されると、彼女にはまた母子の幸福がもどってきます。そして、この幸福感は、自分にこもりがちであった心を開かせ、他の付添いの婦人とも親しく言葉を交すまでに至ります。最初は異邦人としてほうり出された日常生活の場に、彼女はゆっくりと根を下ろし始めるのです。しかし、そのことは同時に、Joeの場合にみられた如く、昔の友人達との隔りを大きくしてゆくことになります。そして、このことが終章のGeorgeとの再会の場面で、結局Octaviaのことは打ち明けないまま、別れることの主な理由なのです。

　Georgeとのことがあって以来、特にOctaviaが生れてからは、幾度となくGeorgeを思うRosamundですが、ホモ的なGeorgeに愛を期待できないと思い、愛の押しつけになることを懸念する彼女は、そのつど会い度いという衝動を抑えてしまいます。ところがクリスマスの前夜、Octaviaの風邪薬を買いにでかけた薬局で偶然Georgeと出合うのです。 Rosamundは彼をOctaviaに会わせます。

　　　'She's beautiful,' said George.
　　　'Yes, isn't she ?' I said.
　　　But it was these words of apparent agreement that measured our hopeless distance, for he had spoken for my sake and I because it

was the truth.... There was one thing in the world that I knew about, and that one thing was Octavia.... George, I could see, knew nothing with such certainty. I neither envied nor pitied his indifference, for he was myself, the self that but for accident, but for fate, but for chance, but for womanhood, I would still have been. (172)

このように隔てられてしまったGeorgeに、Octaviaのことを話しても意味のないことです。ここには、母であることに確かな存在を得たRosamundと相変らず根なし草的な生き方をつづけるGeorgeとの対照が鮮かに語られています。ここにはまた、確かな生の證しを得た者の自信があふれています。

　この作品の随所にみられるRosamundのユーモアはこの自信とゆとりから生れます。例えば、妊娠をふり返って、次のように客観化して笑うことのできる精神です。

I walked around with a scarlet letter embroidered upon my bosom, visible enough in the end, but the A stood for Abstinence, not for Adultery. (18)

妊娠は男性と関係をもつことを拒みつづけたことの報いというのです。又、前に、Rosamundの胎内で胎児が重要な意味をもつものとなったと述べましたが、そこには次のような表現も見出すことができるのです。

...it did not seem the kind of thing one could have removed, like a wart or a corn. (66)

Rosamund は、このようなユーモアによって、憐憫と道化の意識をまじえながら自己の体験をこまかく語ってゆくのです。そして Rosamund の自己確認に至る過程を、彼女独特の見事な語り口にのせられて追体験する読者の脳裏には、語り手 Rosamund をふくむ総体としての Rosamund の映像が生々しく刻みこまれることになるのです。

　このようなからくりで造形される Rosamund は確かにせん細な感受性と鋭い知性に恵まれた魅力ある女性です。しかし、さめた眼で見直してみると、いやなところも眼につくようです。ごう慢とさえいえるような自信、鼻につく自我意識、図々しさ等々です。Drabble の研究家 Myer 女史は、Rosamund は結局作者によって弾劾されていると述べています。

> …far from displaying a mean female chauvinism and endorsing Rosamund's decision to rear an illegitimate child alone, Margaret Drabble is judging her. Ultimately poor Rosamund, so brilliantly created, so sympathetically analysed and understood, stands condemned.[5]

Drabble が、自己と一定の距離を保って Rosamund を造形しているのは事実です。しかし、Rosamund の性格・行動の形態そのものが作者の糾弾を示すものだとすれば、果してそうであるか否かは読者の Rosamund に対する反応次第です。そして私には、Rosamund はやはり愛すべき女性なのです。又、Drabble が客観的糾弾の視点を作品中に与えているということであれば、一般的に云って、作者が一人称小説の「私」を批判する視点を設定することには技法的無理が伴います。作者の「私」に対する直接的見解はすべて「私」の自

己に対する見解につつみこまれてしまうからです。この技法上の問題を解決する方法としては、「私」の相手に直接話法で長広舌をふるわせるとか、「私」のことを述べた他人の書簡類を直接読者にみせるとかの工夫が考えられますが、そのような試みはこの作品ではなされていません、もっとも Rosamund が彼女をモデルとした Lydia の小説を盗み読みする場面 (92–4) がありますが、その内容は直接ひろうされることなく、Rosamund によって伝えられ、更に、この挿話の趣旨は小説家がいかに尤もらしいつくり話を書くかということを皮肉るものとなっています。それから、このような一般的技法上の問題よりもまず、Drabble が Rosamund 糾弾の視点を作品中に設けることは、私がさきほどあとずけた読者をいや応なしに「私」の視点に引っぱり込み、「私」の視点から「私」を追体験させるという作品の基本的構成を壊すことになります。このようにみてくると、作者が Rosamund を糾弾しているとはとても思えないのです。Drabble の意図は、そんなことではなくて、Rosamund という人物を生の形でまるごと読者に提供し、その判断はいっさい読者にゆだねるということではないでしょうか、云いかえれば、Rosamund を創造した作者の胸には、"Who's to doom, when the judge himself is dragged to the bar?" (445) という Ahab の叫びにも似た思いが去来していたのではないでしょうか。

注
1. Valerie Grosvenor Myer は、Drabble に関する著書の冒頭で次の如く述べている。Margaret Drabble is the most contemporary of novelists: a whole generation of women readers identifies with her characters, who

they feel represent their own problems. Myer, 13.
2. 本稿を書き終えたところで、*The Realms of Gold* が最近出版されたことを知った。Eric Korn の書評によれば、Drabble としては珍しい実験的手法の試みが、複数の視点によって、なされているようである。TLS 1975, 1077.
3. 1967 年、BBC の "Novelists of the Sixties" という番組のインタヴューに答えて、Drabble は次の如く述べている。
   > I don't want to write an experimental novel to be read by people in fifty years, who will say, ah, well, yes, she foresaw what was coming. I'm just not interested. I'd rather be at the end of a dying tradition, which I admire, than at the beginning of a tradition which I deplore. Bergonzi, 65.
4. Frederick R. Karl は現代の作家の状況について次の如く述べる。
   > Faced with the buzzing confusion of a society that offered no conclusions or resolutions, the writer would be tempted to withdraw from the large world into the little one. But the result of such indulgence would be finely wrought insignificant novels, or intelligently presented minor fictions, or sharply etched small books. Karl, 327.
5. Myer, 176.

引用文献

Bergonzi, Bernard. *The Situation of the Novel*. London: Macmillan, 1970.

Drabble, Margaret. *The garrick Year*. Harmondsworth, Middlesex: Penguin Books, 1969.

―――. *The Millstone*. Harmondsworth, Middlesex: Penguin Books, 1971.

Karl, Frederick R. *A Reader's Guide to the Contemporary English Novel*. Rev. Ed. New York: Farrar, Straus and Giroux, 1972.

Korn, Eric. "Archaeology Begins at Home." Rev. of *The Realms of Gold* by Margaret Drabble. *Times Literary Supplement* 26 September 1975: 1077.

Melville, Herman. *Moby-Dick*. Ed. Harrison Hayford and Hershel Parker. New York: Norton, 1967.

Myer, Valerie Grosvenor. *Margaret Drabble: Puritanism and Permissiveness*. London: Vision Press, 1974.

Ⅱ　白鯨を求めて

WHAT IS MOBY DICK ?

I

Moby Dick is a whale and the protagonist of the work. This is an overwhelming impression I have when I read *Moby-Dick*. He may be a sign of something but he is no more a sign than Ahab. He has his substance in himself. Where does such a monster breach from? I try to find the root of his life and pave the way to understand what he stands for.

The narrator of *Moby-Dick* is Ishmael. Moby Dick is born of his narration, which is roughly divided into two parts: the story and the information. The information supports the story and makes it a great work. Fortunately, we find a budding form of Ishmael's narration in "The Town-Ho's Story," where Ishmael tells a story about a sailor's revenge against his cruel officer and the listeners ask him for information about the happenings in the story. For instance, Ishmael says 'Canallers' but they cannot understand the word until Ishmael gives the information about it. The purpose of his information is to introduce to the listeners the world of the story and make them believe that the world of the story is one with the world they actually live in. Don Pedro cries: "I see! I see! No need to travel! The world is one Lima." (215) And at the end of the story Ishmael swears by the Bible: "I know it to be ture; it happened on this ball." (224) As you see here, the common basis of communication in the Town-Ho's Story is an actual fact and the structure of Ishmael's narration is very simple. In the case of *Moby-Dick* as a whole, however, it is more complex and elaborate. While the basic structure of the story and the information is the same, the latter's function is different. It metamorphoses the story from the actual world to another world. Let me offer an example.

In "The Line," Chapter 60, Ishmael introduces the whale line to us. First he reports the facts about it, as if he were a lecturer of cetology, though not without such humor as: "the boat looks as if it were pulling off with a prodigious great wedding-cake to present to the whales," or "In these instances, the whale of course is shifted like a mug of ale, as it were, from the one boat to the other." (239) Then we find that he puts stress upon such a fact as: "Thus the whale-line folds the whole boat in its complicated coils, twisting and writhing around it in almost every direction." "All the oarsmen" seem, he continues, "as Indian jugglers, with the deadliest snakes sportively festooning their limbs." In such a situation, just suppose a horrible moment when the harpoon is darted. You may say: "like the six burghers of Calais before King Edward, the six men composing the crew pull into the jaws of death, with a halter around every neck." (240) After that, Ishmael, convincing us that there is no way to escape this peril, concludes with this analogy: "All men live enveloped in whale-lines." (241)

In this way the meaning of the whale-line becomes richer as the story proceed, while retaining its own substance. See "The Deck" in

Chapter 127. There you will find the line-tubs upon which a coffin is laid. And Ahab's comment, "See! that thing rests on two line-tubs, full of tow-lines." (432) It is this line that drags Pip out of the boat into madness, (345–347) and further it is this line that catches Ahab by his neck as if it were a snake manipulated by the hands of Death. (468) Through this process, a thing becomes a living thing whose meaning never ceases growing. This is a symbol in the sense that it is at once a fact and a perpetual extension of meaning.

This symbolic technique is found everywhere throughout the work. Especially in the chapters on cetology (including the narration about whale-fishery), wit, satire, humour, analogy, simile, metaphor etc., almost all the techniques are used for this purpose. Besides, the most outstanding fact we cannot miss is that Ishmael's view-point is always focused on the whale and it is likely that anything that has any connexion with it never fails to be mentioned. As a matter of course, all associated meanings seem to be interlaced into an organic body, 'whale.' Ishmael remarks:

> I am horror-struck at this antemosaic, unsourced existence of the unspeakable terrors of the whale, which, having been before all time, must needs exist after all humane ages are over. (380) ....
>
>   Wherefore, for all these things, we account the whale immortal in his species, however perishable in his individuality. He swam the seas before the continents broke water; he once swam over the site of the Tuileries, and Windsor Castle, and the Kremlin. In Noah's flood he despised Noah's Ark; and if ever the world is to be again flooded, like the Netherlands, to kill off its rats, then the eternal whale will still survive, and rearing upon the topmost crest of the

equatorial flood, spout his frothed defiance to the skies. (384–385)

These figures of whales carry our minds back to the gods in the Ancient Greece. Moby Dick appears among them with such a grand and sublime beauty:

> A gentle joyousness—a mighty mildness of repose in swiftness, invested the gliding whale. Not the white bull Jupiter swimming away with ravished Europa clinging to his graceful horns; his lovely, leering eyes sideways intent upon the maid; with smooth bewitching fleetness, rippling straight for the nuptial bower in Crete; not Jove, not that great majesty Supreme! did surpass the glorified White Whale as he so divinely swam.
> On each soft side—coincident with the parted swell, that but once leaving him, then flowed so wide away—on each bright side, the whale shed off enticings. (447)

To present this glorious appearance of Moby Dick, Melville provides a very ingenious style. It is like this: we cannot actually see the Whale until we reach the last three chapters, although all through the book we are chasing him in our imagination. Just turn back to the first chapter, and you will already see there the phantom of Moby Dick alluring Ishmael: "one grand hooded phantom, like a snow hill in the air." (16) Then we hear "the monstrousest parmacety" (69) devouring Ahab's leg. And after a long sustained pause, Ahab's sudden proclamation of his revenge on Moby Dick. Hence, the identification of the Whale with Ahab's goal. This means that the sustained expectancy for Moby Dick goes along with the tragic tension of Ahab, who is also described with this style as shown later.

Now I think you had some understanding about how a whale changes himself into a mythic whale Moby Dick, and how a world of whales is formed encircling him. That world might be called 'myth' in that it has an organic vitality and impenetrability against reason and that each component in it has a sort of mythic synecdoche. According to Ernst Cassirer the mythic synecdoche is explained as follows: "Every part of a whole is the whole itself; every specimen is equivalent to the entire species. The part does not merely represenit the whole, or the specimen its class; they are identical with the totality to which they belong; not merely as mediating aids to reflective thought, but as genuine presences which actually contain the power, significance, and efficacy of the whole." [1]

For an illustration I will pick up some specimens of 'whale-myth.' See the tail, the movement of which is the sign of the "Free-Mason." (317) See the spout, which is the Spirit-Spout: "on such a silent night a silvery jet was seen far in advance of the white bubbles at the bow. Lit up by the moon, it looked celestial; seemed some plumed and glittering god uprising from the sea." (199) See the Pacific, which is the womb of this "sweet mystery": "And meet it is, that over these sea-pastures, wide-rolling watery prairies and Potters' Fields of all four continents, the waves should rise and fall, and ebb and flow unceasingly; for here, millions of mixed shades and shadows, drowned dreams, somnambulisms, reveries; all that we call lives and souls, lie dreaming, dreaming, still; tossing like slumberers in their beds...." (399)

I am afraid I am too much obsessed with whales. Some may claim:

I see your 'whale-myth' but what does it matter with human beings? Perhaps that is the irritation felt by Ahab. First question arises here. Aren't there any human inhabitants in the myth? Yes, there are some but, no need to add, they are all mystic figures. Among them Fedallah and the three pagan harpooners are first to be mentioned.

Fedallah: "He was such a creature as civilized, domestic people in the temperate zone only see in their dreams, and that but dimly." (199) It is none but Fedallah that follows Ahab like a shadow throughout.

Queequeg: A bosom friend of Ishmael, yet he "in his own proper person was a riddle to solve." (399) If you compare Queequeg in his coffin with the dying whale, you will see their kinship.

> 〔Queequeg〕 How he wasted and wasted away in those few long-lingering days, till there seemed but little left of him but his frame and tattooing. But as all else in him thinned, and his cheekbones grew sharper, his eyes, nevertheless, seemed growing fuller and fuller; they became of a strange softness of lustre; and mildly but deeply looked out at you there from his sickness, a wondrous testimony to that immortal health in him which could not die, or be weakened. And like circles on the water, which, as they grow fainter, expand; so his eyes seemed rounding and rounding, like the rings of Eternity. (395)
>
> 〔the whale〕 It was far down the afternoon; and when all the spearings of the crimson fight were done : and floating in the lovely sunset sea and sky, sun and whale both stilly died together; then, such a sweetness and such plaintiveness, such inwreathing orisons curled up in that rosy air, that it almost seemed as if far over from the deep green convent valleys of Manilla isles, the Spanish land-breeze, wantonly turned sailor, had gone to sea, freighted with these

vesper hymns. (409)

The scenes represent their eternal fertility.

Tashtego: He looks like "a son of the Prince of the Power of the Air." (107)

Dagoo: "There was a corporeal humility in looking at him; and a white man standing before him seemed a white flag come to beg truce of a fortress." (108)

If we recall further the last scene of the Pequod, we find there the heroic figures of the dying harpooners. "...fixed by infatuation, or fidelity, or fate, to their once lofty perches, the pagan harpooners still maintained their sinking look-outs on the sea." (469)

It is no wonder why Ahab baptized his harpoon with their blood "in nomine diaboli." (404) Ahab needs their vigour and strength to cope with Moby Dick. Compared with these demons even Ahab seems somehow powerless and playful.

When we turn our eyes from these pagans to the whites, they will seem mere bubbles floating on the surface of the myth. They cannot penetrate that surface, and so they cannot have vigour. As an aid to my comment I point out the difference of style with which the mates and the harpooners are described in "Knights and Squires," Chapters 26-27. (102–108). While the mates are drawn with a comic touch, the harpooners are with an epic-style.

The whites are alienated from 'whale-myth.' Ahab alone clearly sees this fact and he seems to have such a fear that the real source of life is deep in that inscrutable myth. To follow the way how Ahab engages himself in it, we may as well set another chapter.

II

 Ishmael's narration has two view-points; narrator-Ishmael's and actor-Ishmael's. Until now we have mainly followed the former's, but in tracing Ahab we must follow the latter's. Not to mention of, 'whale-myth' independently treated above is brought to the full revelation along with Ahab's action which makes up the main-plot.

 The story of the main-plot is very simple. A whale bites off Ahab's leg and he tries to revenge himself upon the whale and chases it round the world until at last he is killed by it. In whale-fishery it is not unusual for a whale to hurt or kill men and it is usually considered as an accident. And yet Ahab tries to kill the whale even at the cost of both his life and the Pequod. What impels him to this course of action?

 Now we are to follow Ahab and we can expect that he too comes to the stage as a mystic figure. But he is different from the pagans in that he has reason against mysticism and he can never abandon it even in his madness. As was just glanced at, Ahab's characterization is produced in the same style as that of Moby Dick.

  Ahab's first outline is drawn by Captain Peleg. Briefly speaking: He lost his leg by the whale. His name is *Ahab*, which is said to be prophetic by "the old sqaw Tistig." (77) He is the most skillful whale-man. Summing up, "He is a grand, ungodly god-like man." (76) On the way back from the Pequad Ishmael finds himself filled "with a certain wild vagueness of painfulness concerning him." He felt a strange awe of Ahab but he could not know what it was. "But I felt it," Ishmael comments, "and it did not disincline me towards him; though I felt impatience at what seemed like mystery in him, so imperfectry as he was known to me then." And though he says that "for the present dark Ahab slipped [his] mind," (77) the dark seed dropped by him never goes out of our minds and we shall unawares see Ahab's whale go side by side with the white phantom in the loomings in the first chapter.

The next dark hint is given by a begger-like stranger, whose name is known to be *Elijah*. "Elijah!" Ishmael thinks walking away from the ominous figure, who follows him still for a while. "This circumstance, coupled with his ambiguous, half-hinting, half-revealing, shrouded sort of talk, now begat in [him] all kinds of vague wonderments..." and he recalls in his mind all that has connexion with the Pequod—Captain Ahab—his leg lost—Peleg's information—the voyage with Queequeg "and a hundred other shadowy things," (88) Here, we may recall the fact that the Pequod was selected by the direction of Yojo, Queequeg's god.

The third hint is given on the next morning when they go aboard. "There are some sailors running ahead there, if I see right," says Ishmael to Queequeg, "it can't be shadows...." Then they are suddenly addressed again by Elijah, who reminds them of the foregoing shadowy figures with a dark meaning and sends them the following farewell words: "Good-bye to ye. Shan't see ye again very soon, I guess ; unless it's before the Grand Jury." (90–91)

With this sustained tension Ahab's figure is formed in our imagination and with it the main-plot is carried through till his appearance. The Pequod sets sail on Christmas Day and she takes her course to the south and it is a long time before we see Ahab actually.

His appearance is narrated as follows:

> It was one of those less lowering, but still grey and gloomy enough mornings of the transition, when with a fair wind the ship was rushing through the water with a vindictive sort of leaping and melencholy rapidity, that as I mounted to the deck at the call of the forenoon watch, so soon as I levelled my glance towards the taffrail, foreboding shivers ran over me. Reality outran apprehension; Captain Ahab stood upon his quarter-deck. (109)

Now examin this style of narration, and with it alone you will see how it has a letent strength which points towards Ahab and how Ahab comes alive with a mythic power as a result.

Ishmael observes Ahab's features:

> He looked like a man cut away from the stake, when the fire has overrunningly wasted all the limbs without consuming them, or taking away one particle from their compacted aged robustness. His whole high, broad form, seemed made of solid bronze, and shaped in an unalterable mould, like Cellini's cast Perseus. Threading its way out from among his grey hairs, and continuing right down one side of his tawny scorched face and neck, till it disappeared in his clothing, you saw a slender rod-like mark, lividly whitish. It resembled that perpendicular seam sometimes made in the straight, lofty trunk of a great tree, when the upper lightning tearingly darts down it, and without wrenching a single twig, peels and grooves out

> the bark from top to bottom, ere running off into the soil, leaving the tree still greenly alive, but branded. (109–110)

In spite of the fact that Ahab now reveals himself before us his mystery never diminishes. What is his overbearing grimness? Isn't it likely that his rod-like mark is the same as Cain's brand?

"Not a word he spoke," Ishmael narrates, "nor did his officers say aught to him." (111) Sometimes, however, we may hear him mutter to himself: "It feels like going into one's tomb, for an old captain like me to be descending this narrow scattle, to go to my grave-dug berth." (112) This silence pregnant with something ominous reminds me of a type of the demoniacal defined by Kierkegaard in *The Concept of Dread*. The demoniacal threatens to do something but that something is never to be foreseen because of his shut-upness from others.[2]

We are arrested in such a dreadful moment. Just at that time Ahab declears his cause for chasing Moby Dick:

> All visible objects, man, are but as pasteboard masks. But in each event—in the living act, the undoubted deed—there, some unknown but still reasoning thing puts forth the mouldings of its features from behind the unreasoning mask. If man will strike, strike through the mask! How can the prisoner reach outside except by thrusting through the wall? To me, the white whale is that wall, shoved near to me. Sometimes I think there's naught beyond. But 'tis enough. He tasks me; he heaps me; I see in him outrageous strength, with an inscrutable malice sinewing it. That inscrutable thing is chiefly what I hate; and be the white whale agent, or be the white whale principal,

I will wreak hate upon him. (144)

From a view-point of common sense it is undoubtedly a crazy conceit, as shown in Starbuck's opposition: "Vengeance on a dumb brute! that simply smote thee from blindest instinct! Madness!" (144) And yet nobody can resist Ahab before his demoniac power. Now, Ahab, mates, harpooners and sailors all swear: "Death to Moby Dick! God hunt us all, if we do not hunt Moby Dick to his death!"[3] (146) With these barbarous cries the Pequod settles her course to the Whale.

In the following two chapters, "Moby Dick and The Whiteness of the Whale," Ishmael further elucidates the cause of the hunt: Ahab suffered from the loss of his leg and through the suffering he changed himself, as it were, into some living instrument aimed at Moby Dick. "...yet Ahab's larger, darker, deeper part remains unhinted." (161) To keep the metaphor of 'instrument', the operator of the instrument remains in ambiguity in spite of Ishmael's effort.

As to the crew's cause too, we are informed with the same ambiguity: "...the White Whale as much their insufferable foe as his; how all this came to be—what the White Whale was to them, or how to their unconcious understandings, also, in some dim, unsuspected way, he might have seemed the gliding great demon of the seas of life,—all this to explain, would be to dive deeper than Ishmael can go." (162) Ishmael himself "could see naught in that brute but the deadliest ill." (163)

The answer may be found in the whiteness of the Whale. With various examples Ishmael shows how intensely the white gives us

II-1 What Is Moby Dick?

awe and terror. From his remarks we can pick up these words: "...not yet have we solved the incantation of this whiteness, and learned why it appeals with such power to the soul; and more strange and far more portentous—why, as we have seen, it is at once the most meaning symbol of spiritual things, nay, the very veil of the Christian's Deity; and yet should be as it is, the intensifying agent in things the most appalling to mankind." (169) And from some point of view the world itself comes to be shrouded with this whiteness. "...pondering all this, the palsied universe lies before us a leper.... And of all these things the Albino whale was the symbol. Wonder ye then at the fiery hunt?" (170)

In this way all the ambiguities drive anyone who tries to solve the riddle of the hunt on towards one point: What is Moby Dick? And this is of course the motive which drives Ahab on towards his goal.

At all events, Ahab set his determination to kill Moby Dick and in doing so he became the instrument of something unknown. He pursues while being pursued. The dark hints about Ahab suggest his fate. Above all Fedallah, one of the demons of 'whale-myth' mentioned above, performs the most effective role in setting a fatal seal on Ahab. While the narrator deviates from the main-plot, Ahab's fate is mainly woven with the informations about Moby Dick given by the whale-ships which cross their wakes with the Pequod's. Furthermore, among other premonitions we may count such happenings: the spirit-spout alluring them for ever; (199–202) the fish running away from the Pequod when she runs across the Albatros; (203–204) the squid, the vast white monster; (236–238) the life-buoy made by a coffin; (430–431) Ahab's hat "slouched heavily over his eyes" (438) like Jonah's slouching hat, being carried away and dropped into the deep by a black hawk. (440–441)

Despite these ill forebodings Ahab never alters his course. He sticks to hunting the Whale with the frenzy of monomaniac. Yet on rare occasions, we may see another aspect of his gleaming out of darkness. For example, you will see it in the chapter "The Symphony." Now he has come to the last battlefield. "It was a clear steel-blue day. The firmaments of air and sea were hardly separable in that all-pervading azure." (442) Whether nature melted his hardness or not, he recalls his days and home left far behind. He addresses Starbuck: "Close! stand close to me, Starbuck; let me look into a human eye; it is better than to gaze into sea or sky; better than to gaze upon God." This is the most pathetic scene in the work and we see here Ahab's humanity. Starbuck replies: "Away with me! let us fly these deadly waters! let us home!" (444)

After all, however, Ahab cannot submit himself to Starbuck's persuasion. Already he seems to have lost himself somewhere: "Is Ahab, Ahab? Is it I, God, or who, that lifts this arm?" (445) And as if it were his role to replace Ahab's vacant mind, Fedallah is standing beside him. To change such a course of Ahab is now perhaps beyond the reach of mortal abilities, not to speak of Starbuck's. Well, let us consider the point from another angle.

Ahab's action is expressed metaphorically as 'seaward' and the imagery of 'sea' and 'land' appears recurrently throughout the work. Therefore it is useful to consider what these images have to do with the point.

On the day when the Pequod sets sail Ishmael praises Bulkington's spirit of independence: "Know ye now, Bulkington? Glimpses do ye seem to see of that mortally intolerable truth; that all deep, earnest thinking is but the intrepid effort of the soul to keep *the open independence of her sea*; while the wildest of heaven and earth conspire to cast her on *the treacherous, slavish shore?*" This Bulkington is another Ahab. So these words may as well be the farewell gift to the Pequhd. To one who seeks "the highest truth" "*the land* [seems] scorching to his feet." "For worm-like, then, oh!" Ishmael continues, "who would craven crawl to *land*!" (97; emphasis added) As a result the Pequod is, once she sets sail from shore, never to touch the land. After that the land does not appear but in minds.

The sea is rough but there are sometimes such calms when the sailors are apt to take it for the land. At those times the whales are likened to the mowers as seen in the chapter "Brit": "As morning mowers, who side by side slowly and seethingly advance their scythes through the long wet grass of marshy meads; even so these monsters swam, making a strange, grassy, cutting sound; and leaving behind them endless swaths of blue upon the yellow sea." (234) Or, the waves are taken for the cats: "At such times, under an abated sun; afloat all day upon smooth, slow heaving swells; seated in his boat, light as a birch canoe; and so sociably mixing with the soft waves themselves, that *like hearthstone cats* they purr against the gunwale; these are the times of dreamy quietude...." And moreover: "These are the times, when in his whale-boat the rover softly feels a certain filial, confident, *land-like* feeling towards the sea; that he regards it as so much flowery earth; and the distant ship revealing only the tops of her masts, seems struggling forward, not through high rolling waves, but throhgh the tall grass of a rolling prairie.... The long-drawn virgin vales; the mild blue hill-sides; as over these there steals the hush, the hum; you almost swear that play-wearied children lie sleeping in these solitudes, in some glad May-time, when the flowers of the woods are plucked." (405-406; emphasis added) These are the times too when Ishmael prays: "Would to God these blessed calms would last." (406) And from these dreamlike quietudes is formed the symphony where Ahab's humanity gleams out.

Yet we must also remember that these are the times when: "lulled into such an opium-like listlessness of vacant, unconcious reverie is this absent-minded youth [man at the mast-head] by the blending cadence of waves with thoughts, that at last he loses his identity; takes the mystic ocean at his feet for the visible image of that deep, blue, bottomless soul, pervading mankind and nature.... There is no life in thee, now, except that rocking life imparted by a gentle rolling ship; by her, borrowed from the sea; by the sea, from the inscrutable tides of God."

Then Ishmael's warning follows at once: "But while this sleep, this dream is on ye, move your foot or hand an inch; slip your hold at all; and your identity comes back in horror. Over Descartian vortices you hover. And perhaps, at mid-day, in the fairest weather, with one half-throttled shriek you drop through that transparent air into the summer sea, no more to rise for ever. Heed it well, ye Pantheists! (140) Here, turn your eyes back to the image "hearth-stone cats," and you will see there the wave which looks like "a velvet paw but conceals a remorseless fang." (405) The dream-like land in the sea is quite as treacherous as the "slavish shore." Under the calms the horrors of Moby Dick lurk: "And thus, through the serene tranquilities of the tropical sea, among waves whose hand-clappings were suspended by exceeding rapture, Moby Dick moved on, still withholding from sight the full terrors of his submerged trunk, entirely hiding the wrenched hideousness of his jaw." (448)

So long as such Moby Dick swims Ahab cannot harmonize himself with the symphony of nature, metaphorically 'land' in the sea. That is the reason why though these soothing scenes "did seem to open in him his own secret golden treasuries, yet did his breath upon them prove but tarnishing." (406)

When the Pequod ran across the Bachelor, which was the only successful whale-ship of all the Pequod met: "And as Ahab, leaning over the taffrail, eyed the homeward-bound craft, he took from his pocket a small vial of sand, and then looking from the ship to the vial, seemed thereby bringing two remote associations together, for that vial was filled with Nantucket soundings." (408) For Ahab the land was the thing which had been left in the past where mortals can never return. For him there was no other possible way than to go 'seaward' hunting Moby Dick.

The course is unmovable. It is tragically settled and a pattern of tragedy may be applied to it. But that tragedy is maimed, for it has no epiphany (the final revelation of the meaning of the hero's action).[4] So long as Moby Dick lives Ahab must hunt him for ever; he cannot admit any ultimate but to hunt the Whale, whether Devil or God. Therefore his death means nothing but an abrupt end of his tragedy, an accident but not the catharsis. None the less he is heroic enough, for such an impression that he is selecting the only existence possible as a human being is too strong. In this sense he is an ungodly, godlike hero.

As we have traced till now all the ambiguities and riddles seem to focus on one point, Moby Dick. The White Whale is, as it were, the deus ex machina. That very god, however, disappears accompanying Ahab at the last moment, and the Pequod too is gulped down into the yawning deep. What is left behind now? Where are we taken to? The sea is still veiled with the myth.

"Now small fowls flew screaming over the yet yawning gulf;" Ishmael narrates, "a sullen white surf beat against its steep sides; then all collapsed, and the great shroud of the sea rolled on as it rolled five thousand years ago." (469) If we feel catharsis, it would be this eternal song of sea-dirge and further the conviction that there must be some one who might chant the hymn over such tragedy even thought it is unheard by mortal ears.

III

Before entering the conclusion it will be well to listen to Father Mapple's sermon.

The sermon is "a story of the sin, hard-heartedness, suddenly awakened fears, the swift punishment, repentance, prayers, and finally the deliverance and joy of Jonah." (45) What was the sin of Jonah? He disobeyed God and sought to flee from Him, for he feared the command that he should "preach the Truth to the face of

Falsehood." Inducing a lesson from this, Father Mapple lays stress upon the following point: "Woe to him who would not be true, even though to be false were salvation!" (50) and "Delight is to him, who gives no quarter in the truth, and kills, burns, and destroys all sin though he pluck it out from under the robes of Senators and Judges. Delight—top-gallant delight is to him, who acknowledges no law or lord, but the Lord his God, and is only a patriot to heaven." (51)

Here, we see that to seek Truth is the most sublime duty of human beings. To seek Truth is to believe in God. There is no conflict between both commands. God's existence is never to be doubted. Then recall how Ishmael encouraged Bulkigton who went to the sea to seek Truth. Let me cite here the words which follow the former quotation: "Terrors of the terrible! is all this agony so vain? Take heart, take heart, O Bulkington! Bear thee grimly, demigod! Up from the spray of the ocean-perishing—straight up, leaps thy apotheosis!" (98) And recall that Bulkington was another Ahab.

Did Ahab's apotheosis leap straight up? Surely, Ahab sought Truth. To seek Truth was, however, no longer to believe in God but to ask if God exists or not. That is to say to seek Truth became to hunt Moby Dick. And how damned the hunt was what we have seen now. What should I consider such a hunt? Is there any moral meaning in it?

Lawrance Thompson's commentary on Ahab's hunt is as follows: "Boldly stated, then Melville's underlying theme in *Moby-Dick* correlates the notions that the world was put together wrong and the God is to blame, that God in his infinite malice asserts a sovereign tyanny over man and that most men are seduced into the mistaken view that this divine tyranny is benevolent and therefore acceptable;

but that the freethinking and enlightened and heroic man will assert the rights of man and rebel against God's tyranny by defying God in thought, word, deed, even in the face of God's ultimate indignity, death."[5]

As you see here, Thompson's view is that Moby Dick is the symbol of the malicious God. It is certain that Moby Dick is not benevolent. But who can decide that he is malicious? It is certain again that Ahab saw in Moby Dick an inscrutable malice. But who can be sure of asserting that Ahab did not commit an error in the hunting? Ahab might have dragged the crew into the Hell. We must not forget that Moby Dick is divine as well as devilish. In so far as Truth remains a riddle, no one can judge the deeds of human beings. We are certain only of the fact that man can retain his life and vigor and strength as long as he keeps struggling for Truth.

For some reasons Ahab found himself powerless, meaningless and, that is to say, alienated from God. Around him there stretched far and wide the ocean of 'riddle.' He felt himself surrounded by something inscrutable, 'wall' beyond which he felt the thing he lost was lurking. To regain his power, meaning, God, he had to strike, strike the wall and wade through the mythic ocean until he lost himself there.

For Ahab to live was to hunt Moby Dick. Now, I venture my conclusion: Moby Dick is the symbol of what human beings are living for.

Notes
1. Feidelson, 65.
2. kierkegaard, 105–117.
3. Starbuck alone turns away from the excitement.
4. About the concept of tragedy I owe to Francis Fergusson, *The Idea of a Theater*.
5. Thompson, 242–243.

Works Cited

Feidelsen, Charles, Jr. *Symbolism and American Literature*. Chicago: U of Chicago P, 1953.

Fergusson, Francis. *The Idea of a Theater*. Garden City, N.Y.: Doubleday, 1949.

Kierkegaard, Soren. *The Concept of Dread*. Princeton: Princeton U P, 1957.

Melville, Herman. *Moby-Dick*. Ed. Harrison Heyford and Hershel Parker. New York: Norton, 1967.

Thompson, Lawrance. *Melville's Quarrel with God*. Princeton: Princeton U P, 1952.

The Resurrection of Ishmael

I

Moby-Dick, beginning with the words "Call me Ishmael" (12), takes an autobiographical form, and so it is a prerequisite that Ishmael survives the wreck of the Pequod. The circumstances of his rescue are told in the Epilogue,[1] where we find an extract from the Book of Job: "And I only am escaped alone to tell thee." (470) This is the phrase repeated every time a messenger reports Job's calamity[2] and it reminds us of the fact that Ishmael is another messenger who comes to us with the report of Ahab's catastrophic disaster. As you see here, his main function is to be a reporter. Perhaps, the problem of his survival may be simply solved as a means to save the narrator and nothing more.

This solution, however, seems to be brought about too easily, for even such a means has its own meaning in the context of a novel. Certainly, there is something more in the survival of Ishmael. Generally, the survival is regarded as the symbol of salvation in contrast to the damnation of Ahab. Here is a representative opinion. Howard P. Vincent remarks:

> With this epilogue of Ishmael's rescue, the great spiritual theme of

> *Moby-Dick* is rounded off. Ishmael had started for the South Seas in a state bordering on suicide, alone and angered at life. Ishmael learned the law of aloneness and the law of companionship, the psychological duality. But Ishmael has also learned the law of acceptance, to accept what Fate has in store for him, not to fight it in the manner of Ahab. And now afloat with his coffin he has achieved spiritual rebirth, symbolically pictured. The 'Epilogue' deals with the metaphysics of resurrection. Ishmael has, in Keats's phrase, experienced a 'dying into life.'[3]

While Ahab remains exclusive and rebellious, Ishmael comes to know friendship and the law of acceptance. Presupposed here is a Christian doctrine that supports the spiritual growth of Ishmael and in the end redeems him from the seas of damnation. Not to go so far as Christianity, it is common that some virtue—friendship, wisdom or suchlike—is taken as the law of morality according to which the characters are discussed and judged as to whether their deeds deserve their ends. It follows that Ishmael is saved because he obeys the law, whereas Ahab is condemned because he violates it.

But, to take the matter from such a viewpoint, we must differentiate clearly the sailor-Ishmael on the Pequod from the narrator-Ishmael in the present, and further to contrast this figure with Ahab's. This is most troublesome, for those two figures of Ishmael are subtly fused together and, what is worse, the character who is set against Ahab is not Ishmael but Starbuck. If Ishmael were against Ahab, he should cause some conflicts with Ahab. In fact, there is no one but Starbuck who tries to confront "the fiery hunt" (170) of mad Ahab. Moreover, there is a barrier coming from the nature of the first person narration. As a whole the individual image of Ishmael is so obscure that, if we follow the way of asking if his personality deserves salvation or not, we will be lost in a labyrinth. We have to go back to the Epilogue where the narrator deals with his survival.

Ishmael tells us that from the great vortex caused by the sinking Pequod a coffin life-buoy, "*rising with great force…shot length-wise …fell over, and floated by* [*his*] *side. Buoyed up by that coffin, for almost one whole day and night,* [*he*] *floated on a soft and dirge-like main…. On the second day, a sail drew near, nearer, and picked* [*him*] *up at last.*" (470) The fact that Ishmael is saved by the coffin after the White Whale and the Pequod turn out to be the hearses realizing Fedallah's prophesy for Ahab is important. Besides, 'coffin' is the recurrent imagery which weaves its death-motif throughout the work. A coffin life-buoy, this ironical object is likely to unfold the riddle of Ishmael's salvation.[4]

II

Somehow Ishmael finds himself weary of his life on shore and finds himself "involuntarily pausing before *coffin warehouses,* and bringing up the rear of every *funeral*" (12; emphasis added) he meets. To drive off such spleen he decides to go whaling and starts for "Cape Horn and the Pacific." (16) But the grim air haunts him further. The night of New Bedford, where he is to embark for Nantucket, shows an awfully dismal aspect. "Such dreary streets!

blocks of blackness, not houses, on either hand, and here and there a candle, like a candle moving about in a *tomb*." Then, after some failures he comes upon an inn, "*The Spouter-Inn*," and finds that the name of the landlord is *Peter Coffin*. "*Coffin?*—*Spouter?*—Rather ominous in that particular connexion," he thinks trembling with cold like another *Lazarus*. And yet here is "the very spot for cheap lodgings." (18–19; emphasis added) Then he enters there to find another *Jonah* behind the bar made of *the jaws of the whale*. (21; emphasis added)

From this brief survey we can see how Ishmael is haunted by 'coffin'. Let me give here another example which comes when Ishmael and Queequeg, after landing at Nantucket, stand looking at the sign of the chowder-restaurant: "It's ominous," Ishmael thinks. "A Coffin my Innkeeper upon landing in my first whaling port; tombstones staring at me in the whalemen's chapel; and here a gallows! and a pair of prodigious black pots too! Are these last throwing out oblique hints touching Tophet?" (64) Thus, 'coffin' becomes the seed from which the death-imagery grows up.

As we glanced in the above example Ishmael pays "a Sunday visit" (39) to a Whaleman's Chapel at New Bedford. There are many dead whalemen buried without the bodies in the chapel. Looking over them he suffers the dread from the "bitter blanks in those black-bordered marbles which cover no ashes! What despair in those immovable inscriptions! What deadly voids and unbidden infidelities in the lines that seem to gnaw upon all Faith, and refuse resurrections to the beings who have placelessly perished without a grave." His fancies wander about those helpless souls and he feels the fear that the same fate may be his own. But he grows merry again, for "Faith, like a jackal, feeds among the tombs, and even from these dead doubts she gathers her most vital hope." (41) Then Faith resurrects in his soul and he is to attend the sermon of Father Mapple.

While 'coffin' appears as an image of death it is also accompanied, as seen above, by such imagery as 'Lazarus', 'Jonah', which suggest the Christian salvation. We can say that already here grows in the association of these images a germ of salvation, 'death into life.'

Ishmael, under an obsession with death, is seeking to be saved from it. If he can be saved, whence does Ishmael's salvation come? Father Mapple's sermon has two mainpoints: one is repentance and the other is obeying God at any cost. (44–51) Could this God give sanction to the fate of Ishmael?

Shaking off his pale fears by Faith and encouraged by the sermon, he goes aboard the Pequod. But as early as at the first lowering for the whale his faith breaks down. What a business that he should "break his own back pulling himself back-foremost" (196) into the whale's jaw that means nothing but death! What a fate that he should some day come face to face with Moby Dick in such a state? To get through "this business of whaling—a speechless quick chaotic bundling of a man into Eternity," (41) he spins a sort of philosophy called "free and easy sort of genial, desperado philosophy," (196) with which he "takes this whole universe for a vast practical joke," and he "bolts down all events, all creeds, and beliefs, and persuasions, all hard things visible and invisible, never mind how knobby; as an ostrich of potent digestion gobbles down bullets and gun flints." (195) And it is with this attitude that he observes "this whole voyage of the Pequod, and the great White Whale its object." (196) Isn't it that this Ishmael is the same as he who, as Father Mapple warns, "while preaching to others is himself a castaway?" (50) Moreover, to escape the apprehension of death he makes up his will beforehand. Then he locks up his "death and burial" in his sea-chest and he pretends to have survived himself. All his days after, he thinks, will be "as good as the days that Lazarus lived after his resurrection." (197) Isn't it that this Ishmael is the same as he who, as Father Mapple warns, "would not be true, even though to be false were salvation?" (50)

  In brief, that fortitude which is, as seen in the sermon, indispensable to bear God's providence fails Ishmael, who has resigned himself to "those stage managers, the Fates." (16) He is but a looker-on on board the Pequod. Reviewed thus from God in the sermon Ishmael's salvation is just an ironical matter as much as "Delight," the name of the whale ship defeated by Moby Dick. (441–442) In the sermon "Delight" is offered to him whom God may bless. (50–51) Ishmael cannot share in that blessing.

   If his salvation cannot come from Christianity, our attention must turn elsewhere. Here looms out a heathen, Queequeg, for it is his coffin that saves Ishmael. The coffin (the symbol of death) is made for him and then changed into a life-buoy (the symbol of life) according to his suggestion. Why should Queequeg play such a conclusive part in the metamorphosis of 'coffin' into 'life-buoy'? It will be better that we have a brief survey of his character beforehand.[5]

II-2 The Resurrection of Ishmael

There are many episodes about him in the work. Let us pick up some among them. First there comes a picture of the event that happens when Starbuck's crew, to which Ishmael and he belong, pass a whole night on the half-drowned boat after the failure of the first lowering just mentioned above. Left alone in the darkness of the rising sea there is nothing for them but to light the lamp for help. The lamp is handed to Queequeg. "There, then," Ishmael narrates, "he sat, holding up that imbecile candle in the heart of that almighty forlornness. There, then, he sat, the sign and symbol of a man without faith, hopelessly holding up hope in the midst of despair." (195) Hopeless as it seems, Queequeg holds up a lamp of hope in the darkness. It may be expected that the lamp can throw light on the way to salvation.

Queequeg, Ishmael's bosom friend, is called "soothing savage." He has a strange bewitching power that attracts Ismael when they first meet. Ishmael narrates:

> I began to be sensible of strange feelings. I felt a melting in me. No more my splintered heart and maddened hand were turned against the wolfish world. This soothing savage had redeemed it. There he sat, his very indifference speaking a nature in which there lurked no civilized hypocrisies and bland deceits. Wild he was; a very sight of sights to see; yet I began to feel myself mysteriously drawn towards him. And those same things that would have repelled most others, they were the very magnets that thus drew me. I'll try a pagan friend, thought I, since Christian kindness has proved but hollow courtesy. (53)

Already here in the early part of the story Queequeg is holding his hands out to help the desolate heart of Ishmael who was cast away from the civilized world.

The next two incidents may be added as relevant examples that show another aspect of his redeeming power. The first happens on the seaway for Nantucket. Queequeg saves from the sea a young fellow so bravely and skillfully that from that time Ishmael cleaves to him "like a barnacle" (61) till the last. The second happens in the working of bailing out oil of the whale's head. By a queer accident Tashtego drops into the head, which too, to make the matter worse, sinks into the deep while retaining him within. This "coffined" Tashtego is delivered by Queequeg "performing his agile obstetrics on the run." (290) These are the events in which Queequeg literally saves human beings.

Tracing the figure of Queequeg, we have an impression that he is more than a human. Such impression comes, however, not only from him but also from the other savages on the Pequod such as Tashtego and Dagoo, not to speak of Fedallah. They are all full of some mystic vitality.[6] That quality of Queequeg is shown most vividly in the following scene.

When the Pequod draws near Japan it is found that some oil in the hold is leaking. To plug it Queequeg works hard and falls into a strange illness and in some days draws close "to the very sill of the door of death." But, the more he wastes physically the more his spiritual strength glows up. Ishmael narrates:

> How he wasted and wasted away in those few long-lingering days,

till there seemed but little left of him but his frame and tattooing. But as all else in him thinned, and his cheekbones grew sharper, his eyes, nevertheless, seemed growing fuller and fuller; they became of a strange softness of lustre; and mildly but deeply looked out at you there from his sickness, a wondrous testimony to that immortal health in him which could not die, or be weakened. And like circles on the water, which, as they grow fainter, expand; so his eyes seemed rounding and rounding, like the rings of Eternity.... So that—let us say it again—no dying Chaldee or Greek had higher and holier thoughts than those, whose mysterious shades you saw creeping over the face of poor Queequeg, as he quietly lay in his swaying hammock, and the rolling sea seemed gently rocking him to his final rest, and the ocean's invisible flood-tide lifted him higher and higher towards his destined heaven. (395-396)

Here, we see that a heroic savage is dying into his heaven. And as a means of conveyance to that holy place a canoe-shaped coffin is ordered. For a dead warrior in his race is, Queequeg says, placed in his canoe and so left "to be floated away to the starry archipelagoes; for not only do they believe that the stars are isles, but that far beyond all visible horizons, their own mild, uncontinented seas, interflow with the blue heavens; and so form the white breakers of the milky way." So, "some heathenish, coffin-colored old lumber …cut from the aboriginal groves of the Lackady islands" (396) is chosen and from these planks the coffin is to be made.

When the coffin is finished Queequeg lies in it by way of trial and murmurs "Rarmai" meaning "it is easy." (397) Compare this serenity of Queequeg before death with the agitated commotion of

Ishmael at it. For Queequeg death is by no means his journey's end but his new start, and the coffin is nothing but a comfortable vehicle for "his destined heaven." (396)　In this way, the coffin is now first substantially brought about on the scene, not as an ominous thing but as a hopeful thing.

After every preparation has been made, however, miraculously he recovers from his death-bed for the strange reason that he cannot die yet because some duty on shore is left undone　Then he regains his full strength in less than a few days and his coffin, now useless, becomes his sea-chest and on its lid is copied a part of his tatooing which is said to be "a complete theory of the heavens and the earth, and a mystical treatise on the art of attaining truth" written by "a departed prophet and seer of his island." (399)

There comes a chance for the coffin to change itself into a life-buoy when the old life-buoy is thrown out vainly to help "the first man of the Pequod that mounted the mast to look out for the White Whale, on the White Whale's own peculiar ground," (429)　and it is replaced by his coffin according to Queequeg's hint "by certain strange signs and inuendoes."

Now, the coffin becomes a life-buoy. But the propriety of the step is only known to Queequeg. The others are either doubtful or indifferent about it.

"A life-buoy of a coffin!" cries Starbuck.

"It will make a good enough one," says Flask, "the carpenter here can arrange it easily." (430)

But the carpenter, who is as omnipotent and "unprincipled as the gods," (432)　works at it all grudgingly. Catching a sight of the coffin being made into a life-buoy, Ahab says to himself:

> "There's a sight! There's a sound! The greyheaded wood-pecker tapping the hollow tree! Blind and dumb might well be envied now. See! that thing rests on two line-tubs, full of tow-lines. A most malicious wag, that fellow. Rat-tat! So man's seconds tick! Oh! how immaterial are all materials! What things real are there, but imponderable thoughts? Here now's the very dreaded symbol of grim death, by a mere hap, made the expressive sign of the help and hope of most endangered life. A life-buoy of a coffin! Does it go further? Can it be that in some spiritual sense the coffin is, after all, but an immortality-preserver! I'll think of that. But no. So far gone am I in the dark side of earth, that its other side, the theoretic bright one, seems but uncertain twilight to me. (432–433)

Now, the strange life-buoy hangs at the Pequod's stern, and then by chance it causes some wicked laughter when the Pequod sails away from the wrecked Delight mentioned above. "Ha! yonder! look yonder, men!" comes a cry from the ship. "In vain, oh, ye strangers, ye fly our sad burial; ye but turn us your taffrail to show us your coffin!" (442)

It appears that a coffin is a coffin after all is said and done. And yet the very coffin, when Ahab's Pequod sank deep, floats up and saves Ishmael. In fact it proves to be "the expressive sign of the help and hope of most endangered life." (433)

III

Now, we have seen how 'coffin' becomes 'life-buoy' and what Queequeg does in the process of becoming, from which can be drawn the rich implications of Ishmael's survival. To set them in brief conclusive words, however, tends to lessen their richness. So, I can only draw here a draft about them.

It will be allowed to say that if Ahab comes to damnation led by Fedallah, Ishmael comes to salvation led by Queequeg. And we may as well say that Queequeg is an agent of the benevolent god as say that Fedallah is an agent of the malicious god. Queequeg can possibly be an incarnation of something that may save human beings. Ishmael himself feels there lurks in Queequeg some power that could save him. But he cannot be sure of it, he cannot believe in it, for he cannot have a clear sight of what Queequeg is in spite of there being such intimacy as between them.

The mysterious being of Queequeg is symbolized by his tattooing which has been occupying Ishmael's attention since the first moment of their encounter. (28–29) The twisted tatooing that covers his whole body reveals, as mentioned already, "a complete theory of the heavens and the earth." And further Ishmael continues: "so that Queequeg in his own proper person was a riddle to unfold; a wondrous work in one volume; but whose mysteries not even himself could read, though his own live heart beat against them; and these mysteries were therefore destined in the end to molder away with the living parchment whereon they were inscribed, and so be unsolved to the last." (399)

Thus the truth is shrouded in an impenetrable veil, which also veils the secret of Ishmael's survival. And, so long as this veil cannot be lifted, we must restrain ourselves from concluding that his survival symbolizes the Resurrection. In other words, it still remains as an event that shows nothing more than a facet of the mysterious universe whose symbol is Moby Dick.

This essay began with reference to a phrase in the Book of Job, so it seems well to end with an allusion to the Bible. While Ishmael, cast away from his father Abraham, wanders with his mother Hager in the wilderness of Beersheba and is saved by God's well,[7] our Ishmael, having a disillusion at the Christian land, wanders with Ahab hunting Moby Dick in the heathen sea and is saved by such a coffin as reviewed now.

Notes

1. Moby Dick was first published in England on 18 October, 1851, and this edition did not include the Epilogue. On the other hand, the American edition published soon after it on 14 November, 1851, had the present form. Because of such a short interval between the both publications and because of Melville's careful preparation for Ishmael's survival, however, it is difficult to conceive of the Epilogue as an after-thought. "The omission of the Epilogue in the English edition remains unexplained." (Mansfield and Vincent, 831)
2. Job i, 15–17, 19.
3. Vincent, 390–391.
4. On this subject I learned much from R. E. Watters. His remarks on the

coffin are very suggestive. He turns our attention to "the very means of Ishmael's salvation," the coffin life-buoy. After he has enumerated the various images of 'coffin' he concludes as follows: "So, in its own way, the coffin-lifebuoy-treatise becomes one with the doublooon and the ship and the white whale—and they all symbolizes the universe, incorporating Nature's 'cunning alphabet whereby selecting and combining as he pleases, each man reads his own peculiar lesson according to his own peculiar mind and mood'." (86)

I cannot follow him, however, when he comments on Ishmael's survival as follows: "Ishmael was saved because he alone had learned anything from all their experiences, because he had, in effect, solved *his* problem, had triumphed over the symbolic white whale and the universe." (84-85) Perhaps I may be wrong, but I cannot think that Ishmael has solved his problem, even if it is "his own peculiar" problem; Ishmael's curiosity about the White Whale remains unsatsfied to the last.

5. On the problem of Queequeg's character I owe much to James Baird. In his elaborate study on primitivism, *Ishmael*, Baird points to the momentous function Queequeg plays in saving Ishmael. By Queequeg, he says, Ishmael was "taught wisdom, particularly the wisdom of selflessness and the wisdom of how to accept God, and of how to die." (229)

6. See the three harpooners in "The Candles" for example:

   Relieved against the ghostly light, the gigantic jet negro, Dagoo, loomed up to thrice his real stature, and seemed the black cloud from which the thunder had come. The parted mouth of Tashtego revealed his shark-white teeth, which strangely gleamed as if they too had been tipped by corpusants; while lit up by the preternatural light, Queequeg's tatooing burned like Satanic blue flames on his body. (415–416)

7. Genesis xxi, 9–21.

Works Cited

Baird, James. *Ishmael*. Baltimore : Johns Hopkins, 1956.

Mansfield, Luther S. and Howard P. Vincent. "Explanatory Notes," *Moby-Dick*. Ed. Luther S. Mansfield and Howard P. Vincent. New York: Hendricks House, 1952. 569–832.

Melville, Herman. *Moby-Dick*. Ed. Harrison Heyford and Hershel Parker. New York: Norton, 1967.

Vincent, Howard P. *The Trying-Out of* Moby-Dick. Boston: Houghton Mifflin, 1949.

Watters, R. E. "The Meanings of the White Whale," *Discussions of* Moby-Dick. Ed. Milton R. Stern. Boston: D. C. Heath, 1960. 77–86.

Pierre in Contrast to Ahab

Pierre was written immediately after the completion of *Moby-Dick*. Both Ahab and Pierre seem to be meant to be tragic heroes. But their aspects are quite different from each other. Where does the difference come from? This simple question has led me to an analysis of the structure of *Pierre* in relation to *Moby-Dick*. The scene of *Pierre* is American domestic life in contrast to the whales and sea of *Moby-Dick*; and while *Pierre* is narrated in a conventional form by an omniscient author, *Moby-Dick* is narrated by an actor-narrator, Ishmael, who recollects, organizes and tells his experience with the first-person narrator's immediacy.

Ishmael's narration is, as it were, a magician's wand. When touched with it, everything is turned into the magic channel through which the reader's attention is directed to the converging point, Moby Dick, the object of Ahab's hunt. Let me show, as an example, the description of the whale-line. First, the factual information is given: its material, size, length, weight, where it is stored, how it "folds the whole boat in its complicatd coils," and so forth. Then the description becomes metaphorical. Reminding us of the sudden perils the crew will be involved in when the harpoon, to which the line is attached, is darted, Ishmael tells us that they look like "Indian jugglers, with the deadliest snakes sportively festooning their limbs," and moreover, that they look like pulling "into the jaws of death, with a halter around every neck." (240) But when the line "silently serpentines about the oarsmen before being brought into actual play," its appearance is tame and peaceful. Yet, in this "graceful repose," Ishmael says, the most awful aspect of the line exists, just as the real terror of the storm exists in the calmness before it. And Ishmael warns:

> All men live enveloped in whale-lines. All are born with halters round their necks; but it is only when caught in the swift, sudden turn of death, that mortals realize the silent, subtle, ever-present perils of life. And if you be a philosopher, though seated in the whale-boat, you would not at heart feel one whit more of terror, than though seated before your evening fire with a poker, and not a harpoon, by your side. (241)

Now the whale-line, a common thing in the whale fishery, becomes a specimen of horror lurking in peaceful repose. And it is this line that catches Ahab round the neck by its fatal turn. Thus Ishmael's narration magnifies and enriches the symbolic meaning of Moby Dick and strengthens the plot of Ahab's hunt for the Whale.

　The case is different with *Pierre*. The narrator is not an actor but a critical bystander, and his attitude toward Pierre is ambivalent, half derisive and half sympathetic though, as the story draws near the end, the sympathy prevails over the derision. The story is Pierre's tragic pilgrimage for the Truth and it consists of two main plots arranged in sequence and one subplot. The first main plot shows

Pierre as a rescuer and it occupies the first two-thirds of the story. The second main plot dealing with Pierre as a writer occupies the remaining one-third. The subplot which runs parallel with the second main plot handles Lucy's rejoining Pierre in New York and it is introduced to wind up the story.

The story opens with the romantic world of Saddle Meadows where Pierre has been brought up. Though he loses his father when he is young, Pierre, handsome and healthy, now indulges in idylic happiness of love. He loves his mother and Lucy, his fiancée, and he is loved by them. The author suggests, however, that their happiness is too dream-like to be real and he covertly hints some ominous premonitions: the sad face which occasionally haunts Pierre's imagination, for instance. The premonition comes true by the sudden appearance of Isabel, allegedly his father's illegitimate daughter. His deceased father has been to Pierre the "personification of perfect human goodness and virtue," (79) and has been revered as a god in his heart. Because ascending the steps leading to God has only been possible when guided by the sacred image of his father, the shock he gets from his father's sin is all the more fatal. And as other evidences—the words, "My daughter!—God! God!—My daughter!" (82) from his dying father; his father's portrait resembling her face; and his aunt's tale about the portrait—seem to confirm Isabel's letter revealing her identity, the foundation upon which his whole morality has been based collapses and everything that has seemed to sanctify his existence becomes dubious. The author narrates:

> Then he staggered back upon himself, and only found support

in himself. Then Pierre felt that deep in him lurked a divine unidentifiableness, that owned no earthly kith or kin. (105)

Responding to that divinity though undefinable in his heart and believing it to be God's calling, Pierre recklessly decides to rescue Isabel disowning "a mortal parent" and spurning "all mortal bonds." (125)

Here the tragic figure of Pierre as a rescuer becomes clear but the author's critical eye upon him is too severe for the figure to develop into heroic size. Pierre is fundamentally characterized as an "infatuated young enthusiast." (212) Pointing out the profound mysteries surrounding Pierre's existence, the author emphasizes "oversights," "inconsistancies," "preposterousness" in Pierre's judgement by which he comes to his final resolution. Pierre is warned by the author:

> Ah, thou rash boy! are there no couriers in the air to warn thee away from these imperilings, and point thee to those Cretan labyrinths, to which thy life's cord is leading thee ?" (206)

Pierre is too obviously fated. Even before he reads Isabel's letter he has a dim feeling "that not always in our actions, are we our own factors," (58) and when the letter convinces him of her identity, the author invokes the "Three Weird Ones" for revealing the secret of his fated fortune:

> ...What threads were those, oh, ye Weird Ones, that ye wove in

II-3 Pierre in Contrast to Ahab

the years foregone; that now to Pierre, they so unerringly conduct electric presentiments, that his woe is woe, his father no more a saint, and Isabel a sister indeed ? (81)

And Pierre who has finally stood at the threshold of his career as a tragic hero is disparaged:

...now we behold this hapless youth all eager to involve himself in such an inextricable twist of Fate, that the three dextrous maids themselves could hardly disentangle him, if once he tie the complicating knots about him and Isabel. (206)

Moreover, the sacredness by which Pierre justifies his action toward Isabel cannot escape the author's critical eye. His suggestion that it is tainted with an element of erotic desire is all too clear. When Pierre casts his first glance at her face, the author says, the face "bewilderingly allured him, by its nameless beauty, and its long-suffering, hopeless anguish." (56) And the allurement of the face for him "did not so much appear to be embodied in the mournful person of the olive girl, as by some radiations from her, embodied in the vague conceits which agitated his own soul," (59) and already before Pierre went to meet her "he was assured that, in a transcendent degree, womanly beauty, and not womanly ugliness, invited him," (127) and though for him "Isabel wholly soared out of the realms of mortalness," (167) his erotic passion betrays itself when he holds her in his arms:

> ...he imprinted repeated burning kisses upon her; pressed hard her hand; would not let go her sweet and awful passiveness.
> 　Then they changed; they coiled together, and entangledly stood mute (226)

　Relentless as the author's analysis is, Isabel is fortunately spared it, which helps build up her mystery and it is this mystery that mainly advances the story in the plot of Pierre as a rescuer. Deceiving the world by sham marriage, Pierre and Isable leave Saddle Meadows for New York with another hapless girl, Delly. In the carriage on their way Pierre happens to read a pamphlet saying that God's virtue reversely corresponds to human virtue, that those who follow the way of God on the earth will eventually involve themselves "in strange, *unique* follies and sins," (250) and that "A virtuous expediency… seems the highest desirable or attainable earthly excellence" (252) for people. His suspicion that he has made a wrong choice becomes strong. Arriving in the city at night, they are coldly rebuffed by his cousin, Glen, whose welcome he has expected, and the police station, the only shelter they can take from a midnight street, is filled with prostitutes and drunkards. With a help of his old friend, Charlie, Pierre settles in an apartment house with the two girls and a few days later his incestuous relationship with Isabel is consummated. And simultaneously Isabe1's mysterious allurement, which has forced him to follow his way of God, disappears and she finally turns out to be a common jealous girl. As a result the plot of Pierre as a rescuer, deprived of the impetus, becomes too weak to carry the story except by giving a few pieces of information. For instance, a letter comes from Saddle Meadows reporting the death of Pierre's mother, Pierre's disinheritance and Glen's new inheritance of Saddle Meadows, and Lucy's new engagement with Glen.

Having turned his back upon the world, Pierre has sought God's way in rescuing Isable and has been disillusioned again. In the process, however, he seems to have found the truth about reality. This consciousness gives shape to the new plot of Pierre as a writer, which gradually replaces the weakening old plot. To earn a living in New York Pierre begins to write a novel but the milieu surrounding him is not favorable for him because he has decided, contrary to the expectation of the publishers, to write a truth-telling novel instead of a romantic novel. In addition, telling the truth is not so easy a task as young Pierre imagines. The author criticizes Pierre's attempt as immature and sophomoric. To know the truth, the author says, Pierre has to explore "the soul of a man" which is as "appallingly vacant as vast." Pierre's fond optimism is severely criticized:

> …because Pierre began to see through the first superficiality of the world, he fondly weens he has come to the unlayered substance. But, far as any geologist has yet gone down into the world, it is found to consist of nothing but surface stratified on surface. To its axis, the world being nothing but superinduced superfices. (335)

In due time Pierre willy-nilly has to realize "the everlasting elusiveness of Truth" (399) and he has to see that "Silence is the only Voice of our God." (239) He feels that his Titanic thews have been cut by "the scissors of Fate" and he feels himself to be "a moose, hamstrung." (398) He knows he is drowning in the sea but the knowledge is no use for him because "the sea is the sea, and these drowning men do drown." (357) Having been lost in a tantalizing maze and having been driven to the cul-de-sac, Pierre's heroic soul has now been smothered and for that smoldering soul there is no exit to flare up but in a dream:

> ...no longer petrified in all their ignominious attitudes, the herded Titans now sprung to their feet; flung themselves up the slope; and anew battered at the precipice's unresounding wall. Foremost among them all, he saw a moss-turbaned, armless giant, who despairing of any other mode of wreaking his immitigable hate, turned his vast trunk into a battering-ram, and hurled his own arched-out ribs again and yet again against the invulnerable steep. (407)

That armless giant is Enceladus and Pierre sees in him "his own duplicate face." (407)

Pierre's action becomes so solipsistic and lacking social extension and, in terms of plot, so narrow and weak that another plot must be introduced to wind up the story. Lucy, having recovered from the mental disorder caused by Pierre's 'marriage', decides to help Pierre and giving him advance notice in a letter comes to live in his apartment. This newly introduced plot, which runs parallel with the main plot as mentioned above is carried by the conventional technique of a romance. The theme is an anticlimax, a repetition of the plot of Pierre as a rescuer. Lucy sees her way of God in Pierre

II-3 Pierre in Contrast to Ahab

and gets disillusioned just as Pierre does with Isabel. Involved with the incidents accompanying her action, Pierre commits murder and is taken to prison. Lucy and Isabel visit him in the prison and Lucy, believing lsabel's confession that she is his sister, dies from the shock; while Pierre and Isabel commit suicide by taking poison.

The above analysis will show that *Pierre*, too as *Moby-Dick*, has two strings of narration: one is to represent the hero's action and the other is to give commentary on it. In contrast to *Moby-Dick*, however, the narrator often frustrates the hero's action. The author is sometimes so critical of Pierre and sometimes so sympathetic that we have the impression that he is creating him as a caricature of the tragic hero on the one hand and as a genuine tragic hero on the other. The author himself seems to have anticipated some incoherence in Pierre's characterization while writing the story. We have the following paragraph in *Pierre*:

> Easy for me to slyly hide these things [the author's information about Pierre's psychology], and always put him before the eye as perfect as immaculate; unsusceptible to the inevitable nature and the lot of common men. I am more frank with Pierre than the best men are with themselves. I am all unguarded and magnanimous with Pierre; therefore you see his weakness, and therefore only. In reserves men build imposing characters ; not in revelations. He who shall be wholly honest, though nobler than Ethan Allen; that man shall stand in danger of the meanest mortal's scorn. (127)

The above quotation reminds me of how reservingly Ahab is characterized. The information about him is very sparingly given:

first, Captain Peleg's mention (69; 76–7); then some foreboding in Ishmael's mind (77); and Elijah's ominous prophecy (86–8; 91); finally the long delayed appearance of Ahab on the quarter deck (109) with the mystery veiling him to the last. This well-controlled technique of premonition, delay and realization produces the heroic figure of Ahab. But it can only be achieved by repressing the impulse to reveal the truth. Melville must have been conscious of it not only when he wrote *Pierre* but also when he was writing *Moby-Dick*. Melville's famous essay, "Hawthorne and his Mosses," was written in the summer of 1850 when *Moby-Dick* was in progress. It is not so much a critical article about Hawthorne's short stories as the confession of his own view of literature. In this essay Melville questions the world's view of the value of Shakespeare, saying that it does not lie in being a mere dramatist but in being "the profoundest of thinkers":

> ...it is those deep far-away things in him; those occasional flashings forth of the intuitive Truth in him ; those short, quick probings at the very axis of reality:—these are the things that make Shakespeare, Shakespeare. Through the mouths of the dark characters…he craftily says, or sometimes insinuates the things, which we feel to be so terrifically true, that it were all but madness…to utter, or even hint of them…. And few of his endless commentators and critics seem to have remembered, or even perceived, that the immediate products of a great mind are not so great, as that undeveloped, (and sometimes undevelopable) yet dimly-discernible greatness, to which these immediate products are but the infallible indices. In Shakespeare's tomb lies infinitely more than Shakespeare ever wrote.[1]

II-3 Pierre in Contrast to Ahab

This quotation reflects not only Melville's unrepressible desire to tell the truth he thinks he has grasped but also the insurmountable difficulty he finds in telling it. It is true that this difficulty was caused partly by pecuniary concerns[2] and partly by the inhibition he would have felt imposed by society, but it can safely be inferred that it was mainly caused by the nature of the truth, the nature of Melville's perception of reality itself.

Man usually lives in the conventional structure of reality and the reality he experiences is usually interpreted by culturally defined symbols. But Melville was too religiously skeptical to be comfortable in the system of meanings defined by the established culture, which seemed to him fundamentally incompatible with his experience of reality. This skepticism, as T. Walter Herbert, Jr. points out, had a deep relation with the religious conflict his young mind absorbed from "the opposing theories of Unitarianism" and Calvinism "during the early nineteenth century" in America.[3] And when Melville visited Hawthorne at Liverpool on his journey to Israel in 1856, Hawthorne gave in his journal the following observation about his religious attitude:

> Melville, as he always does, began to reason of Providence and futurity, and of everything that lies beyond human ken, and informed me that he had "pretty much made up his mind to be annihilated;" but still he does not seem to rest in that anticipation; and I think, will never rest until he gets hold of a definite belief. It is strange how he persisits—and has persisted ever since I knew him, and probably

long before.... He can neither believe, nor be comfortable in his unbelief; and he is too honest and courageous not to try to do one or the other.[4]

Melville was forced to explore "the ultimate structure of reality"[5] upon which his interpretation of experiences was to be based. But the deeper he explored, the more he seems to have been convinced of "the everlasting elusiveness of Truth" as is Pierre. And dispossessed of the frame of reference Melville must have been exposed to the chaos of reality and he must have felt his existence being threatened by its inscrutableness just as Ahab finds himself being threatened by the inscrutable wall of Moby Dick "shoved near to" (144) him.

Despite the fact that Melville had to acknowledge the disordered reality and because he had to acknowledge it, he had to try the harder to seek for a definite order in it. From this paradoxical situation, I suppose, was born his tragic vision of a human being as a quester fated to grasp an ungraspable object. If a quester of this kind is to attain his greatness, the ungraspable object has to keep the illusion of being graspable. Melville solved this problem by transforming the inscrutable reality into a tangible and assailable form of the Whale. In other words, he was able to create the heroic figure of Ahab by transforming the reality into a fictional form. But to achieve this artistic success he had to repress his impulse of telling the truth and had to follow carefully the rule the fiction demanded.

When he was writing *Pierre* he was more ambitious and reckless to tell the truth of reality:

> Save me from being bound to Truth, liege lord, as I am now. How shall I steal yet further into Pierre, and show how this heavenly fire was helped to be contained in him, by mere contingent things, and things that he knew not. But I shall follow the endless, winding way—the flowing river in the cave of man; careless whither I be led, reckless where I land. (126)

But it was to introduce the disorder of reality from outside into a fiction which should have its own order if it was to have coherence in its meaning, and further it was to divest 'the ungraspable object' of 'the illusion of being graspable.'

As is shown in Melville's referring to *Pierre* as "a rural bowl of milk"[6] in his letter to Sophia Hawthorne on January 8, 1852, when he had just started to write the novel, he evidently began it as "a regular romance."[7] But "the complex web of life" was, apparently to Melville, woven with "the more thin than gossamer threads" which were impossible "to unravel, and spread out, and classify." (166) Melville's perception of reality was too profound and amorphous to be shaped into a well-made romance. Besides he was too true to reality to circumscribe and modify it so that it could be accommodated to a coherent structure of fiction. This preoccupation with telling the truth of reality resulted in producing the frustrated hero of *Pierre* by bringing disruption into the structure of the novel.

Notes
1. Melville, "Hawthorne and His Mosses," *Moby-Dick*. 541–42.
2. In June, 1851, Melville wrote to Howthorne: "What I feel most moved to write, that is banned—it will not pay." *Letters*, 128.
3. Herbert, *Moby-Dick and Calvinism*. 5–6.
4. Leyda, *The Melville Log*. 529.
5. Herbert, 6.
6. *Letters*, 146.
7. In his letter to Richard Bentley on April 6, 1852, Melville tries to improve the terms of publication of *Pierre* and says that *Pierre* is "…a regular romance, with a mysterious plot to it, & stirring passions at work, and withall [*Sic*], representing a new & elevated aspect of American life…." *Letters*, 150.

Works Cited

Herbert, T. Walter, Jr. *Moby-Dick and Calvinism*. New Brunswick, N. J.: Rutgers UP, 1977.

Leyda, Jay. *The Melville Log*. New York: Harcourt, Brace and Co., 1951.

Melville, Herman. *The Letters of Herman Melville*. Ed. Merrell R. Davis and William H. Gilman. New Haven: Yale UP, 1960.

——— *Moby-Dick*. Ed. Harrison Hayford and Hershel Parker. New York: Norton, 1967.

——— *Pierre*. Ed. Henry A. Murray. New York: Hendricks House, 1957.

"Benito Cereno" における恐怖

　"Benito Cereno" は Melville の作品の中でも特に毀誉褒貶の激しい作品であるが、Newton Arvin は次の如く非難している。

> ...and nothing is more expressive of the low pitch at which "Benito" is written than the fact that with one incident in his original Melville takes no liberties whatever: the scene of the actual mutiny on the *San Dominick*, which might have been transformed into an episode of great and frightful power, Melville was too tired to rewrite at all, and except for a few trifling details, he leaves it all as he found it, in the drearily prosaic prose of a judicial deposition.[1]

成程、San Dominick 号上の黒人暴動の場面が即物的な裁判記録としてではなく、リアルに活写されておれば、此の作品は確かに迫力あるドラマに変貌したことであろう。しかし、"Benito Cereno" とは全く異った作品に変質したであろうことも確かである。そして素直に此の作品を読んでゆくとき、吾々はそこに描れているものが暴動の事実ではなく、実は暴動と云う事件によってひき起された恐怖であることに気付くのである。先づその恐怖が如何に見事に表現されているかを跡づけ、次にその恐怖の対象についてのいくらかの考察を試みてみたい。

I

　初めに黒人暴動事件のあらましを述べておく。スペイン商船 San Dominick 号の船長 Don Benito は友人 Don Alexandro の所有する黒人奴隷多数を載せ、チリーのヴァルパライソからペルーのカヤオへ向う。途中黒人の暴動が起り、Don Alexandro を始めとする白人の大半が殺害され、船は黒人に占有される。暴動の首謀者 Babo は Benito 船長を強迫し黒人の国セネガルへ向う様に命じる。逃れる機会を摑み度いと思う Don Benito は水の補給と云う名目で——事実水も糧食も極度に不足している——チリー沖の孤島サンタ・マリヤ島を目指して船を進める。しかし、凪と暑気と水不足に悩まされ航海は困難を極める。思いもよらない多数の日程を費したあと、ようやく或る明け方サンタ・マリヤ島沖にたどり着き、そこでアメリカ船 Bachelor's Delight 号に出会う。暴動の発覚を恐れる Babo は実に巧妙な隠ぺい工作を行い、更にアメリカ船の奪取をも画策する。そこへアメリカ船の船長 Delano が訪れ San Dominick 号の荒廃ぶりに驚く。彼は早速水や食糧補給の手配を行い、自ら水先案内の役を務める。しかし風と潮流の具合が悪く、湾内にうまく停泊させることが出来るのは既に夕方のことである。Delano 船長は早朝から薄暮までほぼ 12 時間近く San Dominick 船上に滞在することになるが、暴動の事実を発見することが出来ない。事件を知るのは Don Benito が、San Dominick 号を離れんとする Delano のボートに飛び移る時である。Delano 船長はただちに迅速果敢なる指揮を行い、黒人暴動を制圧する。黒人達はリマに護送され、裁判を受け、処刑される。此の様にして事件は解決する。しかし、此の事件によって Don Benito の心に生じた傷は遂に癒ゆることなく、三ヶ月後リマ郊外の修道院で死ぬ。

以上の事件から「恐怖」を描き出してゆくため Melville は、作者の視点とは別に、もうひとつの視点を用意する。Delano 船長の視点である。そしてトップ・シーンから Delano 船長が San Dominick 号を離れるまでの作品の主要部は主として此の視点から語られる。

II

作品は San Dominick 号がサンタ・マリア島沖に姿を現わす場面で幕を開く。そして吾々は Delano 船長の視点から怪しげな船 San Dominick 号へ近づいてゆく。朝靄が立ち込め全てが灰色にいろどられたその朝の異様な雰囲気を作者は次の様に描写する。

> The morning was one peculiar to that coast. Everything was mute and calm; everything gray. The sea, though undulated into long roods of swells, seemed fixed, and was sleeked at the surface like waved lead that has cooled and set in the smelter's mould. The sky seemed a gray surtout. Flights of troubled gray fowl, kith and kin with flights of troubled gray vapours among which they were mixed, skimmed low and fitfully over the waters, as swallows over meadows before storms. Shadows present, foreshadowing deeper shadows to come. (46)

次第に輪郭を明らかにしてくる白い船影には船籍を示す旗もなく、その航法も、湾内へ入ろうとしているのか沖へ出ようとしているのか、実に不確かである。そして、Delano 船長の捕鯨用ボートが更に近づくにつれ次の様な相貌を露わす。

ないと思われ、安堵へと変わる。しかし恐怖は又直ぐにぶり返す。此の様にしてDelanoの心は「不安」―「恐怖」―「安堵」のリズムを繰り返すことになる。この繰り返しはDelano船長がSan Dominik号を離れるまで続く。彼の不安を的確に描写している文として次の例を挙げておく。

> Trying to break one charm, he was but becharmed anew. Though upon the wide sea, he seemed in some far inland country; prisoner in some deserted château, left to stare at empty grounds, and peer out at vague roads, where never wagon or wayfarer passed. (74)

　吾々がSan Dominick号を見るのは此の様な「不安」―「恐怖」―「安堵」のリズムを通してである。San Dominick号には「何か恐るべきもの」がひそんでいると云う読者の不安は益々高まらざるを得ない。そしてこの不安と緊張がほぼその極点にまで高められたとき、不安の正体である黒人叛乱の事実が明るみに出され、舞台は急転直下暴徒制圧の場面へと移行する。[3] そしてその場面の直後に作者はDon Benitoの法廷における供述書を挿入し、ここで読者はSan Dominick号事件の全貌を知らされることになる。[4]

　黒人叛乱の事実を知るとき、Delano船長は最早や不安におののく人ではなく、勇敢な行動の人である。彼の恐怖は覆われた「事実」に対するものであり、「事実」を覆うベールがはぎ取られ「事実」が明るみに出されれば跡形もなく消え失せるような性質のものである。ところがここで吾々は事件が解決したあとも依然として恐怖におののき遂にはその恐怖のために死んでゆく人物Don Benitoを見出す。Don Benitoの恐怖は何か？

III

　これまで吾々は Delano 船長の視点から San Dominick 号を見てきた。事実、その様な見方を強制される仕組みになっている。しかし作者は決して Delano 船長の見方を全面的に肯定している訳ではない。むしろ否定的なのである。此の作品は、別の観点からみれば、Delano 船長のような人物には「如何にものが見えないか」と云うことが暴露される物語であるとも云える。ここで Delano 船長に関する次のような作者の意見が想起される。

> …Captain Delano's surprise might have deepened into some uneasiness had he not been a person of a singularly undistrustful good nature, not liable, except on extraordinary and repeated incentives, and hardly then, to indulge in personal alarms, any way involving the imputation of malign evil in man. Whether, in view of what humanity is capable, such a trait implies, along with a benevolent heart, *more than ordinary quickness and accuracy of intellectual perception*, may be left to the wise to determine. (47)

そして「人並ならぬ知的感受性」の持主として、Don Benito の像が浮び上ってくる。人並ならぬ知的感受性の持主であるが故に人並ならぬ恐怖にとらえられるのである。だがその恐怖の実体はと問われるとき吾々は途方に暮れざるを得ない。San Dominick 号事件に対する Don Benito の心の反応が殆ど説明されていないからである。ただいくらかの手掛りを与えてくれるものに、黒人をリマへ護送する San Dominick 号上で交される Delano 船長と Don Benito との次の様な対話がある。

"You generalize, Don Benito; and mournfully enough. But the past is passed; why moralize upon it? Forget it. See, yon bright sun has forgotten it all, and the blue sea, and the blue sky; these have turned over new leaves."

"Because they have no memory," he dejectedly replied; "because they are not human."

"But these mild trades that now fan your cheek, do they not come with a human-like healing to you? Warm friends, steadfast friends are the trades."

"With their steadfastness they but waft me to my tomb, señor," was the foreboding response.

"You are saved," cried Captain Delano, more and more astonished and pained; "you are saved; what has cast such a shadow upon you?"

"The negro."

There was silence, while the moody man sat, slowly and unconsciously gathering his mantle about him, as if it were a pall. (116)

救い出されてからもなお此の様な暗い影を与えるものは何かと問われて、唯一言 'the negro' と答え、まるで棺衣をまとうかの様にゆっくりと外套に身をつつむ Don Benito の姿。それは 'the negro' の与える恐怖感に捉えられて生命力を失ってゆく Don Benito の象徴的な姿と云えよう。

'the negro' とは勿論叛乱の首謀者 Babo のことである。Babo は年齢約 30 歳の小柄なセネガル出身の黒人であるが、その悪魔的な頭脳の働きには Iago を思わせるものがある。そして事実彼の所業には悪魔的としか形容しようのない残酷さがある。しかし、全体として見た場合、彼の行為が自由を求める奴隷の戦いであることは否定出来ない。[5] そして悪魔的と思える個々の所業も此のような戦いでは止

むを得ないものと見なすべきであろう。では Don Benito は此のような黒人奴隷の解放運動におののいているのであろうか？ だがこのような事実関係からのみ Babo の叛乱を解釈しようとすれば吾々には次の様な結論が得られるだけである。

> ...the tale ["Benito Cereno"] seems a plummet-like drop from the unconditionally democratic peaks of *White-Jacket* and *Moby-Dick*—an "artistic sublimation" not, as Schiffman maintains, of anti-slaveryism, but rather of notions of black primitivism dear to the hearts of slavery's apologists....[6]

Babo が 'black primitivism' の形象化であることは確かであろう。しかし Melville における 'black primitivism' の意味は決して 'slavery's apologists' の云う意味と同質なものではない。"Benito Cereno" における黒人を世間的現実における黒人と直結させるには作品の詩的密度は余りにも高いのである。

作者は作品の結末において Babo を次の如く描写している。

> Some months after, dragged to the gibbet at the tail of a mule, the black met his voiceless end. The body was burned to ashes; but for many days, the head, that hive of subtlety, fixed on a pole in the Plaza, met, unabashed, the gaze of the whites; and across the Plaza looked towards St. Bartholomew's church, in whose vaults slept then, as now, the recovered bones of Aranda; and across the Rimac bridge looked towards the monastery, on Mount Agonia without; where, three months after being dismissed by the court, Benito Cereno, borne on the bier, did, indeed, follow his leader. (116–117)

Babo の持つこの異様な神秘的な力は何か？ この異様な力こそ Don Benito を恐怖させるものではないだろうか？ この疑問を解くには吾々は更に Melville 文学における「黒人」の意味を問わなければならない。

　San Dominick 号上で不安におびえる Delano 船長が嬰児に乳をふくませている黒人の母親を見て次の様に考え、ほっと安堵する場面がある。

> There's naked nature, now; pure tendernness and love.... (73)

此の考えが如何に見当違いであるかは黒人の女達が実は男達以上に残忍であったことによって明らかとなるが、この一例からも推察出来る如く Melville の作品では黒人は——文明社会にはいり込んでしまっている黒人コックや黒人給仕等を除けば——'uncivilized nature' の象徴として描かれる。その典型的な例は *Moby-Dick* の Dagoo であろう。彼は次の如く描写されている。

> ... a gigantic, coal-black negro-savage, with a lion-like tread—an Ahasuerus to behold.... Dagoo retained all his barbaric virtues, and erect as a giraffe, moved about the decks in all the pomp of six feet five in his socks. There was a corporeal humility in looking up at him; and a white man standing before him seemed a white flag come to beg truce of a fortress. (107–108)

ここで注目すべき事は、Dagoo は畏怖の対象ではあっても決して恐怖の対象ではないと云うことである。*Moby-Dick* では畏怖の対象であった黒人のイメィジが何故恐怖の対象に転化したのか？ 云い換

えるならば処女作 Typee 以来 Melville の作品に流れている原始的なものに対する「憧れ」が何故 "Benito Cereno" に至って「恐怖」とならねばならなかったのか？ ここに黒人 Babo の意味を解く鍵がひそんでいるように思われる。Melville が "Benito Cereno" を含む一連の短篇小説を雑誌に連載し始める直ぐ前の作品である Moby-Dick 及び Pierre を中心として此の問題を考えて見よう。

IV

　Melville はよく「悪」を描く作家と云われる。あたかも「悪」を弾劾する正義漢であるかの如く語られることさえある。だがそのような正義漢 Melville が見られるのは Redburn と White-Jacket ぐらいではないだろうか？ 他の作品に現れた作者の魂はむしろ善悪判断の基準喪失に悩み、その基準を求めてあがいていると云えよう。云い換えれば善悪の根本原理としての神が求められていると云えよう。Ahab に次のような言葉がある。

　　I like a good grip; I like to feel something in this slippery world that can hold, man. (390)

　白鯨の遊弋する世界、それは異様な生命力をみなぎらせる世界であるが、それは又同時に善悪のけじめが失われた「すべすべとする世界」である。そして白鯨はそのような世界の象徴である。だが白鯨と云う壁を打ち破ればそこから「何か意味あるもの」が姿を現わすに違いない。白鯨の彼方にこそはこのすべすべとする世界のなかで己れをぐっと摑まえてくれるもの——神——が存在する筈だ。此の考

えが妄執となって Ahab は白鯨を追跡する。しかし　この狂的追跡も徒労に終り神は遂に姿を現わさない。Melville はこの様な作品を執筆しながら、つまり Ahab と白鯨と云うイメィジで神の問題を考えながら次第に神の不在と云う不安を強めていったのではないだろうか？

此の不安がより一層はっきりとした形で現われるのが Pierre である。此の作品で作者は神を求める者に対して次のような警告を与えている。

> ...we learn that it is not for man to follow the trail of truth too far, since by so doing he entirely loses the directing compass of his mind; for arrived at the Pole, to whose barrenness only it points, there, the needle indifferently respects all points of the horizon alike. (194)

そして主人公 Pierre が最後に到達するのは善悪の根本原理は「無」であると云う結論である。

> ...a nothing is the substance, it casts one shadow one way, and another the other way; and these two shadows cast from one nothing; these, seems to me, are Virtue and Vice. (322)

神の證しが得られないとき Melville を取り巻く世界は人間の追跡を拒絶する白鯨によって象徴される世界となる。それは測り知ることの出来ない力に支配される世界である。云い換えれば、神に支配されざる 'nature' の世界であり、神を拠り所とする人間には全く得体の知れないものである。そしてその「得体の知れないもの」は吾々の「外」にあるばかりではなく、吾々の「内」にもある。(Pierre で

は心の内奥が探られ、Melville はその正体が不可解なものであることを発見する。）此の様に「内」も「外」も何か得体の知れないものに支配されていると感じるとき、吾々は無限の恐怖を覚えるのではないだろうか？　そして此の様な恐怖の対象の 'artistic sublimation' が Babo ではないだろうか？

　ここで冒頭の場面から作品のイメィジを整理してみよう。不安をはらんだ灰一色のなかに怪しい船が現われる。次第にその輪郭が定まるとき、それは風雨に漂白された修道院のようであり、舷檣に垣間みる黒い人影は黒衣の修道僧のようである。そして更に近づくとき，吾々が既に見たような San Dominick 号が姿を現わす。不思議なことに船首像は覆われている。だが実はそこには Babo によって殺され、Babo によって白骨とされた Don Alexandro の白骨像がアメリカ大陸の発見者 Columbus の像——それは白人にとっては希望の象徴と云えよう——に代る新しい船首像として飾られているのである。そしてこの白骨の船首像の下には 'Follow your leader' と白く描かれている。これは命令に従わない場合、白人は全て Don Alexandro と同じ運命をたどると云う Babo の警告である。そして作品の結末は "Benito Cereno, borne on the bier, did, indeed, follow his leader." (117) となるのである。此の様なイメィジのなかに、今や神を拠り所として生きる人間にとっては無限の恐怖の対象となった 'nature' の前に没落してゆくキリスト教文明の姿を見ることはさほど難しいことではないように思われる。

注
1.　Arvin, 239.

2. 引用文中の斜字体は，作品名と船名を除き，すべて筆者の手による。
3. 此のサスペンスの盛り上げ方は *Moby-Dick* の手法によく似ている。つまりかの膨大なる作品の大部分は白鯨に対する畏怖の念を高めるために費され、白鯨はその最後の三章に至って始めて姿を現わすのである。
4. 法廷における Don Benito の供述書は Newton Arvin も指摘する如く、底本である Amasa Delano の『世界周航記』所載の供述書を殆どそのままに写したもので、そこに Don Benito の視点を認めることは難しい。Delano, 87–95.
5. 当時農場においてばかりではなく海上においても黒人奴隷の暴動は頻発し、このような暴動は自由を求める戦いとして奴隷制度廃止論者の強い支持を受けた。更に、Melville が捕鯨船 Acushnet 号に乗り込んで南海へ向った 1841 年には黒人奴隷の暴動に関して「奴隷として故郷から連れ去られる黒人達が自由を求めて立ち上る時、彼等は自由を彼等から奪わんとする何人をも殺す権利を持つ。」と云う画期的な最高裁判所の見解が示されている。以上は Sidney Kaplan に拠る。詳しくは次の論文を参照されたい。Kaplan, 167–78.
6. Kaplan, 177.

引用文献

Arvin, Newton. *Herman Melville*. New York: Viking, 1963.
Delano, Amasa. "A Narrative of Voyages and Travels…Round the World." *Melville's Benito Cereno*. Ed. John P. Runden. Boston: D.C. Heath, 1965. 87–95.
Kaplan, Sidney. "*Benito Cereno*: An Apology for Slavery?" *Melville's Benito Cereno*. Ed. John P. Runden. Boston: D.C. Heath, 1965. 167–178.
Melville, Herman. "Benito Cereno." *Piazza Tales*. Ed. Harrison Hayford, Alma A. MacDougall, G. Thomas Tanselle and Others. Evanston and Chicago: Northwestern UP / Newberry Library, 1987. 46–117.
———. *Moby-Dick*. Ed. Harrison Hayford and Hershel Parker. New York:

Norton, 1967.
———. *Pierre*. Ed. Henry A. Murray. New York: Hendricks House, 1957.

Ⅲ　ポストモダン管見

エドワード・オールビー
——幻想の破壊と生の再生——

I

　エドワード・オールビー（Edward Albee）は 1928 年 3 月 12 日首都ワシントンで生まれた。[1] 生後二か月の時孤児院から引き取られ、リード・オールビー夫妻の養子となった。祖父の名を取りエドワード・フランクリン・オールビーと名付けられた。祖父は全米各地に寄席演芸のチェーン劇場を持つキース＝オールビーの共同経営者の一人であった。オールビーはニューヨーク州ウエスト・チェスターの大邸宅で何不自由なく育てられた。父リードと母フランシスとの間には、その後のオールビー劇に登場する父と母との関係に似たものがあったらしい。オールビーは祖母に溺愛された。

　恵まれた家庭環境にもかかわらず、オールビーは気むずかしい少年に育ち、学校嫌いであった。初等学校の課程を修了すると、ニュージャージー州の名門校ローレンスヴィルへ進学したが、出席不良のため退学となり、母の希望で転入した軍隊式訓練を特色とする高校でも同様な結果となった。結局、コネティカット州のチョート校を卒業し、ハートフォードのトリニティ・カレッジに入学するが、そこでも文学や演劇以外には身が入らず、一年半で退学した。

　幼い頃からブロードウェイでの観劇に親しみ、また劇場関係者の出入りが多かった家庭環境のせいもあってか、オールビーは文芸活

動では早熟であった。6歳の頃から詩を創り、12歳で三幕ものの笑劇を書き、15歳から17歳にかけて二編の小説を書いた。更にチョート時代には学校の文芸誌に一幕もののメロドラマを載せ、大学時代にはマックスウェル・アンダーソンの『王たちの仮面』（The Masque of Kings）のフランツ・ヨーゼフ皇帝役で舞台に立った。またオールビーは音楽にも関心が強く、11歳から12歳の頃は作曲家になることを夢みた。[2]

　トリニティ・カレッジを退学したオールビーは両親の家に帰り、そこから一年余り音楽番組のシナリオ・ライターとしてマンハッタンの放送局に通ったが、1950年、創作に専念するために独立を決意し、家を出た。グリニッチ・ヴィレッジでのアパート暮らしが始まった。その前年祖母がオールビーを受取人として預けた10万ドルの信託預金から、週50ドルを受取ることができ、これが生活の支えとなった。不足分はさまざまな仕事で補った。広告会社、レコード店、本屋、食堂等で働き、またウェスタン・ユニオンの電報配達員として街を歩き廻った。このグリニッチ・ヴィレッジでの九年間は、『動物園物語』（The Zoo Story, 1959）のジェリーを思わせるみじめな生活であったとオールビー自身は語っているが、実情は大分違っていたらしい。友人のウィリアム・フラナガン（William Flanagan）によれば、かなり快適なアパート暮らしであったようだ。

　オールビーは最初は詩作に専念したが、1953年ソーントン・ワイルダーに会って戯曲を書くことを勧められ、劇作に転向した。当時の演劇を志すアメリカの青年たちに衝撃的影響を与えたのが、ヨーロッパの不条理演劇であった。オールビーはその頃に特に影響を受けた劇作家として、ジャン・ジュネ（Jean Genet）、サミュエル・ベケット（Samuel Beckett）、ウジェーヌ・イヨネスコ（Eugène Ionesco）、ベルトルト・ブレヒト（Bertolt Brecht）等の名を挙げている。[3] 一

方、当時のオールビーに詳しいフラナガンはオールビーがテネシー・ウィリアムズに心酔していたことを述べている。

　芸術家仲間と語り明かすヴィレッジでの生活は刺激に富むものではあったが、オールビーにとって創作に適した環境ではなかった。[4] 長い歳月の間、何ひとつまとまったものが書けないオールビーは、しだいに絶望感を深めていったと考えられる。そのような心境を一人の青年に託し、一気に一幕ものの戯曲を書き上げた。30歳の誕生日を迎えた1958年のことで、題名は『動物園物語』であった。『動物園物語』は、当初アメリカ国内では上演の引き受け手がなく、翌年9月28日、ベルリンで初演された。ベケットの『クラップの最後のテープ』（*Krapp's Last Tape*）と二本立で上演された初演は絶讃を博し、その後ドイツ国内では12の都市で上演された。1960年1月14日、プロヴィンスタウン劇場がアメリカでの初演を行ない、オールビーは一躍オフ・ブロードウェイの寵児となった。

II

　『動物園物語』の舞台はセントラル・パークの日曜日の昼下がり。幕が開くと中年の紳士がベンチに腰をおろして本を読んでいる。いかにも裕福そうなピーターである。そこへ疲れ切った感じの青年が現われ、声を掛ける。絶望と孤独にあえぐジェリーである。二人の対話は、対話と言うよりは、ジェリーの一人芝居の形で進行する。ピーターは嫌悪を覚え、対話を避けようとするが、ジェリーはそれを巧みに引き止める。ジェリーはまずピーターから家庭の事情を聞き出し、それが幸福という名の幻想にすぎないことをあばく。次に自分の身の上や身の廻りの悲惨な現実を訴える。更に、孤独な人間

が孤独からの脱却をいかに激しく求めるものであるかを、犬との「対話」を例として語る。ジェリーの住むアパートの管理人が犬を飼っている。犬はジェリーを攻撃する。ジェリーは犬にハンバーガーを与え、懐柔をはかる。犬の攻撃はやまない。ジェリーは犬の毒殺をはかる。犬は危く一命をとりとめる。犬の攻撃はやむ。犬とジェリーとの間には一種の対話が成立する。この語りの迫真性にピーターは動揺し、立ち去りかける。ジェリーはそれを引き止め、次には言語的手段に代えて、物理的手段の「対話」を試みる。ピーターと並んでベンチに腰をおろし、まずくすぐる。次に力ずくでピーターをベンチから押しのけようとする。ついにピーターも怒る。ベンチをめぐる二人の争いが始まる。「対話」の手段はますます暴力的になる。最後に、ジェリーが投げ与えたナイフを拾って身構えるピーターに向かってジェリーは突進し、みずからナイフに突き刺されて死ぬ。一方事の意外な結末に驚いて走り去るピーターにとって、日曜日の公園のベンチに象徴される幸福は永久に消える。

　ジェリーはピーターとの「対話」を求めた。半ば自嘲的ではあれ、ピーター（＝ペテロ）を諭すキリストに自己を見立てるジェリー[5]にとって、その目的は単に自らの孤独からの救いにあるのではなく、ピーターを覚醒させることにあった。そして、今やジェリーは自らの生命を犠牲として、ピーターとの「対話」を完全なものとし、ピーターの目を覚まさせることができた。少なくともジェリーにはそう思われたに違いない。死に臨むジェリーには、時折激痛に表情をゆがめながらも、安らぎと微笑がある。更に、死に瀕しながらも、ナイフの柄からピーターの指紋を拭きとり、証拠となる恐れのある本を忘れないようにと注意をする。このような思いやりさえ示すジェリーの安らぎは、死を賭して目的を達成したという満足感から生まれている。

しかし、この安らぎも真の安らぎではなく、単なる自己満足に由来するものではないかという疑問が観客には起きる。ジェリーの死は、ほんとうに死に値するのか。「対話」の成就は結局何をもたらしたのか。ピーターの覚醒には一体どのような意味があるのか。人間と人間との結びつきが死を媒介としてしか存在しえないものとすれば、そのような現実に直面するピーターにどのような未来があるのか。このような疑問が起きてくる。結局ジェリーの死は無駄死にすぎなかったのではないか。そのことが意識をかすめるのか、ジェリーの最後の言葉となる「ああ、神よ」は、ピーターが驚きと悲しみの感嘆詞として繰り返す「ああ、神よ」をまねるあざけりとも祈りともとれる口調で言われる。

このように結末部ではあいまいさが見られるが、ナイフに向かって突進するまでのジェリーの行動には、いささかのためらいも見られない。「対話」は成就されなければならないのである。ピーターの幻想は破壊されなければならないのである。そして、この劇の面白さはその幻想破壊の過程のスピードと激しさにある。ピーターのみならず、観客もジェリーのすさまじいエネルギーに圧倒されるのである。

以上で明らかなように、既にこの第一作において、我々はオールビーの最も基本的な主題を明確に見ることができる。幻想は、その結果の如何を問わず、破壊されなければならないという主題である。そして、その問題点についても読み取ることができる。すなわち、「幻想破壊」が、破壊されなければならないという倫理的命題として主張されることである。言いかえれば、幻想破壊の結果あるいは効果が観客に一任されることなく、幻想の打破による再生という一定の方向性をもって暗示されることである。この問題点は、『ヴァージニア・ウルフなんかこわくない』（*Who's Afraid of Virginia Woolf?*,

1962）や『小さなアリス』（*Tiny Alice*, 1964）において、より増幅された形であらわとなる。

III

　既に述べたように、オールビーはイヨネスコやベケットに代表されるヨーロッパ不条理劇の影響の下に、劇作家への道を歩み出した。特に初期の一幕物にはその影響が濃厚に見られ、またデビュー作の『動物園物語』はベケットの『クラップの最後のテープ』と二本立で上演されたというような事情もあって、初期のオールビーにはアメリカ不条理演劇の旗手というレッテルが貼られた。しかし、オールビー劇は不条理劇とは本質的に違った性格を持っている。オールビー劇の中で、最も不条理劇的性格を持つと言われる『アメリカの夢』（*The American Dream*, 1961）を取り上げ、両者の相異を明らかにしたい。

　この作品には、イヨネスコの『禿げたソプラノ歌手』（*La Cantatrice chauve*, 1950）の影響が随所に見られる。例えば構成においても、中産階級の典型的な家庭に来客が突然目的もなく訪れ、波瀾が起き、人間関係のおかしさが暴露されるという趣向は同じである。しかし、両者の根本的相異を示すものは、オールビーの場合におけるおばあちゃんの存在である。このおばあちゃんは『砂場』（*The Sandbox*, 1960）に既に登場している。『砂場』の主要人物は母さんと父さんとおばあちゃんで、脇役として死の天使を務める青年と音楽を奏でる楽士が登場する。父さんは母さんの尻にしかれ、何でも母さんの言いなりである。死期を迎えて浜辺に連れて来られたおばあちゃんが砂場で遊んでいる。時々しんらつな言葉で娘夫婦の悲し

みの欺瞞性をあばく。やがて砂場に横たわり、青年に看取られて死んでゆく。ここでおばあちゃんは、現代のおかしな状況を批判する価値基準となっている。『禿げたソプラノ歌手』にはそのような価値基準はない。愛や論理性や言語など、従来人間の在り方の尺度となると考えられてきたあらゆるものが、いかに無意味なものであるかがあばかれ、人間存在の不条理性が明らかにされる。

　『アメリカの夢』における現代の審判者としてのおばあちゃんの役割は、静的な『砂場』の場合に比べて、より積極的である。『アメリカの夢』の主要人物は『砂場』と同じように母さん、父さん、おばあちゃんで、その三者の関係も同様である。それに訪問者として、パーカー夫人と青年が加わる。まず母さんと父さんの無意味な関係が決まり文句の対話で提示される。二人はおばあちゃんを養老院へ送るための迎えの車を待っているようだ。おばあちゃんは荷造りをしながら、二人に対して鋭い批判を浴びせる。そこへパーカー夫人が訪れる。しかし夫人は何のために来たのか分らない。この趣向は『禿げたソプラノ歌手』の消防士の訪問と似ている。ただ夫人の場合は度忘れのようだが、消防士の場合は本人は分っているつもりなのに、実際は何のために来たのかさっぱり要領を得ないのである。それから、消防士の来訪目的は結局最後まで分らないが、パーカー夫人の場合はおばあちゃんによってその目的を示唆され、養子縁組協会から派遣されてきたことになる。やがて美貌の青年が訪れる。青年もまた来訪の目的が分らない。おばあちゃんはこの青年にアメリカの夢という役割を与える。青年は昔、母さんと父さんの養子となり、若くして死んだ少年と双生児の兄弟であることが判明する。少年は母さんの気に入らないという理由で、気に入らない部分を次々と切り取られ、死んでいったのである。更に、美貌の青年が実はこの兄弟の死とともに人間の心を失い、今では有能なだけの一

種の機械人間になってしまっていることも明らかになる。おばあちゃんはパーカー夫人と示し合わせて、青年を母さんと父さんの新しい養子とする。美貌の青年であるアメリカの夢を養子に迎えて大喜びする母さんと父さんを陰ながら見て、おばあちゃんがめでたし、めでたし、これでおしまいと観客に挨拶をし、幕となる。

　このように『アメリカの夢』では、おばあちゃんは失われた価値を代表するとともに、乱れた論理の糸を紡ぎながら、現代のアメリカの病根が物質主義的快楽のみを追求し、アメリカの理念を忘れているところにあると解説する。しかも、このおばあちゃんは明らかに作者の主張を代弁している。このような解説が舞台の上でまともに演じられることは不条理劇では考えられない。演じられるとすれば、イヨネスコの『授業』(*La Leçon*, 1951) に見られるように、いかにおかしなものであるかを示すためである。あるべき人生など存在しうるはずのない世界において、その現実に気付くことなく、「あるべき人生」を生きているつもりの人間のおかしさが、不条理劇では描かれるのである。

　不条理劇は人間存在を形而上的に捉え、それは本来不定形で無秩序なものと考える。これに対して、オールビーは人間存在を特殊な相の下で捉える。現代の混乱と無秩序は、現代という特殊な条件の下で生まれたと考える。すなわち、幻想にあざむかれ真実を見失っているところに現代の状況の原因があると考える。幻想を打破し、真実に目を開けば価値ある人生が可能になるという信念あるいは願望が少なくとも初期のオールビーにはある。もしこのような見方が正しいとすれば、すべての価値基準を幻想にすぎないものとして排除する不条理劇の手法を、オールビーが取り入れたことは、不幸なことであったと言わなければならない。『ヴァージニア・ウルフ』における架空の息子や『小さなアリス』における模型が劇評界を戸

惑わせたのは当然と言える。単に新奇な技法というだけではなく、理念的に相容れないものが入り込んでいるのである。

IV

　幻想の打破による再生という図式が最もよく当てはまるのが、オールビーの代表作とされる『ヴァージニア・ウルフなんかこわくない』である。『動物園物語』以来、『砂場』、『ベッシー・スミスの死』(*The Death of Bessie Smith*, 1960)、『アメリカの夢』と次々に大胆な手法で劇界に旋風を起こしたオールビーは、この作品において初めて多幕物を手掛けた。三幕物の伝統的手法に基づく『ヴァージニア・ウルフ』は、1962年10月13日、ブロードウェイのビリー・ローズ劇場で初演された。二年間のロング・ランとなり、オールビーはアメリカ国内のみならず世界的にも最も有名な劇作家の一人となった。

　『ヴァージニア・ウルフ』の舞台はニューイングランド地方の小さな大学の構内住宅の居間。登場人物はマーサとジョージ、それに来客として登場するハニーとニックの二組の夫婦。マーサは52歳、大柄で小肥りの精力的な女性で、夫の勤める大学の総長の娘である。痩身のジョージは妻より6歳年下で、歴史学の助教授、髪は既に白くなりかかっている。マーサとジョージの関係は基本的にはこれまで見てきた母さんと父さんの関係を引き継ぐもので、その意味では、この劇は父さんの反乱とも言える。将来は大学総長である父のあとを継ぐものと思っていた期待を、夫の無能ぶりに裏切られたマーサとジョージとの間には、激しい愛憎関係があり、その関係がゲーム化されることによって夫婦の絆はかろうじて保たれている。

このゲームの基本的な型は、怒り——ののしり合い——機智に富んだ冗談——笑い——仲直りである。最も分りやすい例を、ジョージが持ち出してみんなを仰天させるショットガンの場面[6]に見ることができる。ジョージが怒る。憎しみを込めてマーサの後頭部に銃の狙いをつける。振り向くマーサ。ジョージは引金を引く。ポンと銃口から中国風のパラソルが開く。笑いと仲直り。といった具合である。そしてこのようなゲームの極め付きとして、二人の間には架空の息子がもうけられ、今や21歳の誕生日を迎えようとしている。マーサとジョージの二人だけの間では、このゲームは円滑に進行する。マーサのルール違反にもジョージは寛容である。しかし、ハニーとニックという第三者を迎え入れる時、ゲームは必然的に変質する。その変質の例も、ショットガンの場合に見ることができる。仲直りの部分である。マーサがキスを求める。ジョージは客を気にしてしぶる。マーサはあきらめない。二人のキス。マーサがジョージの手を取り乳房に当てる。ジョージは体をふり離し、ブルー・ゲームかとなじる。マーサは怒る。となり仲直りは成立しない。

　二人だけの間では架空の息子という幻想を育ててきたゲームが自壊作用を起こし、幻想破壊ゲームへと変質する。「亭主をこきおろせ」、「お客をやっつけろ」、「かみさんにのれ」、「子育て」という形で展開される真実暴露ゲームである。このような変質を予感するのか、ジョージは来客を迎え入れる前に「息子」のことはしゃべるなとマーサに注意し、この注意はその後も繰り返される。「息子」は二人の間では真実の幻想性を保ちえても、いったん第三者に露顕すれば、その幻想性はたちまち崩壊するということをジョージは意識していたとも言える。

　幻想育成が幻想破壊へと変質する『ヴァージニア・ウルフ』は、第一幕「愉快なゲーム」、第二幕「魔女たちの祭り」、第三幕「悪魔

払い」の三幕で構成され、マーサとジョージのすさまじい闘いが、アルコールを武器としながら、深夜から夜明けまで続く。導入部の第一幕は闘いの準備期間となる。ここでは今述べたようなゲームの変質過程が提示されるとともに、プライバシーに関することを第三者に暴露し、相手を攻撃するというマーサの戦略が示される。第二幕はジョージとニックの親密な対話の場面で始まる。この対話によって、次の「亭主をこきおろせ」と「お客をやっつけろ」の二つのゲームの展開に必要な情報が提供される。

　「亭主をこきおろせ」で自分が最も大切にしている部分を嘲笑され激怒したジョージは反撃に転じ、ニックとの対話で仕入れたばかりの情報をもとにして、ニック夫妻のお上品な仮面をはぎとり、その醜さをさらけ出す。これが「お客をやっつけろ」である。この段階に至るとマーサとジョージの緊張関係は極度に高まり、両者は全面対決となる。マーサは、ジョージに最後の止めをさす手段として、ニックを誘惑する。ジョージが明らかに冗談として口にした「かみさんにのれ」を、マーサは実際に演じようとするのだ。ジョージは嫉妬にかられる。しかし、ここで嫉妬を示せば全面屈服である。ジョージは耐える。マーサとニックは寝室へ消える。ジョージは耐え切れなくなって手にしていた本を投げる。それが玄関のチャイムにあたりチャイムの音。その音で目を覚ましたハニーが浴室から姿を現わし、「誰が来たの？」ときく。この問いにヒントを得て、ジョージはマーサとの愛の幻想である「息子」を殺すことを決意する。

　第三幕は、「息子」の死を予感するのか、マーサの哀感に満ちた感傷的な言葉で始まる。やがてジョージが現われ、全員が揃ったところで「子育て」のゲームが始まる。初めはいやがっていたマーサも、しだいに「息子」の幻想に魅せられてゆき、誕生日から生い立ちを語り出す。この間、それと並行してジョージは弔いのお経を唱える。

あらかじめ「息子」の事故死を聞かされていたハニーは、耐えられなくなり、「止めて」と叫ぶ。ハニーを証人として、ジョージは「息子」の事故死を知らせる電報が配達されたとマーサに告げる。二人の「息子」を一方的に殺すことはできないはずと抗議するマーサに対し、ジョージは「息子」のことをしゃべるなという掟が破られた以上一方的に殺すことは可能だと反論し、「息子」の死は確定する。

ハニーとニックが帰ったあと、それまでの二人の絆であった「息子」も失い、二人だけになったマーサとジョージは言葉もとぎれとぎれに静かにゆっくりと語り合う。最後にジョージはマーサに向かって「ヴァージニア・ウルフなんかこわくない」と低くそっと歌う。マーサは「こわいわ、わたし」とつぶやく。ジョージはゆっくりとうなずき、幕となる。ヴァージニア・ウルフとは幻想をはぎとられたあとの世界を象徴する。そのような世界に立ちすくむマーサ。それを静かにいたわるジョージ。夜明けも近いこの最終場面には、真実に基づく二人の新しい生き方が暗示されている。幻想の破壊による生の復活が示唆されているのである。

確かに、ジョージとマーサの最後の場面には希望を予感させるものがある。21年間「息子」を育み、ただその「息子」を絆としてのみ存在を続けることができた夫婦が、その「息子」を殺し、しかも希望を予感させる。この不思議な舞台の謎を解くためには、「息子」殺しのプロットを更に検討する必要がある。そこで我々は、これもまたひとつのゲームとして演じられていることに気が付く。ジョージを司祭とするマーサの悲劇というゲームである。「息子」のことをしゃべってはならないという掟を破るのがマーサのヒューブリスであり、「息子」殺しがそのネメシスとなる。フランシス・ファーガソンの悲劇のプロット[7]に従えば、プロローグでヒューブリスが明らかとなり、「亭主をこきおろせ」や「お客をやっつけろ」のゲー

ムがアゴンに当たる。クライマックスはニックを誘惑する場面であり、マクベスの「人生は歩く影にすぎない」を思わせる哀感に満ちた第三幕の開幕部がパトスに相当する。「息子」殺しと結末部がエピファニーとなる。このように悲劇の古典的なプロットがほぼ完璧なまでに踏襲されている。結末部の救済感は実はマーサの悲劇というこの疑似古典悲劇によってつくり出された疑似カタルシスにほかならない。悲劇のパロディとして実に見事であるが、そのパロディ性が最後まで貫徹されていないところが惜しまれる。もっとも結末部までパロディ化されると「悪魔払い」は不完全となり、作品の主題がくずれることになる。

V

　『ヴァージニア・ウルフ』のすぐあとに書かれた『小さなアリス』の上演ほど物議をかもした劇は珍しい。演劇史上最高の冒険的試みの一つだという賛辞から、アメリカの舞台史上これほどの堕落を示したものはないという酷評に至るまで実に賑やかである。[8] フィリップ・ロス（Philip Roth）に至っては同性愛者の妄想にすぎないときめつけている。[9] この劇の舞台に宗教的寓意を観てとった劇評家も勿論いるが、「10年劇評をやっているが、これほど面喰らったことはないね」[10] という言葉に代表されるごとく、作品の意味に首をひねった者が多い。主役のジュリアンを演じたジョン・ギールグッド（John Gielgud）自身、作者の真意をつかみかねて、「私の役は自分が何をやっているのか、その意味を問い続けることだったから気楽なものだった」と自嘲気味に述懐している。[11]
　このような反響を気にしたのか、オールビーは、劇評担当の記者

団に対して、作品のプロットを次のように説明している。

  平修道士が教会と金持ちの婦人との契約上の実務処理のために上司によって派遣される。平修道士は自分の考える神と世間の擬人化された神とに折り合いをつけることができず、まだ僧侶の資格を取っていない。平修道士はそれまで悩み苦しんできた問題のすべてが、中心部にも、たえず変貌する表層部にも含まれている境遇に巻き込まれることになる。性的ヒステリーと宗教的エクスタシーとの関係や、奉仕の無私と殉教の華やかな栄光との矛盾の問題である。最後に平修道士は自分が主張してきたもの、すなわち、人によってつくられた代用品としての神との結合ではなくて、抽象としての神との結合を受け入れざるをえなくなる。神であれ、アリスであれ、それが何と呼ばれようと、彼は純粋抽象としての神にゆだねられる。そして結局、見方によって次の二つのうち一つが起きる。抽象としての神が姿を現わし、現実のものとなるのか、それとも死に臨む者が最後に自らをあざむく必要に迫られて、存在しないと知りながら幻影をつくり出し、信じるのか。[12]

適切な要約である。いくらか補足すれば、登場人物は平修道士のジュリアン、その上司の枢機卿、金持ちの婦人のミス・アリスのほかに弁護士と執事がいる。ジュリアンが派遣されて住むことになるミス・アリスの館(やかた)は実はアリスの神殿でありミス・アリスは弁護士や執事とともにアリスに仕えている。何も知らないジュリアンはまず館の構造に驚く。館の図書室にはその精密な模型があり、その模型の同じ箇所にも同じような模型があり、更に……というように館は無限に、より小さな館を入れ子構造として含んでいる。そして実は、館はそのような模型の複製と説明される。いずれが実物でいずれが複製か分らなくなる。なお、館の次元と各模型の次元では、チャペルの火事によって明らかになるように、同じ現象が発生している。ジュ

リアンはこのような不思議な世界にはいり込んでしまったのである。

　教会とミス・アリスとの契約が、実は莫大な献金と引き替えにジュリアンをアリスへの生贄とするものであることもジュリアンは知らない。ジュリアンはひたすら神への奉仕を願っている。しかしジュリアンの信仰心には性的妄想が不可分に結びついている。このようなことが観客に示されたあと、ジュリアンはミス・アリスに誘惑され、二人は結婚する。しかし、ミス・アリスはアリスの身代わりにすぎない。ジュリアンはミス・アリスを介して、アリスと結婚したことになる。このことを認めないジュリアンは弁護士に射たれ、アリスとの結婚という現実を受け入れることを強要される。図書室に一人残されたジュリアンは館の模型に背をもたせかけ、十字架上のキリストの姿勢で死んでゆく。死の間際、模型の中を移動する灯り、次第に大きくなる心臓の鼓動に似た音、舞台に広がる影によって、ジュリアンは何ものかの接近に気が付く。死の瞬間には音は耳をろうするばかりになり、影は舞台一面に広がる。最後にジュリアンは、「神よ、アリスよ、私はあなたの心を受け入れる」と微かなほほ笑みを浮かべながら唱え、息が絶える。

　この作品の面白さは、神の実体がアリスというおどろおどろしきものとして具象化され、神の幻想を打ち砕くところにあるようだが、舞台の焦点は必ずしもそこに定められてはいない。ロスの指摘するホモ・セクシュアル的関係の過剰を問題としているわけではない。これはジュリアンの宗教感情にひそむ性倒錯的妄想の背景的説明として納得がいく。問題はこれまでにも指摘したように、最終場面である。ジュリアンの最後の描き方である。作者は執拗なほど写実的に、ジュリアンの戸惑い、絶望、苦悶、哀願、あきらめなどを強調する。更にジュリアンは「神はわれを見捨て給いしや」と十字架上

のキリストを演じ、しかもそれはパロディ化を許さない深刻な悲劇として演じられる。すなわち、ジュリアンの求める神とアリスとの乖離が強調される。既に観客はその神の実体がアリスであることを知っている。この悲劇的アイロニーから喚起される情感は、感傷的悲哀以外のなにものでもない。

　オールビーにとって、幻想の死は生の復活を意味するものであった。いかに苦しくても真実に向かって進めば、そこから生の可能性が生まれてくる。少なくとも意図としては、それが『ヴァージニア・ウルフ』が語るものであった。しかし、『小さなアリス』において、幻想の死によってあらわにされる世界はアリスというおどろおどろしき世界である。そのような世界を受け入れるジュリアンに復活の予感はない。この作品の焦点は、不条理な世界に直面した人間のおののき、苦しみ、悲哀を語ることにあるようだ。

VI

　物事はある時点を過ぎれば勝手に変えられないのに、人間はいつでも変えることができるという幻想にとらわれている。これが『微妙なバランス』（*A Delicate Balance*, 1966）を構想する原点になったように思うとオールビーは語っている。[13] これをビグズピーの

> ベケット劇のアイロニーは彼の人物が物事はあるようにしかありえないということを認めないところにあり、オールビー劇のアイロニーは彼の人物が物事は変えることができるということを分っていないところにある。[14]

という言葉と重ね合わせると、『微妙なバランス』はベケットの世界に近づくことになる。実際、この作品にはこれまでの作品とは違った変化が現われる。悲劇的激情は部分的なエピソードとなり、全体として風習喜劇調になる。どうにもならないのに騒ぎ立てる人物たちにはどこかベケット的なおかしさがある。これまでの、特にジェリーやジュリアンの場合に見られたような作者と人物との過度の密着も、この作品では消える。そして、このような傾向が以後の作品を通して全般に見られることを考えれば、『微妙なバランス』はオールビー劇の転回点を示すものとしても重要な意味を持つ。

　作品構成にも新しい趣向が導入される。始めと終わりに、同じ言葉で始まる詠嘆調のセリフが同一人物によって語られ、不条理劇によく見られる循環形式となる。家族と訪問者という構成は従来の型を踏襲するものであるが、おばあちゃんに当たる批判的人物が虚無的な考えの持ち主であるところが新しい。なお、これまで息子に恵まれなかったオールビー劇の夫婦に、今回は幼くして亡くなった息子があり、失われた希望を象徴する。以上のことからも分るように、幻想の破壊による再生という構図を当てはめるとすれば、再生の可能性はもはやなく、失われた希望への詠嘆がそれに代わる。

　登場人物は、アグネス、50代後半の主婦。トバイアス（トービー）、その夫、いくらか年上。アグネスの妹クレア、アルコール依存症で、いわば観客席に位置する虚無的な批判者。トバイアス夫妻の娘で、四回目の結婚に失敗して帰ってくるジュリア、家族対訪問者の関係では中間的存在。訪問者として、トービーの無二の親友ハリーとその妻エドナ。この訪問によって微妙なバランスがくずれる。場面は郊外の高級住宅の居間。金曜日の夜から日曜日の早朝にかけての出来事。アグネスの詠嘆的セリフで幕が開き、アグネス、トービー、クレア三人の相互関係が明らかにされる。トービーとクレアとの間

には義理の兄妹以上の関係が暗示され、熱がさめた夫婦と妻の妹との微妙な関係は、アグネスを支点としてバランスを保っている。そこへ、ジュリアから家に帰るとの知らせがはいる。やがて、前触れもなくエドナとハリーが訪れる。ふと不安に襲われたため、親友のトービーを頼ってやって来たのだという。

　第二幕はその翌日の夕食前から始まる。ジュリアは既に帰っており、トバイアス家の微妙なバランスは一触即発で壊れそうになっていることが分る。ハリーとエドナはジュリアの部屋に閉じ籠もったまま。やがて姿を現わすと荷物を取ってくると言って出掛ける。永久に一緒に住むつもりらしい。一同あっけにとられて場面が変わり、同じ日の夕食後。部屋を返せと要求するジュリアを台風の目として、嵐の前の静かさ。エドナとハリーが帰ってくる。その二人から主客転倒の扱いを受け、ジュリアは遂に爆発、父親のピストルを持ち出す騒ぎとなる。

　第三幕は翌朝の７時半、幕が開くとトービーが一人だけ。ほとんどまんじりともせず思案に暮れていた様子。アグネス登場。失われた愛のこと、失われた息子のことなど昔の思い出を交えながら、どう始末をつけるべきかについて話し合うが、結局はお互いに責任回避。そこへクレアとジュリアがそろう。ジュリアは前日のことを後悔してあやまるが、クレアはいつ事が始まるかと野次馬根性まる出し。トービーも遂に一家の主としての決断を迫られ、親友のハリー夫妻を追い出すことはできないと決意を表明する。アグネスは二人は疫病を持ち込んだのよと反論するが、友情の幻想に酔うこの時点のトービーにはあまり苦悩はない。しかし、いよいよ実行の時が来る。トービーとハリーは立ったまま二人だけで向かい合う。最初はさりげない社交的会話。次第に話は決着をつけなければならないところにくる。トービーの動揺と苦悶が始まる。ついに抑制を失い、

ヒステリー状態となる。低音部と高音部が交互に繰り返される嘆きと絶叫のアリアの中で、「いてくれ」と「でていけ」が交錯する。エドナとハリーは去る。微妙なバランスが回復し、アグネスの詠嘆的セリフで幕となる。

　この作品には、架空の息子も、アリスも存在しない。したがって架空の息子の死やアリスとの結婚によってもたらされるような幻想の全面崩壊は生じない。幻想は部分的な亀裂を生じるだけである。ハリー夫妻の訪問によって真実に目覚めるのはトービーだけである。トービーは友情の限界を知り、また自分の家庭がいかに危いバランスの上に保たれているかを知る。しかし他の人物には変化がない。失われた時を求めるアグネスは、相変わらず朝日とともに訪れる秩序の回復を信じている。トバイアス家のバランスが見せかけだけのものにすぎないことには初めから気が付いている観客席のクレアは、相変わらず真実から逃避し、アルコールの世界に安住する。ジュリアも相変わらず。この結末はオニールの『氷人来たる』(*The Iceman Cometh*, 1946) のハリーの酒場を思い起こさせる。白昼夢にふける酔客のなかで、ラリーだけが醒めている最後の場面である。幻想破壊の影響は部分的にしか及ばないと言ったが、それは舞台上の人物に関することであって、この舞台を見る観客は、自分の世界が微妙なバランスに支えられた危い存在でしかないことを知らされることになる。

VII

　『微妙なバランス』がオールビー劇の転回点となることは既に述べた。『箱―毛沢東語録―箱』(*Box* and *Quotations from Chairman*

Mao Tse-Tung, 1968）を起点として、後半の作品が展開されることになる。後半の作品ではトバイアスのアリアに見られたような感情の激発も消え、全体として挽歌的な色調の悲喜劇となる。

『微妙なバランス』はアグネスの詠嘆的なセリフを枠組として持っていたが、『箱―毛沢東語録―箱』では箱が文字どおりの枠組となる。幕が開くと、舞台間口いっぱいに口を開いた黒い大きな箱だけが舞台を占有している。スピーカーを通して、箱の声が現代の状況と芸術の悲哀を挽歌風に奏でる。声が止むと、箱を額縁として『毛沢東語録』が始まる。大きな客船のデッキに四人の人物が姿を見せる。観客に向かって毛沢東語録を語る毛沢東。過去の思い出を託して感傷的な詩を朗唱する老婆。長々と牧師に向かって身の上話を語る長話しの婦人。それを聞く無言の牧師。お互いの間に対話はなく、それぞれの語りは独立している。そしてそれらの語りが交互にはさみ込まれ、全体としてみごとなポリフォニーを奏でる仕組になっている。最後に、再び箱だけが照明を浴び、人物はシルエットとなって、箱の声がほぼ最初と同様の挽歌を奏でる。老婆は過去を、長話しの婦人と無言の牧師は現在を、毛沢東は未来をそれぞれに代表し、全体として現代の状況を象徴する。箱は現代の状況を憂える作者の声を代弁するとともに、『毛沢東語録』のハーモニー、すなわち、現代の混沌から生み出された美が、舞台空間につくり出された幻想にすぎないことを観客に意識させる装置である。『箱』と『毛沢東語録』は本来別箇の作品であるが、初演以来上述のような形で上演され、通常ひとつの作品として取り扱われている。

1980 年 1 月 27 日の『ニューヨーク・タイムズ』（*The New York Times*）の日曜版は、オールビーの最近作『デューブックから訪れた貴婦人』（*The Lady from Dubuque*, 1980）を紹介しているが、その中でオールビーは、作品の着想を得てから誕生させるまでには 10 年

から12年の歳月を要したと語っている。このような長さは例外であろうが、とにかく、オールビーは着想を十分な時間をかけて熟成させ、登場人物が作品の状況を離れても自由に動き廻れるぐらい成長してから、一気に筆を取るタイプの劇作家である。[15]

『臨終』(*All Over*, 1971) と『海の風景』(*Seascape*, 1975) は、このような創作過程の中で、双生児として育まれた。当初の意図では、「生と死」という共通の題名を持つ二つの小品となる予定であったが[16] それぞれ二幕物に成長し、『海の風景』の誕生は『臨終』より4年遅れることになった。

『臨終』の場面は豪華な寝室兼居間。舞台上手にベッドがあるが、衝立にさえぎられて病人の姿は見えない。時間は夜から深夜にかけての臨終までの数時間。主要人物は一家の主人の臨終の場に集まった妻、愛人、親友、娘、息子、それに医師と看護婦。いずれもかなり高齢で、娘と息子も既に中年に達している。主人に愛人ができて、家を離れていた妻と子供たちは20年ぶりにもと住んでいた家で再会したことになる。娘の許可を得て取材の記者とカメラマンが居間に入り、小さな騒動が持ち上がる以外は事件らしいものはなく、臨終を待っているあいだの会話がドラマを構成する。

会話は妻と愛人を主役として展開し、親友と医師が補足的な意見をはさむ。娘はクレアと同じような批判者的立場に立つ。母の欺瞞的な態度を責め、愛人に対しては愛人という名の娼婦にすぎないとなじる。しかし、自分も家庭のある男の「愛人」である娘の発言に説得力はない。息子はただ感傷的に悲しむばかり。妻や愛人と娘とのとげとげしい口論を別とすれば、会話はユーモアさえ交え、全般的に穏やかに進行する。おかしな話に爆笑が起きることもある。しかし、それはヒステリー性の笑いとなる。表面の穏やかさにもかかわらず、常に死が意識され、それが生の空虚さをあばく。妻と愛人

との間にはやさしいいたわり合いが見られるが、内心には主人をめぐるこだわりがある。愛人は臨終の場にのぞみ、愛人という立場を改めて確認し、主人の死とともに訪れる愛の死をあきらめの気持ちで待つ。妻は臨終によって夫は自分の許へ帰って来るという束の間の幻想に酔う。しかし、結局人間は愛されることを愛することしかできない。夫の死後どのような愛が可能だというのか。そのような思いに駆られ、「私は不幸だ」と叫ぶ。その時「御臨終」という医者の声があり、幕となる。愛を主題として、人間存在の虚しさを死によって照らし出したものであるが、全体として挽歌調の感傷性が目立つ作品である。

　『海辺の風景』では、舞台は一転して陽光に輝く砂丘となる。人生の停年を迎えようとするナンシーとチャーリーが語り合っている。一緒に暮らしているというだけの絆で結ばれているような夫婦である。ナンシーは海辺の観光地を放浪しながら余生を送ることを夢みている。チャーリーは何もしたくないと言い、子供の頃もぐった海の底の静かさを懐しむ。時々ジェット機の轟音が空を切り裂く。そんな二人のところへ海から姿を現わした大きな緑色のトカゲの夫婦、レスリーとサラがやってくる。文明と原始的生命との奇妙な対話が始まる。ナンシーとチャーリーはレスリーとサラに文明の説明を試みる。チャーリーの論理的説明は失敗するが、ナンシーの感覚的説明は成功する。両者の間に相互理解が生まれる。チャーリーによって、愛する者との別離の感情を教えられたサラが泣き出す。レスリーが怒ってチャーリーに襲いかかる。女たちに助けられて、チャーリーは危うく難を免れる。文明に危険を感じとるレスリーとサラは海へ帰ってゆく。

　以上のような話であるが、ここで最後の別れの場面に注目したい。ナンシーは、「あなた方はいずれ戻ってこなければならないのです

わ」だから帰らないでと懇願し、助けてあげるのにと言う。どのような方法で、とレスリーが尋ねる。

 チャーリー （悲しげに、照れて）握手をしてということになるかな。君たちも、こういうことをしなくてはならなくなるよ。そのうちに。
 ナンシー （恥ずかしそうに）助けてあげるのに。
    （レスリーは立ち止まる。砂丘を一歩降りてうずくまり、ナンシーとチャーリーをじっと見詰める。）
 レスリー （率直に）分った。始めてもらいましょう。[17]

助けてあげるとは言ったものの、実際に助けてと言われた時、ナンシーにどのような方法があるというのだろうか。文明の進化はジェット機と核兵器と生命の畏縮をもたらしただけではないか。この終幕部の皮肉は実に痛烈である。文明によって畏縮させられたナンシーの生命は、文明以前の生命に触れて、明らかに愛のよみがえりを覚えたことであろう。しかし、それはあくまでもそう感じられただけであって、それもまた幻影にすぎなかったのである。

VIII

『聴く』（*Listening*）には室内劇という副題が添えられている。もともとラジオ・ドラマとして書かれたものであるが、舞台の場合には、小劇場での上演を意図したものであろう。1976年にラジオ・ドラマとして放送され、舞台での初演は1977年である。場面は病院構内の水のかれた噴水池のある庭。登場人物は男と女と若い女。男と女はかつて愛人関係であったらしい。女と若い女の関係は女医と

その患者。若い女は失恋のショックで言語喪失症にかかり療養の身であるが、女医の合図があれば会話の仲間入りができるまでに回復している。しかし、そのためにかえって孤独感が深まっている。そのようなことが明らかにされたあと、男と女の対話が続く。話を聞いてもらえないという若い女の嘆きは無視される。女は男に、夏に毛皮のオーバーを着た婦人に何か見せてあげようと言われ、手首を切って血まみれになった手を見せられた話をする。その時、噴水の池にかがんで、その話を聞いていた若い女が「こんな風に」と血まみれになった手を見せる。池の底にあったガラスの破片で手首を切って、話が理解できたことを示し、会話の仲間入りを求めるのである。既に池の底一面に血は広がっている。この死に瀕した若い女と女との関係には、死によって対話を求めるという意味では、ジェリーとピーターとの関係がある。しかしここには、死を媒介とする結合はない。若い女に「頭がふらつく」と訴えられ、男に「何か手当ては」と促されても、女の態度は「馬がいなくなった馬小屋の戸口を閉めても無駄なことよ」と冷たい。若い女が言語喪失のままでいれば、このような悲劇は起きなかったであろう。現代の状況では言語がいかに危険なものになりうるかを、この作品は語っているように思われる。

　『花占い』(*Counting the Ways*, 1976) の登場人物は架空の息子を失ったあとのジョージとマーサを思わせる男と女である。二人の間にはもはや愛の幻想はない。しかし二人は愛があるかのごとく、お互いに愛の確認を求める。しかし、真剣に求めれば、愛の喪失が確認され二人の関係はおしまいになってしまう。そこで二人は愛の確認をゲーム化する。男と女はこのようなゲームによってしか存在を続けることができない退屈な夫婦である。なお、寄席演芸 (a vaudeville) と副題をつけられたこの作品では、人物は観客に見られていること

を意識した動作を行ない、自己紹介という場面では、俳優が役を離れて自分を紹介する。お芝居はお芝居にすぎないということを観客に意識させるのである。

　同じような方法は『デューブックから訪れた貴婦人』でも用いられる。ただ、この作品では俳優が役を離れて観客に話し掛けるようなことはない。俳優は登場人物として、観客を意識し、しばしば観客に話し掛ける。観客と舞台との垣根が取れ、観客は自分たちも人物の一人となり、劇中劇を観ている感じになる。登場人物は、ジョーとサムの夫婦。それに友人として二組の男女、すなわちルシンダとエドガーおよびキャロルとフレッド。更にデューブックから来た女エリザベスとその連れの黒人の男オスカー。場面はジョーとサムの居間。時間は第一幕が真夜中で、第二幕はその翌朝となる。ジョーは癌にかかり、既に死期が近づいている。薬で抑えているが、時々激痛に襲われる。

　第一幕では「私は誰でしょう」のゲームなどが行なわれる。友人たちはジョーを慰めに訪れているのであるが、ジョーの苦しみが分るはずはなく、結果は逆にジョーを苛立たせ、慰めの場は口論の場となる。客が帰ったあとサムはジョーと二人だけになる。二人は愛を確認する。しかしジョーの死は確実に迫っている。失われゆく最愛のものを最後まで抱きしめておくこと、それがサムのせめてもの願いである。苦痛で絶叫するジョーを抱え、サムは寝室へ退場する。入れ違いにエリザベスとオスカーが登場、幕となる。

　第二幕。エリザベスだけがいるところへ、サムが寝室から降りてくる。サムは「あなたは誰ですか」と尋ねる。第一幕の「私は誰でしょう」のゲームが、現実の場で展開されることになる。間もなくオスカーが登場。エリザベスはジョーの母と言う。あきれるサム。やがて友人たちが登場し、エリザベスはジョーの母としての地位を

確立する。かねがね聞いていたジョーの母とは違うが、偽って母を称する者などいるはずがないという世間の常識に支配される友人たちは、エリザベスを信じ、サムをおかしいと判断するのである。自己の存在を脅かされるサムにとって、最後の拠り所はジョーの証言となる。ジョーが寝室から降りてくる。しかし、死期を迎えたジョーの心は既に現実の世界から離れつつあり、母親が誰であるかなどには関心がない。ただ死への安らかな眠りだけが求められる。友人たちはキャロルを最後にすべて退場。ジョーの心から閉め出されたサムは自己喪失を覚え、ジョーを揺すりながら、「訳を聞かせてくれ」と訴える。それに対してジョーは「私を死なせてほしいだけよ」と答える。ジョーに最後の時が訪れる。オスカーに抱えられ、寝室へ連れ去られる。サムは泣きながらそれを見守るだけである。

　第一幕に次のような場面がある。

サム	（ジョーへ）言葉に気をつけるんだ。ルシアンダが必要な日が来るよ。
ジョー	（笑う）誰に？　わたしに？ （冷静に）そうね。おそらくみなさんすべてが必要な日が来るわ。それから、誰もいらないと思う日が来るのも勿論だわ。それから、そんな日は来ないということも勿論あるわ。 ……
ジョー	（同じ調子で観客に向かって）最近盛んに書かれている本に、そんなことが言われているんじゃありません？　あるところまでくると、最愛の人も必要でなくなるということ。つまり、結び目を解くっていうのね。そうなったらなんにも、必要なものなんてありはしないわ。[18]

ジョーにはこの世との結び目を解く日が訪れたのである。今はの際までジョーとの心の絆を固め、その結合に永遠の愛の証しを願ったサムは、このような死の現実に裏切られたのである。

IX

オールビーにとって、幻想の破壊は生の再生を意味するものでなければならなかった。しかし、生の再生はナンシーの愛の再生に見られるように、幻影という形でしかありえなかった。このような現実認識の深まりが後期の作品を挽歌的にいろどることになったと考えられる。

以上、幻想は破壊されなければならないという命題が、『動物園物語』から最近の作品[19]に至るまで、どのように展開されているかを概観し、前期の悲劇的作品から後期の挽歌的作品への転回をあとづけた。この命題がオールビー劇の長所ともなり、短所ともなっていることを、いくらか明らかにすることができたのではないかと思う。

オールビーの作品には、以上のほかに、**翻案劇**として、『悲しみの酒場のバラード』(*The Ballad of the Sad Café*, 1963)、『マルコム』(*Malcolm*, 1966)、『すべては庭のなか』(*Everything in the Garden*, 1967)、『ロリータ』(*Lolita*, 1981) があり、なお、小品『ファムとヤム』(*Fam and Yam*, 1960) がある。

オールビーは、最近の対談で、すこし生まじめすぎるのではないかという趣旨の質問を受け、自分がユーモアのセンスに富む劇作家であることを強調している。[20] オールビーの作品には確かにユーモアがある。しかし、それが十分に開花するには、倫理的な性格が強す

ぎるようだ。オールビーは、『箱―毛―箱』の序文に次のように書いている。

> 劇作家は二つのことをしなければならない。まず、「人間」（そう呼ばれているもの）の状況について意見を述べること。次に、自分が携わっている芸術形式のあり方について意見を述べること。どちらの場合にも変革を試みなければならない。[21]

オールビーも又、可能性を信じ常に変革を求めてやまないアメリカの夢を、宿命的ににないう者のひとりである。

注
作品の原題名のあとの年数は初演の年を示す。
1. 第一章の伝記的資料は主として Amacher (15-24) による。
2. エドワード・オールビー氏の講演。1975年10月21日、福岡アメリカン・センターにおいて。
3. オールビー福岡講演。
4. Rutenberg, 12.
5. *The American Dream* and *The Zoo Story*, 48.
6. *Who's Afraid of Virginia Woolf?*, 41-42.
7. Fergusson, 126-27.
8. Bigsby, 99.
9. Bigsby, 108.
10. Rutenberg, 113
11. Bigsby, 122.
12. Amacher, 131.
13. Rutenberg, 230.

14. Bigsby, 171.
15. Bigsby, 115.
16. Rutenberg, 236.
17. *Seascape*, 135.
18. *The Lady from Dubuque*, 47.
19. 『デューブックから訪れた貴婦人』以後の作品については、テキストを入手出来ず割愛せざるを得なかった。
20. Wasserman, 1-2.
21. *Tiny Alice*, *Box* and *Quotations from Chairman Mao Tse-Tung*, 124.

引用文献

Albee, Edward. *The American Dream* and *The Zoo Story*. New York: Signet Books, 1963.

―――. *The Lady from Dubuque*. New York: Atheneum, 1980.

―――. *Seascape*. New York: Atheneum, 1975.

―――. *Tiny Alice*, *Box* and *Quotations from Chairman Mao Tse-Tung*. Harmondsworth, Middlesex: Penguin Books, 1971.

―――. *Who's afraid of Virginia Woolf?* Harmondsworth, Middlesex: Penguin Books, 1965.

Amacher, Richard E. *Edward Albee*. New York: Twayne Publishers, 1969.

Bigsby, C. W. E., Ed. *Edward Albee*. Englewood Cliffs, N. J.: Prentice-Hall, 1975.

Fergusson, Francis. *The Idea of a Theater*. Garden City, N. Y.: Doubleday Anchor Books, 1949.

Rutenberg, Michael E. *Edward Albee: Playwright in Protest*. New York: Avon Books, 1970.

Wasserman, Julian N., Ed. *Edward Albee*. Houston: Univ. of St. Thomas P, 1983.

Vonnegut's Desperado Humor in *Slaughterhouse-Five*

I

Slaughterhouse-Five deals with the destruction of Dresden. On February 13-14 in 1945, Dresden, once called the Florence of the Elbe, was burned to the ground in the firestorm caused by the triple air raid of the Allied Air Forces.[1] In the first wave, 244 Royal Air Force bombers participated in the attack at 10 p.m. on the 13th with 4,000–8,000 pound high explosives and numerous incendiaries. About three hours later the second wave was delivered by 1,400 Royal Air Force bombers. And more than 1,000 U.S. Air Force bombers joined the attack around noon the following day, Ash Wednesday.

The fire bombing was carefully planned and executed. The aim was to cause a firestorm. Dresden had rarely been bombed up to then. That it was virtually a virgin city was the reason Dresden was picked as the target. Irving explains:

> While it had been found profitable earlier on in the war to employ a large proportion of incendiaries in attacks, exploiting the latent combustibility of the target, one by one the German cities had

>been attacked, bombed and destroyed, and in the Ruhr there was hardly a city where hundreds of acres had not been turned into an incombustible heap of rubble....
>
>With Dresden the opposite was the case: the target was virtually a virgin city and the full 'Hamburg' treatment could be employed against it: first the windows and roofs would be broken by high-explosive bombs; then incendiaries would rain down, setting fire to the houses they struck, and whipping up storms of sparks; these sparks in turn would beat through the wrecked smashed roofs and broken windows, setting fire to curtains, carpets, furniture and roof timbers.[2]

As a result, Dresden was engulfed by a far bigger firestorm than that of Hamburg in 1943, the first firestorm in World War II. The following quotation illustrates the horror of firestorm:

>The Battle of Hamburg in July 1943 had brought Germany's first-ever fire-storm: 8 square miles of city had burnt as one single bonfire. So horrific was the phenomenon that the Police President had ordered a scientific investigation of the causes of the fire-storm, so that other cities might be warned:
>
>>An estimate of the force of this fire-storm could be obtained only by analysing it soberly as a meteorological phenomenon: as a result of the sudden linking of a number of fires, the air above was heated to such an extent that a violent updraught occurred which, in turn, caused the surrounding fresh air to be sucked in from all sides to the centre of the fire area. This tremendous suction caused movements of air of far greater force than normal winds.

> In meteorology the differences of temperature involved are of the order of 20° to 30°C. In this fire-storm they were of the order of 600°, 800° or even 1,000°C. This explained the colossal force of the fire-storm winds.
>
> The Police President's gloomy forecast was that no kind of A.R.P. precautions could ever contain a fire-storm once it had emerged: the fire-storm was clearly a man-made monster which no man would ever tame.[3]

Dresden's holocaust was monstrous. According to Irving, the "documentation suggests very strongly that the figure [of the victims] was certainly between a minimum of 100,000 and maximum of 250,000."[4] At the time of the air raid, the population of Dresden had increased to more than double the 650,000 inhabitants. Threatened by the advance of the Soviet troops, more and more refugees from the east flooded into Dresden which at that time was regarded as a safe city. That was another reason for the frightening number of deaths.

At the beginning of 1945 the European stage of World War II was coming to a close. The strategic purpose of the Dresden bombing was to quicken the end by terrorizing German people into surrender. From the tactical point of view, the destruction of Dresden was not so significant because it had no important military facilities.

Vonnegut witnessed the destruction of Dresden as a prisoner of war. He miraculously survived with his fellow prisoners in an underground meat locker in the slaughterhouse where they were quartered at night while working at a syrup factory during the daytime. When they came out of the shelter at last, the scenery all around them was like that of the moon's surface.

> It wasn't safe to come out of the shelter until noon the next day. When the Americans and their guards did come out, the sky was black with smoke. The sun was an angry little pinhead. Dresden was like the moon now, nothing but minerals. The stones were hot. Everybody else in the neighborhood was dead. (178)

The prisoners were forced to clean up the collapsed city and Vonnegut was engaged as a corpse miner digging up human bodies under the wreckage.

The war in Europe ended in May and Vonnegut returned home in July after a brief rehabilitation. In the following days, he learned about the atomic bombs dropped on Hiroshima and Nagasaki and, further, about "how ghastly the German extermination camps had been." Learning the extent of terror that human begins were capable of, Vonnegut who used to be an optimist "had a heart-to-heart talk" with himself and became "a consistent pessimist."[5] And his pessimism was further deepend by such later atrocities as in Biafra and Vietnam. To Vonnegut, the destruction of Dresden was the symbol of human terror.

Vonnegut kept thinking about Dresden from the early stage of his writing career. During those years, when he was asked what he was doing, he used to reply that "the main thing was a book about Dresden." (3) Vonnegut thought that this book would be easy to write when he got home from the war because "all [he] would have to do would be to report what [he] had seen." (2) But to report what he saw was not so easy. He was overwhelmed by what he had seen. It is true that Vonnegut survived Dresden. But his survival was physical. He had not quite survived it mentally. He lacked the mental equilibrium and artistical distance necessary to report the terror he had witnessed.

Vonnegut's predicament as a reporter is similar to that of Ishmael who alone escaped to report the tragedy of the Pequod. After the failure of the first lowering for whales, Ishmael says:

> There are certain queer times and occasions in this strange mixed affair we call life when a man takes this whole universe for a vast practical joke, though the wit thereof he but dimly discerns, and more than suspects that the joke is at nobody's expense but his own. However, nothing dispirits, and nothing seems worth while disputing …. That odd sort of wayward mood I am speaking of, comes over a man only in some time of extreme tribulation: it comes in the very midst of his earnestness, so that what just before might have seemed to him a thing most momentous, now seems but a part of the general joke. There is nothing like the perils of whaling to breed this free and easy sort of genial, desperado philosophy: and with it I now regarded this whole voyage of the Pequod, and the great White Whale its object.[6]

With "this free and easy sort of genial, desperado philosophy" Ishmael could, amid the desperate perils of whaling, attain a mental equilibrium which was necessary to follow and narrate the doomed voyage of the Pequod.

Vonnegut as a narrator, too, needed his own "genial, desperado philosophy." To attain it cost him, however, a long, laborious effort as he complains in the first chapter of *Slaughterhouse-Five*:

> I would hate to tell you what this lousy little book cost me in money and anxiety and time. (2)

The book cost him 23 years and six novels according to John Somer.[7] Long in preparation, Vonnegut creates the character Billy Pilgrim as protagonist. And Billy's Tralfamadorian view of time and space has made it possible for the narrator to attain his "genial, desperado philosophy." Hence his success in coping with earthly terrors symbolized by Dresden.

II

Billy Pilgrim is an optometrist but he is almost retired now. His daughter says that he has become senile since his injury in an airplane crash. But subjectively he seems more active than before. He thinks he is now "prescribing correct lenses for Earthling souls," (29) not merely for Earthling eyes. He often "[comes] unstuck in time." (23) When unstuck, he travels through time to the past and to the future as well. His traveling is at random. He never knows where he travels next. And he is obsessed by Tralfamadorian ideas. He believes in what Tralfamadorians believe in.

Tralfamadore is said to be a planet 446,120,000,000,000,000 miles away from Earth. Billy is not only obsessed but in fact possessed by Tralfamadorians. He has been kindnapped and brought to the planet and he is living there in the zoo as a specimen of Earthlings while keeping his life on earth. According to Billy, this is possible because his presence on one planet means his mere micro-second absence from the other owing to a time warp.

Billy participated in World War II as a chaplain's assistant. He was captured by Germans at the Battle of the Bulge and was sent to Dresden as a prisoner of war. Like Vonnegut, Billy saw Dresden burned to the ground. Vonnegut, the narrator, was with him most of the time.

Billy's experience, both mental and physical, occupies the book from Chapter 2 to Chapter 9 and the last half of Chapter 10. (The whole book consists of 10 chapters.) The first chapter and the first half of the last chapter serve as a framework, where Vonnegut talks about himself as narrator. The narration about Billy's experience, which begins with "listen" and ends with "poo-tee-weet ?" (22) thoroughly follows Billy's wayward traveling through time. But the narration about the part of the war story, though it is narrated intermittently, almost wholly coincides with the sequence of actual events. As a result, the war story comes to be interlaced with Billy's Tralfamadorian fantasy without losing its narrative progress toward the end of the war.

On the planet of Tralfamadore, Billy learns Tralfamadorian cosmological determinism. He understands that "[a11] moments, past, and future, always have existed, always will exist." It is an Earthling's illusion that "one moment follows another one…and that once a moment is gone it is gone forever." (27) Naturally death means nothing to Tralfamadorians. When they "[see] a corpse," they just say, "So it goes." For they know that "the dead person is in bad condition on that particular moment, but that the same person is just fine in plenty of other moments." (27)

Free will is out of the question, of course. As a Tralfamadorian scholar explains, "Only on Earth is there any talk of free will." (86) Persuaded by Tralfamadorians, Billy is satisfied that there is no way of preventing wars, of even preventing a Tralfamadorian test pilot from pushing a button to trigger the end of the universe because "[the] moment is structured that way." (117) Any moments are like "bugs trapped in amber," (77) according to Tralfamadorians.

On Earth, Billy has "a framed prayer on his office wall." It comes from Reinhold Niebuhr:[8]

GOD GRANT ME
THE SERENITY TO ACCEPT
THE THINGS I CANNOT CHANGE,
COURAGE
TO CHANGE THE THINGS I CAN,
AND WISDOM ALWAYS
TO TELL THE
DIFFERENCE.

"Among the things, Billy Pilgrim could not change," the narrator comments, "were the past, the present, and the future." (60) Enlightened by Tralfamadorians, Billy is now a Tralfamadorian though he is an Earthling in physical appearance. The physical appearance of Tralfamadorians is preposterous:

> …they were two feet high, and green, and shaped like plumber's friends. Their suction cups were on the ground, and their shafts, which were extremely flexible, usually pointed to the sky. At the top of each shaft was a little hand with a green eye in its palm. (26)

Physically, Tralfamadorians are comic to us but mentally, Earthlings are no less comic to Tralfamadorians who live in a four dimensional world. A guide at the zoo on Tralfamadore, pointing to Billy as a specimen of Earthlings, explains how Earthlings are miserable mentally. The scene is narrated as follows:

> The guide invited the crowd to imagine that they were looking across a desert at a mountain range on a day that was twinkling bright and clear. They could look at a peak or a bird or a cloud…. But among them was this poor Earthling, and his head was encased in a steel sphere which he could never take off. There was only one eyehole through which he could look, and welded to that eyehole were six feet of pipe.
> …. He was also strapped to a steel lattice which was bolted to a flatcar on rails, and there was no way he could turn his head or touch the pipe. The far end of the pipe rested on a bi-pod which was also bolted to the flatcar. All Billy could see was the little dot at the end of the pipe. He didn't know he was on a flatcar, didn't even know there was anything peculiar about his situation.
> The flatcar sometimes crept, sometimes went extremely fast, often stopped—went uphill, downhill, around curves, along straightaways.

Whatever poor Billy saw through the pipe, he had no choice but to say to himself, "That's life." (115)

Billy's experiences, including those in the war, are treated and narrated from this Tralfamadorian point of view. The war story inevitably assumes a comic tone, not to mention the other parts of Billy's story. Dresden no longer overwhelms Vonnegut. He can laugh away the terrors of war. He can gain his equilibrium and distance to cope with the holocaust. And his sense of humor, having been nurtured during the age of the Great Depression and developed through his long career as a writer, is now released to the fullest extent.

Interlaced with and colored by Billy's Tralfamadorian fantasy, the war becomes "the Children's Crusade," (15) not a "glamorous" (14) adventure. Almost all the characters in *Slaughterhouse-Five* are caricatured. Billy the protagonist, "with a chest and shoulders like a box of kitchen matches" looks "like a filthy flamingo." (33) When the bullet from a German sniper just misses him in the road, Billy stands there "politely, giving the marksman another chance." The narrator's comment:

> It was his addled understanding of the rules of warfare that the marksman *should* be given a second chance. (33)

Roland Weary, Billy's war buddy who is "short and thick," "bundled up" with "every piece of equipment he had ever been issued, every present he'd received from home: helmet, helmet liner, wool cap, scarf, gloves, cotten undershirt, woolen undershirt, wool shirt, sweater, blouse, jacket…" looks "like Tweedledum or Tweedledee."(39-40) And his face, hidden with "five layers of humid scarf," suggests "a toad in a fishbowl." (48) Weary is an antitank gunner. His battle scene is represented like this:

> As a part of a gun crew, he had helped to fire one shot in anger— from a 57-millimeter antitank gun. The gun made a ripping sound like the opening of the zipper on the fly of God Almighty. The gun lapped up snow and vegetation with a blowtorch thirty feet long. The flame left a black arrow on the ground, showing the Germans exactly where the gun was hidden. The shot was a miss. (34)

Just at the time they are captured by Germans, Billy and Weary hear three "bangs" far away. The shots sound "inoffensive" to them. But they are fatal to the two American scouts who "ditched" them a little while before. The scouts die this way:

> Now they were dying in the snow, feeling nothing, turning the snow to the color of raspberry sherbet. (54)

After American prisoners are captured and collected, they flow like liquid:

> They were moving like water, downhill all the time, and they flowed at last to a main highway on a valley's floor. Through the valley flowed a Mississippi of humiliated Americans. (64)

While they are carried by boxcars, there is a colonel who dies suffering from pneumonia. He makes a sound "like greasy paper bags" (66) when he inhales. As to this boxcar journey, Vonnegut wrote in his letter to his family from Le Havre in France shortly after "the repatriation":

> …we were loaded and locked up, sixty men to each small, unventilated, unheated box car. There were no sanitary accommodations—the floors were covered with fresh cow dung. There wasn't room for all of us to lie down. Half slept while the other half stood.[9]

The boxcar scene in the book is like this:

> Nobody was to get off until the final destination. To the guards who walked up and down outside, each car became a single organism which ate and drank and excreted through its ventilators. It talked or sometimes yelled through its ventilators, too. In went water and loaves of blackbread and sausage and cheese, and out came shit and piss and language…. Human beings in there took turns standing or lying down. The legs of those who stood were like fence posts driven into warm, squirming, farting, sighing earth. The queer earth was a mosaic of sleepers who nestled like spoons. (70)

At the end of the boxcar journey "the liquid" of Americans, allured by the guards, begins to flow. "Gobs of it [builds] up in the doorway," and "[plops] to the ground" (80–1) if it is alive, but it does not flow if it is dead:

> The hobo could not flow, could not plop. He wasn't liquid anymore. He was stone. (81)

And when the door of Billy's boxcar opens, Billy coughs:

> ...when he coughed he shit thin gruel. This was in accordance with the Third Law of Motion according to Sir Isaac Newton. This law tells us that for every action there is a reaction which is equal and opposite in direction. (80)

The only character that is not drawn as a comic figure is Edgar Derby, a former high school teacher. He is even heroic, but he comes to a comic death. He is ceremoniously tried and executed by a firing squad on the charge of stealing a teapot from the ruins of Dresden.

Needless to say, these comic scenes are not confined to the war story. They are numerous. Readers will find them almost on any page when they open the book. Take the scene of Billy's love affair for example. He is "being unfaithful to his wife Valencia for the first and only time." It is at a party on "New Year's Eve." (46) Billy gets drunk and makes advances to a woman. This disgraceful behavior infuriates the party attendants. Billy tries to escape by car:

> The main thing now was to find the steering wheel. At first, Billy windmilled his arms, hoping to find it by luck. When that didn't work, he became methodical, working in such a way that the wheel could not possibly escape him. He placed himself hard against the left-hand door, searched every square inch of the area before him. When he failed to find the wheel, he moved over six inches, and

> searched again. Amazingly, he was eventually hard against the right-hand door, without having found the wheel. He concluded that somebody had stolen it. This angered him as he passed out.
>
> He was in the back seat of his car, which was why he couldn't find the steering wheel. (47)

Another example of pervasive comedy is the scene of Billy's "wedding night" with Valencia. He is in bed with her "in a delightful studio apartment which [stands] on the end of a wharf on Cape Ann, Massachusetts." "One result" of their night is "the birth of Robert Pilgrim," who is to become "a member of the famous Green Berets." (118) The climax of their romantic honeymoon is rendered this way:

> Billy made noise like a small, rusty hinge. He had just emptied his seminal vesicles into Valencia, had contributed his share of the Green Beret. (118)
>
> ....
> "Would you talk about the war now, if I *wanted* you to?" said Valencia. In a tiny cavity in her great body she was assembling the materials for a Green Beret. (121)

Tralfamadorians dispose of death only by saying, "So it goes" as was mentioned before. "So it goes" appears in the book abundantly. Wherever death is mentioned, whether it is Christ's death or the death of bubbles in a bottle of champane, it is followed by "So it goes" as if it were a rule of punctuation. The narrator is a total egalitarian in terms of evaluating death. The phrase appears one hundred times according to one study.[10] The death is the commonest comic subject in the book.

III

As I mentioned before, Billy's story has a framework, where Vonnegut tells about writing the book. Referring to the book he has just written, he says, "This one is a failure and had to be, since it was written by a pillar of salt." (22) Lot's wife in the Bible looked back where Sodom and Gomorah had been and was turned into a pillar of salt. Vonnegut looked back where Dresden had been and he, too, was tured into "a pillar of salt." This self-criticism shows that Vonnegut is aware that only the Tralfamadorian point of view has made it possible for him to write about Dresden. In other words, he knows that his "genial, desperado philosopy" is based upon his own fantasy, lies. Just as Ishmael in *Moby-Dick*, Vonnegut takes "this whole universe for a vast practical joke," being aware that "the joke is at nobody's expense but his own."

Before concluding, I would like to ask you to listen to the following two remarks. One is made by Vonnegut and the other is made by one of the characters in the book. Vonnegut's remark was delivered to the graduating class at Bennington College in 1970, just a little while after the publication of the book. Vonnegut says:

> Only in superstition is there hope. If you want to become a friend of civilization, then become an enemy of truth and fanatic for harmless balderdash.[11]

And the remark made by Rosewater:

> I think you guys are going to have to come up with a lot of wonderful new lies, or people just aren't going to want to go on living. (101)

Slaugterhouse-five is Vonnegut's "wonderful new lies" which he hopes will make human beings "want to go on living."

Notes
1. The information about the air raid owes to Irving, *The Destruction of Dresden*.
2. Irving, 149.
3. Irving, 174.
4. Irving, 225.
5. *Wampeters, Foma & Granfalloons*, 162.
6. *Moby-Dick*, 195-96.
7. *The Vonnegut Statement*, 222.
8. The original prayer of Reinhold Niebuhr is: "God, give us grace to accept with serenity the things that cannot be changed, courage to change the things which should be changed, and the wisdom to distingush the one from the other." *Bartlett's Familiar Quotations*, 823.
9. Klinkowitz, 98-99.
10. Klinkowitz, 87.
11. Wampeters, 163.

Works Cited

Bartlett's Familiar Quatations. Boston: Little, Brown and Co, 1980.
Irving, David. *The Destruction of Dresden*. London: Gorgi Books, 1971.
Klinkowitz, Jerome. *Slaughterhouse-Five*. Boston: Twayne Publishers, 1990.
Klinkowitz, Jerome and John Somer. Ed. *The Vonnegut Statement*. New York: Delacorte Press / Seymour Lawrence, 1973.
Melville, Herman. *Moby-Dick*. New York: Norton, 1967.
Vonnegut, Kurt, Jr. *Slaughterhouse-Five*. New York: Dell Publishing, 1971.
———. *Wampeters, Foma & Granfalloons*. New York: Delacorte Press / Seymour Lawrence, 1974.

Cat's Cradle を読む

　Cat's Cradle は "Call me Jonah" で始まります。ただちに想起されるのが、『白鯨』の "Call me Ishmael" です。更に、この物語の主要舞台となるサン・ロレンゾ島の最高峰であるマッケーブ山は鯨にたとえられています。

> It was in the sunrise that the cetacean majesty of the highest mountain on the island, of Mount McCabe, made itself known to me. It was a fearful hump, a blue whale, with one queer stone plug on its back for a peak. In scale with a whale, the plug might have been the stump of a snapped harpoon…. (142)

明らかに、『白鯨』の語りのパロディがこの小説の語りの枠組みになっています。ただひとり奇跡的に生還したイシュメイルがピークォド号の悲劇を語るのと同じように、語り手のジョンは *ice-nine* による地球の破滅を語ります。

　ice-nine とは 114.4°F（45.77…℃）を融点とする特殊な氷で、この氷に觸れた水分はたちまち *ice-nine* となって凍結してしまいます。生命の組成分は、その殆どが水分であることを考えるとき、これがいかに危険な物質であるかは容易にお分りになると思います。

　ice-nine はノーベル物理学賞の受賞者であるホェニカー博士によって発明されます。博士は原子爆弾の発明者でもあります。*ice-*

nine 研究のきっかけは海兵隊の将軍によって与えられます。米国海兵隊は創設以来の200年の間湿地帯での戦闘に苦しめられています。将軍は湿地を瞬時にコンクリートのように固めてしまう物質はないものかと、ホェニカー博士に訴えます。その訴えがヒントとなって、常温で安定した氷、すなわち *ice-nine* が生まれます。

　博士の死後、遺されたアンゼラ、フランク、ニュートンの3人の遺児は、彼等の間で *ice-nine* を分けます。その後3人には各方面から誘惑の手が伸びます。そして3人は *ice-nine* と引き換えに、それぞれの幸福を得ることになります。その結果 *ice-nine* はアンゼラを通して合衆国政府に、フランクを通してサン・ロレンゾ国に、ニュートンを通してソ連の手に渡ります。

　ice-nine を手にしたサン・ロレンゾ国の独裁者であるパパ・モンザーノはガンの末期症状で苦しんでいます。その苦しみから逃れるために、*ice-nine* を飲んで自殺を図ります。すると全身がたちまち弓なりに硬直し、*ice-nine* の氷像と化してしまいます。当日は第2次大戦の戦死者慰霊祭の日です。大統領の死は伏せられたまま、式典が挙行されます。そして、その式典の行事として爆撃演習を行っていた戦闘機が、爆弾を装填したまま海に面した宮殿に撃突し、爆発するという事故が起きます。崩れ落ちる宮殿と共に、安置されていたパパ・モンザーノの死体も海に落下します。海は *ice-nine* と化し、無数の龍巻が発生します。このようにして地球上の生命は終末を迎えることになります。

　ice-nine による地球の汚染が始まり、陸地も海も青白い *ice-nine* の結晶によって覆われたなかで、奇跡的な生存を続けるジョンとその仲間の小数の者には、奇妙に静かな6か月の月日が訪れます。サン・ロレンゾ島の宗教であるボコノン教へと回宗したジョンは、その6か月の間にボコノン教の視点から、*ice-nine* による地球破滅につい

ての記録を書き上げることになるのです。

　元々ジョンはフリーのジャーナリストとして、*The Day the World Ended* というルポルタージュを書くために、原子爆弾が広島に投下された日の原爆発明者の言動について取材を続けていたのですが、その過程で *ice-nine* の悲劇に大きく関与することになります。

　ボコノン教によれば、人間はそれぞれ *karass* というチームに編成され、神の意図の実現に努めています。もっとも、自分達が何を実現しようとしているのかは、人間に分る筈がありません。語り手のジョンは次のように説明しています。

> We Bokononists believe that humanity is organized into teams, teams that do God's Will without ever discovering what they are doing. Such a team is called a *karass* by Bokonon, and the instrument,the *kan-kan*, that brought me into my own particular *karass* was the book I never finished, the book to be called *The Day the World Ended*. (11)

『世界が終わった日』はジョンをその所属すべき *karass* に編入するための手段だったのです。更に、それぞれのチームすなわち *karass* には, その行動の軸となるべきものがあり、それは *wampeter* と呼ばれます。

> A *wampeter* is the pivot of a *karass*. No *karass* is without a *wampeter*, Bokonon tells us, just as no wheel is without a hub.
> 　Anything can be a *wampeter:* a tree, a rock, an animal, an idea, a book, a melody, the Holy Grail. Whatever it is, the members of its *karass* revolve about it in the majestic chaos of a spiral nebula. The orbits of the members of a *karass* about their common *wampeter* are

spiritual orbits, naturally. (42)

　また *karass* には常に二つの *wampeter* があります。ある任意の時点をとれば、そのうちの一つは勢力を増しつつあり、他の一つは衰えつつあるとボコノン教は説きます。語り手のジョンは、ホェニカー博士のことでその上司のブリード博士にインタヴューを行い、始めて *ice-nine* のアイディアを耳にしますが、その時こそまさに *ice-nine* が自分の *wampeter* として開花しつつあったことに思い当ります。

> .... I am almost certain that while I was talking to Dr. Breed in Ilium, the *wampeter* of my *karass* that was just coming into bloom was that crystalline form of water, that blue-white gem, that seed of doom called *ice-nine*. (43)

　ホェニカー博士とその3人の子供であるアンゼラ、フランク、ニュートンはジョンの *karass* のメンバーであり、その *wampeter* は *ice-nine* であります。ボコノン教によれば、*ice-nine* による地球の破滅は神の壮大なる意図の一環ということになります。もしそうであれば、人類はその破滅に対して免責を与えられることになります。ホェニカー博士とその家族に代表される人類の愚かさに絶望するジョンはボコノン教に慰めと救いを求めます。

> "What hope can there be for mankind," I thought, "when there are such men as Felix Hoenikker to give such playthings as *ice-nine* to such short-sighted children as almost all men and women are?"
> And I remembered *The Fourteenth Book of Bokonon*, which I had read in its entirety the night before. *The Fourteenth Book* is entitled, "What Can a Thoughtful Man Hope for Mankind on Earth, Given

the Experience of the Past Million Years?
　It doesn't take long to read *The Fourteenth Book*. It consists of one word and a period.
　This is it:
　"Nothing." (164)

更に，教祖ボコノンは次のように説いています。

　"History!" writes Bokonon. "Read it and weep!" (168)

　ジョンがボコノン教に帰依した動機は人間の愚かさへの目覚めであります。その愚かさの典型は、原子爆弾や *ice-nine* のような恐しいものを発明する科学者の無邪気さ、つまり研究の成果に関する倫理的意識の欠如にみられます。そのような科学者の象徴的存在がホェニカー博士であります。例えば原爆の爆発実験が始めて成功し、1個の爆弾で一つの都市のすべてを消滅させてしまうことが証明された日のことです。ある科学者が博士に向って、科学はついに罪を犯しましたねと述べると、それに対して博士は『罪の概念など今では甲冑同様にすたれてしまったものの如く』[2] "What is sin?" (21) と問いかけます。またこの原爆が実際に広島に投下された日のことです。博士はそのことには全く関心がなく、一人であや取りに興じています。更に、オイル暖房は止まり、パイプは凍結し、自動車のエンジンはかからないといった寒い冬の朝のことです。そのような朝は、母のエミリーが亡くなって以来、母親の代りを務める長女のアンゼラにとっては大変な忙しさです。そのような慌しさのなかで、困っている家の者のことにはいささかの関心も示さないで、博士は突然言い出します。

> I wonder about turtles…. When they pull in their heads…do their spines buckle or contract? (20)

　亀といえば、博士が一時亀のことに余りにも熱中し、原爆の研究がお留守になったことがあります。マンハッタン計画の係官は困り果ててアンゼラに相談し、ある晩亀を盗み出してしまいます。博士は亀がいなくなったことには一言も触れず、翌日マンハッタン計画に復帰します。その時の事の次第は次のように表現されています。

> He just came to work the next day and looked for things to play with and think about, and everything there was to play with and think about had something to do with the bomb. (20)

次の引用はホェニカー博士がノーベル賞受賞の際に行ったスピーチの全文です。

> Ladies and Gentlemen. I stand before you now because I never stopped dawdling like an eight-year-old on a spring morning on his way to school. Anything can make me stop and look and wonder, and sometimes learn. I am a very happy man. Thank you. (17)

　この博士自身の言葉にもみられるように、博士は純心無垢な、好奇心にあふれた幼な児の心を持った科学者であります。博士は幼な児が玩具とたわむれるが如く、様々な想念と、思考と実験を通してたわむれるのです。しかし問題は、自分の研究の道義的責任に関しては全く無感覚な科学者の無邪気な研究によって、核兵器や *ice-nine* のような人類の破滅に直結する恐しい武器が生み出されること

です。更に困ったことには、その研究の成果が博士の3人の子供に代表されるような愚かな人類の手に委ねられてしまうことです。

　ice-nine が、3人の子供を通じて、世界の権力者の手中に拡散することは前に述べましたが、その経緯を述べれば人間の愚かさぶりが更にお分りになると思います。まずアンゼラの場合です。父の死後寂しさに苦しむアンゼラをある日、かって父の助手を務め、その後会社を創立したハンサムな青年が訪れます。二人は博士の最後の日々や昔のことを語り合います。その2週間後に二人は結婚します。夫の会社は *ice-nine* という秘密兵器を生産する軍需工場となります。

　アンゼラは6尺豊かな馬面の大女ですが、それと対照的にニュートンはこうもり傘の背丈ほどしかない小人です。ニュートンはハイスクールの時巡業中のソ連ボルゾイバレー団の公演を観に行き、小人のダンサーであるジンカに恋をします。その後コーネル大学に入学したニュートンは、コーネル大学で公演を行ったボルゾイバレー団の楽屋にジンカを訪ね、二人の仲はジャーナリズムに華々しく取り上げられます。二人は婚約を発表し、ケープ・コッドの父の別荘で愛の1週間を過します。その間にジンカは *ice-nine* を手に入れます。ジンカは1週間のアメリカ亡命を破棄し、ソ連大使館に出頭します。ジンカはソ連のスパイだったのです。

　ice-nine を餌として、サン・ロレンゾ国の高官に納まるのがフランクです。フランクは幼い頃から模型造りの天才です。近所のホビー・ショップで専ら模型造りに専念していたフランクは父の葬儀の直後に町を出て、フロリダの模型店に雇われます。しかしその店は模型店とは名ばかりで、実は高級車を盗んでキューバに密輸するギャング団のアジトです。そのことが判明し、フランクもその一味としてFBIの指名手配を受けます。しばらく消息不明であったフランクはその後、キューバを出港した豪華な遊覧船でカリブ海を巡航中に遭

難し、ただひとりサン・ロレンゾ島に漂着します。サン・ロレンゾでは高名なホェニカー博士の子息ということで厚遇され、科学と進歩担当の大臣の要職に就き、次期大統領に目されています。また、モンザーノ大統領の養女で、サン・ロレンゾ随一の美女であるモナの婚約者になります。フランクに破格の待遇を与えたパパ・モンザーノの胸を飾るネックレスのロケットには、フランクから献上された *ice-nine* が納められています。

　ブリード博士から *ice-nine* の話しを聞いて以来 *ice-nine* の悪夢に悩まされていたジョンは、パパ・モンザーノの自殺とそれに続いて起った侍医のフォン・ケーニヒスヴァルトの死によってその恐怖の実態を目撃し、またホェニカー博士の子供達から聞いた話しによって、前述のような *ice-nine* の分配とその後の行方について知ります。たとえパパ・モンザーノの自殺がなくても、また戦闘機の墜落事故がなくても、地球の破滅は必然的な成り行きであったことを思い、ジョンはボコノン教への帰依を深めてゆきます。

　ジョンがボコノン教に始めて接するのは、サン・ロレンゾ島へ向う機中のことです。現代のシュバイツァーといわれるカースル博士の取材旅行をある雑誌社に依頼され、ジョンはサン・ロレンゾ島へ向います。たまたま相席となるのが、サン・ロレンゾ駐在大使として任地に向うアメリカの外交官です。その外交官から、カースル博士の息子のフィリップが書いた『サン・ロレンゾ―その国土、歴史及び国民―』という書物を借用し、ボコノン教のことを知るのです。それからこの飛行機には、フランクの婚約パーティのためにサン・ロレンゾに向うアンゼラとニュートンも同乗しています。

　ボコノン教の教祖の正式名はライオネル・ボイド・ジョンソン（Lionel Boyd Johnson）です。ジョンソンをサン・ロレンゾの訛りで発音するとボコノンとなるのです。ボコノンはトバゴの裕福な黒

人家族に生まれます。ボコノン家の富はボコノンの祖父が海賊黒ひげの埋蔵財宝を発見したことに由来します。英国国教会派のクリスチャンとして育てられたボコノンは、成長すると、淑女のスリッパという風変わりな名前の自家用スループ船でロンドンへ出かけ、高等教育を受けます。しかし第一次大戦の勃発によってその学業は中断され、ボコノンも歩兵として参戦します。毒ガス攻撃を受けて負傷して除隊となり、淑女のスリッパ号で帰路につきます。しかしその途中では、ドイツ海軍の潜水艦に捕えられたり、その潜水艦が更にイギリス海軍の駆逐艦に捕獲されたりの波乱の体験を重ねることになります。結局北米のロードアイランド州のニューポートにたどり着き、そこで終戦を迎えます。ニューポートではラムフォード家の知己を得て土地の有力者と交ります。その後ラムフォード家が所有するセヘラザード号の船長として世界漫遊の航海に出ます。しかしセヘラザード号は霧のボンベイ港で衝突事故のために沈没し、ボコノンだけが助かります。インドには数年間滞在し、その間にはガンジーの信奉者となって独立運動に参加をし、その結果投獄されるなどの体験をします。刑期を終えてトバゴに帰国します。

　ボコノンがサン・ロレンゾ国の初代大統領となるアール・マッケーブと出合うのは、淑女のスリッパ二世号でカリブ海を漫遊中にリケーンに遭い、ハイチの港に避難をした時のことです。当時ハイチは米国海兵隊の占領下にあり、海兵隊を脱走したマッケーブはマイアミまでの乗船を求めます。しかし、マッケーブを同乗させた淑女のスリッパ二世号は、マイアミに着く前に嵐のために遭難します。二人は救命ボートで辛うじて助かります。二人が漂着した島がサン・ロレンゾ島です。1922年のことです。

　二人が漂着した時、サン・ロレンゾの島民の暮しは着のみ着のままの二人よりももっと貧しいものでした。二人はサン・ロレンゾ島

に理想境をつくることを夢想し、島の支配者となることを宣言します。その時島を支配していたカースル砂糖会社は、生産性の低いその島からあっさりと撤退します。理想境を実現するために、マッケーブはサン・ロレンゾの政治と経済の全面的な改革に着手します。ボコノンはキリスト教の僧侶を追放し、新しい宗教を創めます。ボコノンは新宗教創立の心境を土地の民謡のカリプソに託し、次のように謡っています。

> I wanted all things
> To seem to make some sense,
> So we all could be happy, yes,
> Instead of tense.
> And l made up lies
> So that they all fit nice,
> And l made this sad world
> A par-a-dise. (90)

しかしいかなる政治や経済の制度改革も、民衆をみじめな境遇から救い出すことには、一向に役に立ちません。結局宗教のみが人々を幸せにするための唯一の手段であることが明らかとなります。生活の実態が余りにもみじめであるために、真理は『民衆の敵』(118)となるのです。そこでボコノンはますます上手なうそをつくことによって、民衆に希望を与えることに努めます。更に、ボコノンは新宗教に対する民衆の信仰に真の生命と情熱を与えるために、ボコノン教を禁制とすることをマッケーブに要請します。ボコノン教は禁制となり、その信者であることが分れば、腹部をフックという大きなカギ針で貫かれて吊される極刑を受けることになります。マッ

III-3 *Cat's Cradle* を読む

ケーブは独裁者としてサン・ロレンゾ国に君臨し、追放されたボコノンはジャングルの聖者として民衆の心を支配することになります。

　ボコノン教の教義の要諦は上述のことからも分るように *foma*、すなわちうそであります。一例を示せば、ボコノンは太陽系の誕生について次のような面白い教義を展開しています。

> …*Borasisi*, the sun, held *Pabu*, the moon, in his arms, and hoped that *Pabu* would bear him a fiery child.
> 　But poor *Pabu* gave birth to children that were cold, that did not burn; and *Borasisi* threw them away in disgust. These were the Planets, who circled their terrible father at a safe distance.
> 　Then poor *Pabu* herself was cast away, and she went to live with her favorite child, which was Earth. Earth was *Pabu's* favorite because it had people on it; and the people looked up at her and loved her and sympathized. (129-30)

そして、この宇宙進化論に対するボコノン自身の見解は次の通りです。

> Foma! Lies!…. A Pack of foma! (130)

　ボコノン所有のスループ船が淑女のスリッパという奇妙な名前を持っていたことには前に触れましたが、ボコノンは足にこだわります。ボコノン教では足は聖なるものです。ボコノン教の最も聖なる儀式のひとつとして *bokomaru* というものがあります。二人の信者が相対して両足の裏をそれぞれ相手の足の裏と合わせる姿勢をとり、お互いに相手の足裏を押し合うことによって二人の魂を融合さ

せ、法悦の境に至るというものであります。ボコノン教徒となった語り手のジョンは次のように説明しています。

>　　We Bokononists believe that it is impossible to be sole-to-sole with another person without loving the person, provided the feet of both persons are clean and nicely tended.
>　　The basis for the foot ceremony is this "Calypso":
>
>　We will touch our feet, yes,
>　Yes, for all we're worth,
>　And we will love each other, yes,
>　Yes, like we love our Mother Earth. (109)

足の裏（sole）を同音異義の心（soul）に掛けるなど、ヴォネガット特有の露骨な冗談もみられますが、ここには、ボコノン教において最も聖なるものが、人と人との愛であることが示されています。しかし、この愛が神の恩寵として祝福されないところにボコノン教の特質があります。ボコノン教を弾圧する政府の高官でありながら実はボコノン教徒であるフランクは、語り手のジョンに問われて、ボコノン教徒にとって最も聖なるものは神ではなく人間であると答えます。

>　"What *is* sacred to Bokononists?" I asked after a while.
>　"Not even God, as near as I can tell."
>　"Nothing?"
>　"Just one thing."
>　I made some guesses. "The ocean?The sun?"
>　"Man," said Frank. "That's all. Just man." (143)

更に、地球の破滅に立ち合うことになったボコノンは、執筆中のボコノン教の聖典、*The Books of Bokonon* の最終章を次の文で結びます。

> If l were a younger man, I would write a history of human stupidity; and l would climb to the top of Mount McCabe and lie down on my back with my history for a pillow; and I would take from the ground some of the blue-white poison that makes statues of men; and I would make a statue of myself, lying on my back, grinning horribly, and thumbing my nose at You Know Who. (191)

ボコノンによれば、人間は神の意図の実現のために利用される道具にすぎないのです。そして、その意図が何であるのかについては、人間には推し測る術もないのです。神と人間との間には明らかに断絶があります。人間の愛を育むためにボコノンに残された道は、ただより上手なうそをつくことだけです。この宗教観は、1970年にベニントン大学の卒業生に対して与えたヴォネガットの次の言葉と見事に重なります。

> I know that millions of dollars have been spent to produce this splendid graduating class, and that the main hope of your teachers was, once they got through with you, that you would no longer be superstitious. I'm sorry—I have to undo that now. I beg you to believe in the most ridiculous superstition of all: that humanity is at the center of the universe, the fulfiller or the frustrator of the grandest dreams of God Almighty.[3]

ボコノン教とは一言でいえば人間を幸せにするための迷信です。絶

望的な状況のなかで人間に希望を与え、生きる力を与えてくれる迷信です。フィリップのサン・ロレンゾの紹介書で始めてボコノン教に関心を持ったジョンは、その後フランクが所有していた『ボコノンの書』を熟読し、ボコノン教徒となります。そして多年にわたり『世界が終わった日』というノン・フィクションを書くために取材を続けてきたジョンは、皮肉にもサン・ロレンゾ島で地球の最後を体験し、ボコノン教徒として、その記録を遺すことになるのです。

　このようなジョンを語り手とする『ネコのゆりかご』が執筆されたのは 1962 年のキューバ危機の時代であります。米・ソの対立による核戦争の脅威が一触即発の極限にまで高まった時です。ヴォネガットは 1969 年にニューヨークで開催された物理学会に講演者として招かれ、作家の役割について次のように述べています。

> I have taught creative writing. I often wondered what l thought I was doing, teaching creative writing, since the demand for creative writers is very small in this vale of tears. I was perplexed as to what the usefulness of any of the arts might be, with the possible exception of interior decoration. The most positive notion I could come up with was what I call the canary-in-the-coal-mine theory of the arts. This theory argues that artists are useful to society because they are so sensitive. They are supersensitive. They keel over like canaries in coal mines filled with poison gas, long before more robust types realize that any danger is there.[4]

『私をヨナと呼べ』で始まる『ネコのゆりかご』は科学の万能を信じる人間の愚かさに対するヴォネガットの警告であります。『ヨナ書』のニネベの町は悔い改めることにより神の破壊を免れますが、人間がその愚かさを改めない限り、地球は必ず破滅の日を迎えるこ

とをヴォネガットは警告しているのです。

注
1. *Cat's Cradle* からの引用は Kurt Vonnegut Jr., *Cat's Cradle* (New York : Dell Publishing, 1972) である。引用箇所はかっこ内に示す。
2. Kurt Vonnegut Jr., *Wampeters, Foma & Granfalloons* (New York; Delacorte Press / Seymour Lawrence, 1974), 97.
3. *Wampeters, Foma & Granfalloons*, 163.
4. *Wampeters, Foma & Granfalloons*, 92.

Raymond Carver

　"Intimacy" にみられるように、Raymond Carver にはわが国の私小説を思わせるような自伝的傾向がある。明治・大正期の日本と現代のアメリカに何故似たような現象が起きたのか。そこには、近代小説の成立基盤である近代的市民社会の成立前 (Pre-Modern) とその崩壊後 (Post-Modern) というような歴史現象が絡んでいるのかもしれない。比較文学の問題として面白そうだが、年寄りの私にはそこまで立ち入る時間はない。この課題は若い研究者であるみなさんにお任せして本題に入りたい。

　とにかく、Carver は自伝的傾向が強い。そのことからも、Carver の文学を理解するには伝記的要素が重要になる。Carver の人生をたどり、Carver 文学の展開を概観する。[1]

1. Yakima

　1938 年の 5 月 25 日 Carver は Oregon の Clatskanie に生まれる。製材所の工員であった父親の仕事の関係で、1941 年 Washington の Yakima に移り、そこで幼年期と少年期を過ごす。Columbia 川の支流である Yakima 川に沿った Yakima は自然に恵まれ、父親っ子だった Carver は幼い頃から父のお供で、fishing や hunting に親しみ、また父の職場にもよく出入りした。

Carverの小説には地方色や土着性がないといわれるが、それは多分にGordon Lishの編集に起因するものであって、本来のCarver文学はCarverの育ったYakimaの自然にしっかりと根を下ろしている。

　高校生の時二歳年下のMaryann Burkと出会い、二人は恋仲となる。Maryannの高校卒業と同時に結婚する。次々と子供が生まれ、二児の父親となった時Carverはまだ二十歳(はたち)になったばかりであった。Yakima時代を素材とする作品には、"Dummy"("The Third Thing That Killed My Father Off")、[2] "Nobody Said Anything"、"Distance"などがある。"Distance"には新婚の頃が描かれていてほほえましい。

2. Creative Writing Course

　Carverは子供の頃からstory tellerになりたいという夢を持っていた。その夢を育てたのは話し好きの父親であった。高校生の時にはすでに作家志望を固めていた。アメリカの教育制度には独特の作家養成課程がある。CarverはそのCreative Writing Courseによって育てられた。

　Yakima時代、父に費用を出してもらい、Palmer Institute of Authorship in Hollywoodの通信講座を受ける。1958年の夏CaliforniaのParadiseへ引越し、Chico State CollegeのCreative Writing Courseを聴講する。翌年の秋から正規の学生となり、John Gardnerの指導を受ける。添削を中心とするGardnerの授業は懇切を極め、その時の教えがCarver文学の根幹を形成することになる。

　1960年の秋学期からはHumboldt State Collegeへ転学し、Richard Dayの指導を受ける。Dayも大変親切な先生で、アルコール依存症に苦しむCarverの世話など、卒業後もいろいろと面倒を見る。Iowa Writers' Workshopで勉強することを奨めてくれたのもDayである。

1963年の2月、Carverは学士号を得てHumboldt State Collegeを卒業し、同年の9月Iowa Writers' Workshopの修士課程に入学する。創作意欲旺盛で執筆に集中する。Maryannはアスレテイック・クラブの給仕をして、Iowaへ転居したあとの一家の生計を支える。しかし、結局家計の重圧に負けたCarverは一年の課程を修了した段階で中退し、CaliforniaのSacramentoへ引揚げる。

　苦労しながらも、このIowa時代に書き上げた草稿のなかには、"The Student's Wife", "Will You Please Be Quiet, Please?" などの優れた作品がある。

　作家として売り出すまでの二人の生活が如何に苦労の多いものであったか、またそのなかで如何にして作品を書いたかについて、Carverは "Fires" という題のエッセイで次のように回想している。

> She waitressed or else was a door-to-door saleswoman. Years later she taught high school. But that was years later. I worked sawmill jobs, janitor jobs, delivery man jobs, service station jobs, stockroom boy jobs—name it, I did it…. In those days I figured if I could squeeze in an hour or two a day for myself, after job and family, that was more than good enough. That was heaven itself. And I felt happy to have that hour. But sometimes, one reason or another, I couldn't get the hour. Then I woudld look forward to Saturday, though sometimes things happened that knocked Saturday out as well. But there was Sunday to hope for. Sunday, maybe. (*Fires* 35)

3. Debut

　Chico Stateの時代、Gardnerは箱一杯の雑誌を教室に持ち込み、「真

の文学が載っているのはこれらの雑誌です」(*Fires* 44) と学生達に名も無い定期刊行の文芸誌を宣伝した。Carver デビューの推進力となったのが、Gardner の推奨するそれらの 'little magazines' であった。

　Iowa 滞在中の 1963 年に "Furious Seasons" が出版され、1966 年には "Will You Please Be Quiet, Please?" が出版された。何れも Chicago 出版の 'little magazine' である *December* に掲載された。更に、"Will You Please" は 1967 年度の *The Best American Short Stories* に収録されて文学界の注目を浴びた。*December* の編集長は Curtis Johnson で、Johnson は Carver と親交を結び、終生その友情は変らなかった。

　Sacramento では、Carver は Mercy Hospital の用務員として働いたが、専ら創作に力を注ぎ、主たる稼ぎ手は Maryann であった。Maryann は当初レストランの給仕などをしていたが、1965 年の 1 月 The Parents' Magazine Cultural Institute の子供用教材部門の販売員として採用された。才覚に富む Maryann はめきめきと売り上げを伸ばし、同年 3 月末の Maryann の収入は Carver の 2 倍であった。まもなく Maryann は管理職に昇進し、1965 年度の Carver 家の総収入は 11,000 ドルに達した。

　しかし、収入が増えると生活が贅沢になる。派手な交友関係に加えて酒量が増え、結局は収支のバランスが崩れて、1967 年の 4 月、破産の申請をする。[3] Maryann は退職し、車を売り、借りていた豪華な家も明け渡す。住む所に困った挙句、二人はアパートの住み込み管理人となる。このような生活を素材にしたのが "Are These Actual Miles?" ("What Is It?"), "Gazebo" などである。

　妻の才能を妬み、一家の柱としての権威を確立するためには専門職に就くことが不可欠であると痛感した Carver は、図書館専門職員になる計画を立て、1967 年の夏、Iowa University の修士課程に入学する。講義は 6 月 14 日に始まる。しかし、その 3 日後の 17 日

に父が急死し、この計画は挫折する。このような不幸が続いたが、幸運にも7月、Carver は Curtis Johnson の世話により、Palo Alto の Science Research Associates（SRA）の教科書部門の編集者として採用される。Carver 家は Palo Alto へ引越す。

　1968年5月、Carver は Johnson に紹介され、Gorden Lish に会う。当時 Lish は Palo Alto の教材会社で教科書の編集をしていた。オフィスは Carver の勤め先のすぐ近くにあり、二人は Johnson に頼まれて、共に *December* の編集者でもあったが、二人が会うのはその時が初めてであった。その後二人は親交を深める。1969年の10月、Lish は新設された *Esquire* の小説部門の編集長となり、Carver に地方作家から全米の作家への道が開かれる。Carver は Lish に促され、*Esquire* に次々と作品を送るが、最初のうちはなかなか採ってもらえない。

　その間 Maryann は、Palo Alto への転居のあと、1968年の1月にそれまでの学歴を活かして San Jose State College に編入学し、英語教員免許取得のための勉強を続けていた。1970年6月に所定の課程を修了して学士となる。9月には Los Altos High School に英語教師として採用される。

　Carver は SRA を退職し、創作に専念する。1971年に "Neighbors" が初めて *Esquire* に載り、翌年には "What Is It?" が載った。関連して他の一流誌にも載るようになり、Carver は一流誌に作品を発表する作家となった。当然の結果として、方々の大学から声がかかる。1972年には、Stanford, UC Berkley, UC Santa Cruz という三つの有名大学の Creative Writing の講師を兼務した。

4. Extra-Marital Liaison and Alcoholism

　Carverの酒は父親譲りであった。若い頃から酒を楽しんだ。しかし、次第に飲み方が変った。アルコール依存症の徴候が見られるようになった。

　また、アルコールを伴う男女の交友関係のなかではしばしば浮気が起きる。例えば、Stull と Carroll の "Chronology" の 1972 年の記述には、その頃の Carver 夫妻の関係が次のように簡潔に記述されている。

> At Kittredge's party Carver meets Diane Cecily, with whom he begins a sexual liaison that, unlike his earlier flings, continues for several years. His persistent infidelity, coupled with his and Maryann's heavy drinking, leads to violent arguments. (*Stull and Carroll* 967)

　1973 年の秋学期からの一年間、Carver は Iowa Writers' Workshop の visiting fellow として招かれた。同僚に John Cheever がいた。二人はよく一緒に飲んだ。酒屋が店を開く前に、車で店に乗り付けることもあった。Carver は対談のなかで当時を回想している。

> When we were teaching in the Iowa Writers' Workshop in the fall semester of 1973, he and I did nothing but drink. I mean we met our classes, in a manner of speaking. But the entire time we were there—we were living in this hotel they have on campus, the Iowa House—I don't think either of us ever took the covers off our typewriters. We made trips to a liquor store twice a week in my car. (*Conversations* 40)

一方、Maryann はアルコール中毒の恐ろしさを知り、その頃から AA（アルコール中毒治療協会）の会合に通い始める。

　1974 年の 5 月、Carver は Iowa の仕事を終えて Cupertino の家に落ち着く。しかし、久し振りに目にする「わが家」は荒涼とした有様であった。娘は家出をして不在、息子は全くの「他人」で、頼るべき妻は断酒中で冷たかった。われわれは崩壊した「わが家」の惨状を嘆く Carver を "Fires" のなかに見ることができる。

> The time came and went when everything my wife and I held sacred, or considered worthy of respect, every spiritual value, crumbled away. Something terrible had happened to us. It was something that we had never seen occur in any other family. We couldn't fully comprehend what had happened. It was erosion, and we couldn't stop it. Somehow, when we weren't looking, the children had got into the driver's seat. As crazy as it sounds now, they held the reins, and the whip. We simply could not have anticipated anything like what was happening to us. (*Fires* 34)

　出費が嵩み、1974 年の暮れ、二度目の破産申請を行う。翌年の 5 月に一回目の審理があり、そのあと Maryann は、Carver をアルコール依存症から立ち直らせるために、精神科の診療所に入院させる。入院中に Carver はアルコールの禁断症状として激しい発作を起こす。7 月、Carver と Maryann は二人だけの夏季休暇旅行を計画する。その壮行会として友人達が開いてくれたパーティの席上、Carver は酒に酔って Maryann の頭部をワインの瓶でなぐる。9 月、破産処理は終結する。

　年が明けて 1976 年、3 月に *Will You Please Be Quiet, Please?* が出

版されるが、このことについては次章で述べる。同年の秋、Carver は Maryann に付き添われて、アルコール中毒患者の回復施設である Duffy's に入所する。退所のあとは Maryann の看護で回復に努めるが、Maryann の辛抱も限界に達し、二人の別居が始まる。以後二人は別居と同居を繰り返す。この年のクリスマスは、まさに "Serious Talk" に書かれた通りの、悲惨なものであった。

年の暮れの大晦日に、当時同居していた SRA 時代の秘書に連れられて、Duffy's へ再入所する。翌年の 1 月に退所し、2 月からは、Humboldt State 時代の恩師 Day の世話で、単身 McKinleyville に移り断酒に努める。そして 1977 年 6 月 2 日、Carver は最後の酒を飲み、以後酒を断つ。

アルコールと浮気に関連する作品は枚挙にいとまがない。"Where Is Everyone?", "Serious Talk", "Where I'm Calling From", "Chef's House" などが代表的なものである。

5. National Writer

話は少しさかのぼる。1974 年 11 月 Lish は、*Esquire* の編集長としての職はそのままで、McGraw 社に新設された小説部門の発行人に抜擢される。McGraw 社は小説シリーズ刊行の第一回の作家として Carver を選ぶ。この朗報を電話で Lish から受けた Carver は、感激して礼状を書き、「さあ、地球を炎上させてやるぞ」(Sklenicka 272) と喜んだ。

1975 年の夏までには、二人の話し合いによって、載せるべき作品も決まり、出版される本のタイトルも *Will You Please Be Quiet, Please?* となった。Lish は早速編集に取り掛かった。編集の方針は、

個々の作品を整え、全体的に一冊の本としてはっきりとした特色を打ち出すことであった。作中人物が置かれている荒涼とした情況とそこに漂う脅威（menace）が強調され、個々の人物の感情や特定の情況はできるだけ排除された。(Sklenicka 282)

"On Writing" と題するエッセイで、Carver は次のように述べている。

> I like it when there is some feeling of threat or sense of menace in short stories. I think a little menace is fine to have in a story. For one thing, it's good for the circulation. There has to be tension, a sense that something is imminent, that certain things are in relentless motion, or else, most often, there simply won't be a story. (*Fires* 26)

Carver の作品が持つ独特の荒涼とした雰囲気に魅せられて Carver に関心を持った Lish と Carver の二人には、云うまでもなく、相互に引き付けられるものがあったのである。[4]

では、Lish の編集によって、Carver の作品は如何に変容したのか。編集の結果について、Sklenicka は次のように述べている。

> Still, the stoies retain their original form, colloquial tone, humor, and characteristic use of quotidian data to present a reality that is both frightening and seductive. (Sklenicka 282)

更に、Stull と Carroll の "Note on the Texts" には次の記述がある。

> In a letter of September 28, 1975, Carver expressed his thanks for "all the blood, sweat and so on" his editor had invested in the book. He also gave his considered approval of the outcome. "I think, all in all,

you did a superb job w / cutting and fixing on the stories." (Stull and Carroll 980)

　要するに、次に Lish が手掛ける *What We Talk About When We Talk About Love* の場合と比べると、はるかに小規模な「編集」であり、また Carver の称賛する出来映えであったと考えられる。

　しかし、この時点における Carver 家は前章で述べた通り、実に惨憺たるものであった。このように Carver の私生活はどん底であったが、1976 年 3 月 *Will You Please Be Quiet, Please?* が出版されると、作家としての Carver は Lish の天才的な売り込みとも相俟って、一躍全米の新文学を荷う寵児となる。

　1977 年、Carver は 6 月 2 日の記念すべき断酒のあと、別居中の Maryann を McKinleyville に迎え回復に努める。その甲斐があって、1978 年には Vermont の Goddard Collge の冬学期と夏学期に出講する。その間 Carver は Chicago に旅行して Johnson と再会し、更に Iowa に足を伸ばして友人達との旧交を温める。Iowa 滞在中の 3 月に Maryann を Iowa に迎えるが、Maryann は 7 月に California へ帰る。これが二人の離別となる。[5]

　Goddard の夏学期を終えたあとの 8 月、Carver は El Paso へ向かい、Texas University の Writer in Residence となる。年が明けて 1979 年の 1 月、一年余り前の Dallas の学会で初めて会い、その後交際を続けていた Tess Gallagher と同棲を始める。[6]

　1980 年 1 月、Syracuse University の Professor of English となり、Syracuse に赴任する。Carver は同年 2 月、当時 Knopf 社の編集長になっていた Lish に手紙を書き、二冊目の短編集の材料が充分に揃ったことを知らせる。5 月始めに二人はニューヨーク市内で会い、Carver は Lish に原稿を渡す。

Lish は手際良く編集に取り掛かる。6月13日、Fairbanks で開催される学会出席のために、Carver が Gallagher と共にアラスカ旅行に出発しようとする時、Lish からの編集を終えた草稿が届く。それは Carver が手渡したタイプ原稿に、Lish がフェルトペンで編集の書き入れをした草稿であった。本のタイトルは *What We Talk About When We Talk About Love* になっていた。草稿にざっと目を通した Carver は異議をさし挟むことなく、"the collection looks terrific"（Sklenicka 355）と礼状を書き、更にタイピストの浄書のための料金を郵送し、旅行に出発した。

学会が終わって一人 Syracuse へ帰った Carver を待っていたのは、タイプ浄書された原稿ではなく、Knopf 社との契約書であった。Carver は誰に相談することもなく、直ちに契約書にサインをして返送した。（Sklenicka 356）

7月7日、新しいタイプ原稿が届いた。それは明らかに6月13日に届けられた手書き編集の草稿とは別種のものであった。Lish は Carver に断ることなく、二度目の編集を徹底的に行ったのである。語数全体で計算すれば、Carver の原稿の 55% が削減されていた。（Stull and Carroll 991）

Carver は驚愕し、一睡もせずに Lish の最終稿を読み、また6月13日の「草稿」と比較した。翌朝 Lish に宛てて、苦悶と哀訴の手紙を書いた。その書き出しは次の通りである。

> July 8, 8 a.m.
>
> Dearest Gordon,
> I've got to pull out of this one. Please hear me. I've been up all night thinking on this, and nothing but this, so help me. I've looked at it from every side, I've compared both versions of the edited mss—

the first one is better, I truly believe, if some things are carried over from the second to the first—until my eyes are nearly to fall out of my head. (Stull and Carroll 992)

このような哀訴がシングル・スペースで延々と4頁続く。後にこの手紙のことを聞かれたLishには、手紙によって心を動かされたと言う記憶は全くなく、ただ次のように答えている。"My sense of it was that there was a letter and that I just went ahead."（Max 40）

CarverはLishに全幅の信頼を寄せていたが、もともと二人の間には同床異夢のところがあった。CarverがEsquireに登場する時期の編集者としてのLishについて、Sklenickaは次のように述べている。

It was, Lish would later claim, merely the raw material of Carver's stories that interested him. Lish believed that his editorial work on Carver's stories was a creative act in its own right for which he deserved acknowledgment. (Sklenicka 187)

'Captain Fiction' を名乗り、新文学を開拓しているとの自負に燃えるLishが、既に契約書にサインをしたCarverの、このような涙の哀願に耳を貸す筈はなく、What We Talk About When We Talk About Loveは予定通り1981年4月に出版された。若干のマイナスの評価はあったが、全般的には 'minimalism' という新しい文学を確立するものとして迎えられ、好評を博した。不評の多くは、大鉈をふるったLishの強引な編集によるものであった。

Carverはこの出版のあと、編集に関するトラブルは伏せたままLishと袂を分かち、Carver文学の本来の姿を取り戻すために精力を傾注する。削減された作品の復元に努めると共に新作品を次々と発

表し、Carver 文学は円熟期を迎える。

　1983 年の 4 月に詩やエッセイを含む短編集 *Fires* が出版される。このなかには "Distance", "Where Is Everyone?", "So Much Water So Close to Home" の三つの作品の復元版がある。同年の 9 月には、"A Small, Good Thing" の 復元版を載せた短編集 *Cathedral* を世に問う。"A Small, Good Thing" 以外はすべて新作で、それらの作品では Lish が編集した *What We Talk About* とは異質の、より豊かな人間性を持った人物の喜怒哀楽が描かれる。

　当然、次のような二つの疑問が生まれる。一つは、Carver の作品にはなぜ短い版と長い版があるのかという疑問であり、もう一つは、*What We Talk About* 以降 Carver の作風が急激に変るのは何故かということである。この疑問に対して Carver は一貫して、それらの変化はすべて自己の文学の内発的な進展の結果であると答えている。例えば、1986 年の Stull との対談で、*What We Talk About* では骨の髄まで文章を切り詰めたのに、その後の *Fires* でまた元の形に戻したのは何故かと問われた Carver は次のように答えている。

> It had to do with the theory of omission. If you can take anything out, take it out, as doing so will make the work stronger. Pare, pare, and pare some more. Maybe it also had something to do with whatever I was reading during that period. But maybe not. It got to where I wanted to pare everything down and maybe pare too much. Then I guess I must have reacted against that. I didn't write anything for about six months. Then I wrote "Cathedral" and all the other stories in that book in a fairly concentrated period of time. I've said that if I had gone any further in the direction I was going, the direction of the earlier stories, I would have been writing stories that I wouldn't have wanted to read myself. (*Conversations* 182)

Carver の死後ちょうど 10 年が過ぎた時点の話であるが、1998 年 8 月の *New York Times Magazine* に掲載された D. T. Max の暴露記事によって、この疑問は一挙に氷解する。Lish が Carver の原稿に改竄ともいえる編集を行ったことが明るみに出る。そして 2009 年、Stull と Carroll の綿密な考証によって Beginners が出版され、*What We Talk About* の完全な原稿が復元される。

　話を Carver の生前に戻す。1987 年の夏、Carver は四半世紀を超える創作活動の集大成として、自選集のために作品の選定を行う。最新作の 7 篇に加えて、過去の短編集から代表作を選ぶことになった。結局、*Will You Please* から 12 篇、*What We Talk About* から 8 篇、*Fires* から 2 篇、*Cathedral* から 8 篇が選ばれ、新しい作品と合わせて計 37 篇になった。短い版と長い版がある場合にはもちろん長い方の版が選ばれた。選定された作品について、Carver は「これらの物語は私が共に生き、また私を思い出させてくれるものです」(Sklenicka 458) と Maryann に語った。

　Carver は肺癌のため 1988 年の 8 月 2 日になくなる。自選集 *Where I'm Calling From* が出版されたのはその 2 ヶ月余り前の 5 月 25 日、Carver が 50 歳の誕生日を迎えた時であった。著者のサイン入りの特別版には Carver の序文があり、その最後は次のような一節で結ばれている。

> If we're lucky, writer and reader alike, we'll finish the last line or two of a short story and then just sit for a minute, quietly. Ideally, we'll ponder what we've just written or read; maybe our hearts or our intellects will have been moved off the peg just a little from where they were before. Our body temperature will have gone up, or

down, by a degree. Then, breathing evenly and steadily once more, we'll collect ourselves, writers and readers alike, get up, "created of warm blood and nerves" as a Chekhov character puts it, and go on to the next thing: Life. Always life. (*Call If You Need Me* 201–02)

注

1. Carver の伝記に関する資料は主として Sklenicka の *Raymond Carver* 及び Stull and Carroll の "Chronology" に拠る。
2. かっこ内は版によって異なる題名を示す。
3. 破産処理が済み、負債から解放されるのは同年 6 月 13 日である。
4. 1984 年に行われた Carver との対談の記事のなかで、Bruce Weber は Lish の Carver についての見解を次のように紹介している。

    "He's an important writer from any number of standpoints," says Gordon Lish…. "Carver's way of staging a story, staging its revelations, is, I think, unique. Carver's sentence is unique. But what has most powerfully persuaded me of Carver's value is his sense of a peculiar bleakness," a comment that rightly places Carver in the peculiarly bleak tradition of Sherwood Anderson and Carson McCullers. (Bruce Weber, "Raymond Carver: a Chronicler of Blue-Collar Despair." *New York Times Magazine*, 24 June 1984. *Conversations*, 87)

5. 正式に離婚するのは、1982 年 10 月 18 日である。
6. 1988 年 6 月 17 日、二人は Nevada の Heart of Reno Chapel で式を挙げ、結婚する。

引用文献

Carver, Raymond. *Beginners*. Ed. William L. Stull and Maureen P. Carroll. London: Vintage Books, 2010.

———. *Call if You Need Me*. London: Harville Press, 2000.

———. *Conversations with Raymond Carver*. Ed. Marshall Bruce Gentry and William L. Stull. Jackson: University Press of Mississippi, 1990.

———. *Fires*. New York: Vintage Contemporaries, 1989.

———. *The Stories of Raymond Carver: Will You Please Be Quiet, Please? What We Talk About When We Talk About Love, Cathedral*. London: Pan Books, 1985.

———. *Where I'm Calling From*. New York: Vintage Contemporaries, 1989.

Max, D. T. "The Carver Chronicles." *New York Times Magazine* (August 9, 1998): 34–40, 51, & 56–57.

Sklenicka, Carol. *Raymond Carver*. New York: Scribner, 2010.

Stull, William L. and Maureen P. Carroll. "Chronology" and "Note on the Texts" in *Raymond Carver: Collected Stories*. Ed. William L. Stull and Maureen P. Carroll. New York: Library of America, 2009. ("Chronology" 957–978, "Note on the Texts" 979–1004)

Beginners を読む

　2009 年 5 月、編集者 Gordon Lish がフェルトペンで書き入れをした Carver のタイプ原稿に基づき、*What We Talk About When We Talk About Love*（1981）の原稿を復元した *Beginners* が出版された。過剰な Lish の編集によって、Carver の人物は喜怒哀楽を奪われたと言われる。[1] 原稿ではどのように笑い、どのように涙を流したのか、*Beginners* を読み、その実態を検証する。

I

　"Where Is Everyone?" を読む。語り手は「私」である。現在は事情も好転しているが、数年前は失業中でアルコール依存症であった「私」が、当時の惨憺たる家庭の事情をユーモアたっぷりに物語る作品である。ユーモアを感じていただくためには、原文を読んで頂く必要があり、そのために引用が多くなるが、ご勘弁願いたい。

　母を訪ねた日のことが、物語の枠組みとなり、また話を紡ぐ糸ともなっている。冒頭から話はショッキングである。

　　I've seen some things. I was going over to my mother's to stay a few nights, but just as I came to the top of the stairs I looked and she was on the sofa kissing a man. It was summer, the door was open, and the color TV was playing. (11)

そして、「惨憺たる家庭の事情」が次のように要約される。

> A lot has happened since that afternoon, and on the whole things are better now. But during those days, when my mother was putting out to men she'd just met, I was out of work, drinking, and crazy. My kids were crazy, and my wife was crazy and having a "thing" with an unemployed aerospace engineer she'd met at AA. He was crazy too. (11)

「私」はまだ妻に未練たっぷりであるが、二人の関係は冷え冷えとしている。それでも、たまには二人が愛し合った昔のことを語り合うことがある。

> One afternoon we were in the living room and she said, "When I was pregnant with Mike you carried me to the bathroom when I was so sick and pregnant I couldn't get out of bed. You carried me. No one else will ever do that, no one else could ever love me in that way, that much. We have that, no matter what. We've loved each other like nobody else could or ever will love the other again." (15)

しかしそこで、お互いに見詰め合いながら、「私」は二人が掛けているソファーの下にウォッカの瓶を隠していたことを思い出し、用件を言い付けて妻に席を外させ、早速お酒に手を伸ばすという有様である。

　そして、二人が通常話し合うのは、もっと切羽詰まった窮状打開についての話しである。

> But those conversations touching on love or the past were rare. If we talked, we talked about business, survival, the bottom line of things. Money. Where is the money going to come from? The telephone was on the way out, the lights and gas threatened. What about Katy?…. What's going to happen to Mike? What's going to happen to us all? "My God," she'd say. But God wasn't having any of it. He'd washed his hands of us. (15–16)

"My God" 以下の神頼みは正に哄笑に価する。

　妻の浮気の相手は Ross である。Ross は中古車に乗り、同じ女に必死でしがみ付こうとしていること以外にも、いろいろと「私」と共通点を持っている。同じようにアルコール依存症である。そのために NASA を首になっている。しかし、女性関係の派手さは「私」と異なる。二回の離婚歴があり、五人か六人の子供を抱え、「私」の妻以外にも、22 歳の若い女を愛人にしている。そのことを「私」の妻である Cynthia に責められると、Ross は次のように弁解し、当然の成り行きとしてその場は修羅場となる。

> Ross loved Cynthia, but he also had a twenty-two-year-old girl named Beverly who was pregnant with his baby, though Ross assured Cynthia he loved her, not Beverly. They didn't even sleep together any longer, he told Cynthia, but Beverly was carrying his baby and he loved all his children, even the unborn, and he couldn't just give her the boot, could he? He wept when he told all this to Cynthia. He was drunk. (Someone was always drunk in those days.) I can imagine the scene. (16)

またある日のこと、酔った「私」は、本心では妻と子供達を手放すつもりはないのに、嫌がらせで「おまえさんには Cynthia と子供達を養う気はあるのかね」と電話で Ross を問い詰める。その場面は次の通りである。

> I grabbed the phone. "Well, are you going to support them or not?" He said he was sorry for his part in all of this but, no, he guessed he couldn't support them. "So it's No, you can't support them," I said, and looked at Cynthia as if this should settle everything. He said, "Yes, it's no." But Cynthia didn't bat an eye. I figured later they'd already talked that situation over thoroughly, so it was no surprise. She already knew. (16–17)

「私」が Ross と共通点を持っていることは既に述べたが、両者の子供に対する態度は対照的である。Ross は既に見たように子供には生まれる前の胎児に対してさえ愛情を抱くが、「私」は子供に対してはむしろ憎しみを抱き、それが掴み合いにまで発展することがある。

> One afternoon I screamed and got into a scuffle with my son. Cynthia had to break it up when I threatened to knock him to pieces. I said I would kill him. I said, "I gave you life and I can take it away." Madness. (13)

しかし、子供達がそんな父親に屈することはない。自由闊達でたくましい。両親の失策を喰い物にし、喜々として楽しんでいる。

> The kids, Katy and Mike, were only too happy to take advantage

of this crumbling situation. They seemed to thrive on the threats and bullying they inflicted on each other and on us—the violence and dismay, the general bedlam. …they saw craziness on every side, and it suited their purpose, I was convinced. They fattened on it. They liked being able to call the shots, having the upper hand, while we bungled along letting them work on our guilt. (13–14)

冒頭の場面で母の密会に遭遇して面喰った「私」は、時間をつぶしたあと、もういいだろうと母に電話をする。逢引きを盗見されたなどとは思いもしない母は平気なもので、その母との電話は次の通りである。

"I'm not at home," I said. "I don't know where everyone is at home. I just called there."
"Old Ken was over here today," she went on, "that old bastard. He came over this afternoon…. He's just an old braggart, that's all he is. I met him at that dance I told you about, but I don't like him." (19)

その夜は母のアパートに厄介になり、この物語はここで終る。
　このようにこの物語は構成も良く、語り方は、皮肉を交えながら、ユーモアにあふれている。スラングやクリシェが多用され、それも喜劇的効果を高めている。
　Carver はこのようなユーモアによって始めて崩壊に瀕した自己を客観視することができ、更にそれを作品化することによって、アルコール依存症の地獄から立ち直ることができた。[2] その意味でも、この作品は記念碑的な短篇である。
　What We Talk About の最終稿を読んだ Carver が、この短編集に Lish の編集した形で入れるのに最後まで抵抗したのが、"Mr. Coffee

and Mr. Fixit" と改題された "Where Is Everyone?" であった。[3] その理由が分かる。

　Lish はこの作品に大鉈をふるう。削除率は 78% である。[4] 単に削り取られただけではなく、内容の変更も散見される。余りにもそぎ落とされ、Lish の編集に特徴的な簡潔な文体にはなっているが、同時に笑いやユーモアが生まれるゆとりも失われ、結果的に何を狙った作品か分からないものになっている。

　この "Mr. Coffee and Mr. Fixit" には、Carver 党を自任する村上春樹氏も音を上げ、「そういういくつもの事実が、たたみかけるようにばらばらと列挙してあるだけである。まるで悲劇のショウケースのダイゼスト版みたいに…」と解説している。[5]

II

　涙と救いをテーマとする "A Small, Good Thing" を読む。土曜日の午後、Ann は月曜日に八歳の誕生日を迎える息子 Scotty のお祝いのケーキをパン屋に注文に行く。その誕生日当日の月曜日の下校中に、Scotty は自動車事故に遭い入院を余儀なくされる。誕生パーティは勿論キャンセルで、入院後間もなく Scotty は昏睡状態になる。両親は息子の枕許に釘付けになる。

　その日の深夜、父 Howard は入浴と休息を兼ねて一時帰宅する。早々にパン屋からの電話を受ける。ケーキ注文のことなど何も聞いていない父は何のことやら分らず、深夜の突然の電話にただ不気味さを覚える。

　夜中の 12 時を少し廻った頃、Howard は病院に戻る。主治医の回診がある。主治医の診断は最初から「ショックによって意識を失っ

ているだけで、意識はすぐに回復しますよ」というもので、その診断はこの深夜の回診でも変らない。

　しかし、何時までも意識が戻らない息子を見ている Ann の心配は深まるばかりで、そのような妻を夫はいたわる。その時の夫に対する妻の気持ちは次のように表現される。

> Almost for the first time, she felt they were together in it, this trouble. Then she realized it had only been happening to her and to Scotty. She hadn't let Howard into it, though he was there and needed all along. She could see he was tired. The way his head looked heavy and angled into his chest. She felt a good tenderness toward him. She felt glad to be his wife. (61)

この通い合う夫婦の愛は救いのテーマを導入する伏線となっている。

　まだ夜明け前の深夜に Scotty は頭部スキャン検査のため検査室へ移動し、日の出のあと病室へ戻る。火曜日の朝である。その日は午後と夜間の二回主治医の診察があり、二人はベッドの傍に付きっきりで見守るが、Scotty は昏睡から覚めない。

　最夜中を過ぎ水曜日となった日の夜明け前の深夜、Ann は入浴と休息のため一時帰宅する。帰宅して間もない頃電話のベルが鳴る。深夜のことでもあり、パン屋のことなど全く頭にない Ann は、ただ Scotty のことと言って切れた電話の声に脅える。病院に電話を入れ、Scotty の病状に急変がないことを確かめて安堵した Ann は急いで入浴を済ませ、病院へ車を走らせる。

　病院への途中 Ann の不安な心には、二年前の大雨の時の Scotty の行方不明事件のことが回想される。川遊びをしていた Scotty が突然の大雨に出会い、雨宿りをしていて帰宅が遅くなり、大騒ぎへと発

展したことが思い出される。そして同時に、「Scottyの命をお助け下されば、ぜいたくな郊外住宅地の暮しを捨てて、私達が育った小さな町の質素な生活に戻ります」と神に祈ったことも思い出され、現在の苦しみは、神の加護によってScottyが無事であったあとも、相変わらずのぜいたくを続けていることに対する神の罰ではないかとの思いで、不安が募る。

　病室に戻ると夫から「先程神経科の先生と主治医が見え、診断では手術が必要のようだ」と知らされる。そんな話をしている時、突然目を開いた息子にHowardが気付く。しかしその目には何も見えていないようだ。

> "Look!" Howard said then. "Scotty! Look, Ann!" He turned her toward the bed.
> The boy had opened his eyes, then closed them. He opened them again now. The eyes stared straight ahead for a minute, then moved slowly in his head until they rested on Howard and Ann, then traveled away again. (73)

両親の必死の呼び掛けと愛撫も空しく、歯をかみしめた口から最後の息が静かにもれて、Scottyの息が絶える。臨終の場面は悲痛極まりない。

> The boy looked at them again, though without any sign of recognition or comprehension. Then his eyes scrunched closed, his mouth opened, and he howled until he had no more air in his lungs. His face seemed to relax and soften then. His lips parted as his last breath was puffed through his throat and exhaled gently through the clenched teeth. (73)

AnnとHowardは悲しみのどん底に突き落とされる。「大丈夫です」と二人を安心させていた主治医はただひたすらに謝るばかりで、二人の悲しみが薄らぐことはない。主治医の病理解剖の頼みも断り、二人は帰宅する。正午少し前である。
　帰宅後電話のベルが鳴る。受話器を取ったAnnと電話の主との応答は次の通りである。

　　　"Hello, " she said…. "Hello! Hello!" she said. "For God's sake," she said. "Who is this? What is it you want? Say something."
　　　"Your Scotty, I got him ready for you," the man's voice said. "Did you forget him?"
　　　"You evil bastard!" she shouted into the receiver. "How can you do this, you evil son of a bitch?"
　　　"Scotty," the man said. "Have you forgotten about Scotty?" Then the man hung up on her. (75)

例のパン屋からの電話である。事情を知らないパン屋としては、注文したものを取りに来ない無責任な客に対する気の効いたパンチ位の気持で軽く言ったのであろうが、息子の死に直面し悲嘆に暮れる母親にとっては、"Your Scotty, I got him ready for you" とは、まさにのど元に突き付けられた刃にも等しい残酷なものである。
　深夜の12時の直前再び電話があり、ようやくAnnはそれが誕生祝いのケーキを頼んだパン屋からの電話であることに気が付く。度重なる深夜の嫌がらせの電話の主が分かり、激怒したAnnは夫をせき立ててパン屋へ車を走らせる。二人はパン屋と対決し、その場は険悪になる。しかし息子の事故死をパン屋に打ち明けたとたん、Annの高まった怒りは急速に収まり、悲しみの涙がわき出る。

事情を知ったパン屋は同情と後悔の念に打たれ、お詫びと慰めの心を込めて焼き立てのパンをすすめる。真心のこもったパンを食べる二人には、悲痛のどん底から蘇生する思いが込み上げる。物語の最後は次のように結ばれている。

> "Here, smell this," the baker said, breaking open a dark loaf. "It's a heavy bread, but rich." They smelled it, then he had them taste it. It had the taste of molasses and coarse grains. They listened to him. They ate what they could. They swallowed the dark bread. It was like daylight under the fluorescent trays of light. They talked on into the early morning, the high pale cast of light in the windows, and they did not think of leaving. (80)

和やかなおしゃべりはいつまでも続く。パン屋の窓から見える白み始めた夜明けの空は、悲しみからの救いを象徴している。

"The Bath" と改題された Lish の編集では、水曜日の深夜の夜明け前に Ann が帰宅して電話を受けるところで物語は終る。Scotty の生死は不明のままで終り、深夜の電話に象徴される脅威と不気味さのみが強調される。これまで見てきたような涙と救いの情景は、きれいさっぱり拭い取られている。削除率は 78% である。[6]

Carver は成長期に父親がワシントン州のヤキマの製材所の鋸の目立てをする Filer であった関係で、ヤキマの自然の中で育つ。子供の頃から父のお供でフィシュイングやハンティングに親しんでいる。そのような Carver が描く *Beginners* の世界は自ずから、自然の空気に包まれ土の香りに満ちている。また描かれている人物達は情動性に富み、喜怒哀楽の表出が豊かで読者に親しみを感じさせる。しか

しLishの編集では、そのような情緒性の豊かな人間味のある人物は見事にかき消されている。

　Adam MeyerはCarver文学の発展形態を砂時計に譬えた。[7] その比喩を用いれば、砂時計のくびれた部分は、これまで見てきた二つの例でも分かるように、Carver文学の本来的な成長過程によるものではなく、Lishの無理な編集によってもたらされたものである。Carverの詳細な伝記を書いたCarol Sklenickaは、この問題に触れて次の如く述べている。

> A generation of Carver scholars has already made the mistake of assuming that *What We Talk About* represents an extreme minimalist phase in Carver's work from which he began to rebound in his next story collection, *Cathedral*, an interpretation that Carver himself supplied in several interviews. (Sklenicka 362)

注
1. Max, 37.
2. Stull and Carroll, 997.
3. Stull and Carroll, 997.
4. Stull and Carroll, 999.
5. 村上春樹「解題」284.
6. Stull and Carroll, 1000.
7. Meyer, 239–40.

引用文献

Carver, Raymond. *Beginners*. Ed. William L. Stull and Maureen P. Carroll.

London: Vintage, 2010.

―――. *Conversations with Raymond Carver*. Ed. Marshall Bruce Gentry and William L. Stull. Jackson: University Press of Mississippi, 1990.

―――. *Fires*. New York: Vintage Books, 1984.

―――. *The Stories of Raymond Carver: Will You Please Be Quiet, Please?, What We Talk About When We Talk About Love, Cathedral*. London: Pan Books, 1985.

―――. *Where I'm Calling From*. New York: Vintage Books, 1989.

Max, D. T. "The Carver Chronicles." *New York Times Magazine* (August 9, 1998): 34–40, 51, & 56–57.

Meyer, Adam. "Now You See Him, Now You Don't, Now You Do Again: The Evolution of Raymond Carver's Minimalism." *Critique* 30 (1989): 239–51.

Sklenicka, Carol. *Raymond Carver*. New York: Scribner, 2010.

Stull, William L. and Maureen P. Carroll. "Note on the Texts" in *Raymond Carver: Collected Stories*. Ed. William L. Stull and Maureen P. Carroll. New York: Library of America, 2009. 979–1004.

村上春樹　「解題」レイモンド・カーヴァー『愛について語るときに我々の語ること』村上春樹訳. 東京：中央公論新社, 2006. 277–301.

Ⅳ　研究余滴

Kawabata's *Snow Country*

Why can't Shimamura love Komako? Through this question I try to approach *Snow Country*, one of the greatest novels in modern Japan. Shimamura, the hero, is too subtle. We cannot make a clear image of his character and we have the impression that his impotency in love is predestined no matter how the story may develop. It will be better to begin by referring to some other cases of love in Kawabatat's main works. First, *The Izu Dancer* will be reviewed as a typical novel of his early years, then *The Sound of the Mountain* as one typical of his late years. (Chronologically, *Snow Country* comes in the middle between them.)[1]

The Izu Dancer is a story about Platonic love between a high-school student and a young itinerant dancer. 'I', the student, travels Izu Peninsula alone and happens to meet the dancer. With her glossy hair, bright eyes, flowery smile, she is so attractive that he cannot repress his desire to travel with the troupe she belongs to, and when he hears that such dancers often become their patrons' mistresses he is driven to lustful fancy about her. But that fancy is washed away clean one morning when he finds her calling him from a far-off bathroom with her both hands raised high and with nothing on her body. "She is nothing but a child,"[2] he says to himself feeling intense relief, and his affection for her becomes pure and strong. Though something about her hair-do makes her appear to be seventeen or so, she is in fact a girl of fourteen.[3] Mentally and physically, she is now at the turning point from child to girl. Sometimes she is bold like a child, sometimes shy like a girl, and sometimes tender like a mother. And this composite character seems to form her strange attractiveness for him.

In contrast to 'I' in *The Izu Dancer* who belongs to the rising generation, Shingo, the hero of *The Sound of the Mountain*, belongs to the declining generation. He is afraid that the rumbling he sometimes hears from the mountains may be a warning about his death, and now he has long kept himself away from his wife's bed. In his dreams or in his fancy, however, he is haunted by sexual images. They live together with their son's family. Kikuko, their son's wife, is unhappy because her husband takes to drinking and, what is worse, he loves another woman. It seems thet the young couple's marriage is sustained only by physical relations. Shingo consoles her sorrow, but sometimes he is frightened at finding himself strangely drawn to her. Is he seeking in return to get the sorrow of his old age consoled by her affection? When Kikuko joined his family as the bride of his son, he remembers, he found a fresh coquetry in the sort of bashful manner of her movement. Kikuko has a slim beautiful body. This Kikuko somehow reminds him of his wife's elder sister whom he loved in vain in his youth. He married, as it were, on the rebound from that unrequited love. Is such an old wound demanding to be healed by Kikuko, his daughter-in-law? Surely, there is something more than a mere fatherly sympathy in his attitude toward her. It cannot be defined clearly. Only, the following incident may serve to define it. One day Kikuko wears a Noh-mask representing an eternal boy, and it is at this moment that Shingo is most strongly attracted by her. Is he attracted by Kikuko's body behind the mask? Or is he attracted by the mask itself? The eternal boy is, according to an old legend in China, said to drink sacred water and gain strange power which enables him to remain eternally young. We are only sure that he is almost irresistibly drawn to Kikuko with the mask on her face. Muramatsu comments on this point: "Even if Shingo tears off the mask and gets her body behind it, his longing will never be satisfied because the mask of an eternal boy will be there still as if it were pitying him who commits such an act."[4] As is symbolically shown by this incident, here again we can see woman's attractiveness comes from a strange composite. In this case, the composite consists of the following two elements: one is what Kikuko's body symbolizes and the other is what the mask symbolizes.

We have reviewed two of Kawabata's typical works and it seems to me that the nature of childhood is indispensable for a woman to be attractive for a hero in Kawabata's literature. This peculiar structure of woman has a deep relation with his mental structure, more definitely, with his life as an orphan. Kawabata lost his father, mother and grandmother one after another. He was left alone with his grandfather, who was indeed his only near-kin so far as he can remember. In his *Diary of a Sixteen-Year-Old* we can see how strong was his fear that he might be bereaved of this grandfather. The grandfather, however, died soon after the last date of the diary. Kawabata was then taken care of by his uncle's family.

Later, such a state of orphanage compelled him to write many stories dealing with it. Among them we find a rather strange one. It takes a form of the author's letter to his late parents. In that letter he says that he has no memory about his parents and that he thinks he has never had the innocent mind of a child and that therefore it is his secret bliss to play with a little child.[5] Considering that the story is an artistic work there may be some fiction. But I think it was Kawabata's true confession and that the consciousness that he had never had the innocent mind of a child forced him to long for it more strongly than anyone else.

At the age of twenty-three Kawabata loved a girl of sixteen. That was his first love though it was soon frustrated. "The Fire in the South" is a story based on it. The story describes the hero's conception of marriage as follows:

> The marriage Tokio fancied was not to make husband and wife of them, but to make them both return to childhood and to make them play as their innocent minds please. He and Yumiko, both having lost their homes in their earliest days, had not lived with a true childish mind. That buried childish mind he wanted to dig up with her help. All he was thinking about was how to let Yumiko play like a child when they had their sweet home in Tokyo. On the other hand, he was always afflicted with how wrong it must have affected his mind that he had not spent any happy days in his childhood. But from that wound he could be relieved by the marriage, he thought. And for the first time in his life he thought he could see his way brightly shining ahead of him.[6]

Now, you can see the basic pattern of love in Kawabata's literature: Love is an action to regain lost childhood through woman. In other words, a woman is the incarnation of the childhood Kawabata's inner-self is striving to return to. So long as you remain within the limit of Platonic love you can dream such a love. But, once you step across that limit, you must realize this: You are attracted by a woman as the incarnation of childhood, and you approach to her, but when you get her body you are driving away the childhood you are trying to regain. Hence the purified love in *The Izu Dancer*, and the frustration in *The Sound of the Mountain*. Then, let's turn to *Snow Country*.

shimamura is an idler who lives on the money inherited from his parents. As a hobby he is studying dance, formerly Japanese dance but now Western dance. He prefers it to the Japanese dance because, so far as he studies it, he can keep himself aloof from the actual world of dance and freely enjoy his fanciful world of dance which is made from the books and the photographs imported from the West. Living such an idle life, he thinks he tends to lose his honesty with himself and so he frequently goes alone into the mountains wishing to recover it. On his way back from one of these excursions he visits a hot-spring village in the snow country, and there he meets Komako.

Shimamura is struck at the fresh and clean impression she gives him when they meet for the first time. But, as Komako loves him more deeply, the more does he become conscious of the empty feeling in his mind. And, as if it were to fill up that emptiness, there becomes stronger in his mind the image of another girl, whom he first saw in the train on his way to visit the snow country wishing to meet Komako again. That girl is Yoko, who has such a clear voice and such bright eyes that you can hardly believe that they belong to this earth. Above all we get the impression that she is hardly more than a child. As you easily suspect now, Yoko is the symbol of woman Kawabata's heroes are always allured by. But Shimamura must be aware that to love Yoko will result in the same frustration as his experience with Komako. Such a frustrated state of Shimamura's love is most beautifully symbolized in the following scene, where Shimamura glances at Yoko reflected in the train window:

> In his boredom, Shimamura stared at his left hand as the forefinger bent and unbent. Only this hand seemed to have a vital and immediate memory of the woman he was going to see. The more he tried to call up a clear picture of her, the more his memory failed him, the farther she faded away, leaving him nothing to catch and hold. In the midst of this uncertainty only the one hand, and in particular the forefinger, even now seemed damp from her touch, seemed to be pulling him back to her from afar. Taken with the strangeness of it, he brought the hand to his face, then quickly drew a line across the misted-over window. A woman's eye floated up before him. He almost called out in his astonishment. But he had been dreaming, and when he came to himself he saw that it was only the reflection in the window of the girl opposite.[7]

In appearance he is going to see the woman whom only a part of his body remembers, but in reality he is going to see the image of a girl in the window, only a reflection which can never be caught.

About Shimamura's love, the author himself tells us in his postscript to *Snow Country* as follows:

> Komako's love is represented. But can we say that Shimamura's love is represented as well? Can't we say rather that the vacancy in his heart which comes from the sorrow and the regret that he cannot love, none the less throws Komako's pathetic figure into relief?[8]

Notes

1. My analysis owes much to Muramatsu's "Women Figures in Kawabata's literature."
2. *Izu Dancer*, *Zenshu* vol. 1, 208. Translation is mine unless otherwise mentioned.
3. The age is counted in the old Japanese way. In the new way, the girl is twelve or thirteen depending on her birthday.
4. Muramatsu, 327.
5. "Letter to My Parents," *Zenshu* vol. 2, 287–88.
6. "Fire in the South," *Zenshu* vol. 2, 390.
7. *Snow Country*, Tr. Seidensticker, 6–7.
8. Kawabata, "Afterword," *Yukiguni*, 180–81.

Works Cited

Kawabata, Yasunari. *Kawabata Yasunari Zenshu* (The Complete Works of Kawabata Yasunari) 12 vols. Tokyo: Shincho-sha, 1959–62.

———. "The Diary of a Sixteen-Year-Old" (Jurokusai no Nikki) *Zenshu* vol. 1. 7–40.

———. "The Fire in the South" (Nampo no Hi) *Zenshu* vol. 2. 361–408.

———. *The Izu Dancer* (Izu no Odoriko) *Zenshu* vol. 1. 197–226.

———. "The Letter to My Parents" (Fubo e no Tegami) *Zenshu* vol. 2. 285–332.

———. *Snow Country* (Yukiguni) *Zenshu* vol. 5. 263–388.

———. "Afterword." *Yukiguni*. Tokyo: Iwanami, 1957.

———. *Snow Country*. Tr. Edward G. Seidensticker. Tokyo: Charles E. Tuttle, 1957

———. *The Sound of the Mountain* (Yama no Oto) *Zenshu* vol. 8. 145–427.

Muramatsu, Takeshi. "The Women Figures in Kawabata's Literature" (Kawabata Bungaku no Josei-zo) *Kawabata Yasunari—Kindai Bungaku Kansho-koza* vol. 13. Ed. Yamamoto Kenkichi. Tokyo: Kadokawa, 1959. 326–35.

漱石の見た耳納連山

　明治30年の春、漱石は親友菅虎雄が帰省していた久留米に旅行し、その折高良山から発心山まで耳納連山を縦走した。そのとき「高良山一句」以下句稿10句をつくっているが、そのうちの5句が句碑に刻まれている。2011年 の秋句碑をめぐるバスツアーに参加し、漱石の足跡をたどった。しかし漱石が尾根路をススキをかき分けながら山を越えた頃と、雑木林の中の舗装した道を車で駆け抜ける現代との、時の隔たりは余りにも大きいことを痛感せざるを得なかった。

　では漱石が登った山の景観は実際にはどのようなものであったのか。何しろ百年以上も前のことである。それを確かめるのは容易ではない。漱石が遺した資料としては先ほど述べた俳句がある。明治30年4月18日付の子規宛の手紙に、「今春期休に久留米に至り高良山に登り夫より山越を致し発心と申す處の桜を見物致候」(98) とあり、漱石はこの手紙に、句稿51句を添えている。そのうちの10句がこの山越えの報告である。それから、『草枕』の舞台の那古井は熊本の小天温泉をモデルとしているが、那古井に至る山登りを描いた第一章のモデルがこの時の山越えである。(小宮豊隆 325-7、原武 哲『夏目漱石と菅虎雄』148-9) 山越えの俳句と『草枕』を手掛りとし、それを往時の文献などで補強しながら、漱石の見た耳納連山の再現を試みて見たい。[1]

　古代から宿場町として栄え、また高良大社の門前町として賑わっ

た御井の町並みをあとにした漱石は、大鳥居をくぐって表参道を登ったに違いない。御手洗池の太鼓橋を渡ると間もなく第二の鳥居がある。ここから道は岩や石が階段状に敷き詰められた急峻な山道となる。道の両側にはうっ蒼たる杉の大樹が並ぶ。高良山御井寺の第五十世座主寂源が植林した杉と伝えられ、樹齢は漱石の頃既に二百年は優に超えている。後日、『草枕』の主人公に「兎角に人の世は住みにくい」(387) と述懐させた漱石は、この昼なお暗い山路を登りながら何を考えたのであろうか。

　間もなく左手の路傍に、柵で囲んだ馬蹄石と称する石のくぼみがある。神馬のひずめ跡と伝えられるこの石の全体は、その大部分は土に埋もれているが、巨大な岩石である。倉富了一の『高良山物語』には、寂源が植林を始める前の高良山について次の記述がある。

　　　　然らば其の以前の山の相貌は如何であつたらうか、察する所其れ
　　　は東の峯きなる水縄山(みのう)の頂上の様に一本の大木とてもない一面の
　　　草山か、又は突兀(とつこつ)たる岩山であつたと考へねばならない。(8)

この物語に従えば、馬蹄石は「突兀たる岩山」の露頭部であると考えられる。

　このような露頭部は参道に限らず、耳納スカイラインができる前は、漱石がたどったと思われる山路にも随所に見られた。『草枕』は述べる。

　　　　……余の右足は突然坐りのわるい角石の端を踏み損(そ)くなつた。平
　　　衡を保つ為めに、すはやと前に飛び出した左足が、仕損じの埋め
　　　合せをすると共に、余の腰は具合よく方三尺程の岩の上に卸(お)りた。
　　　……路は頗(すこぶ)る難義だ。

土をならす丈なら左程手間も入るまいが、土の中には大きな石
がある。土は平らにしても石は平らにならぬ。石は切り砕いても、
岩は始末がつかぬ。掘崩した土の上に悠然と峙(そばだ)つて、吾等の為めに
道を譲る景色はない。向ふで聞かぬ上は乗り越すか、廻らなければ
ならん。(388-9)

　大鳥居から15町で三の鳥居に着く。ここから本殿境内へ昇る石
段となる。石段は131段である。昇り詰めて振り返ると石段のはる
か彼方に肥前の山が見える。今は何らの痕跡もないが、拝殿の近く
には桜があったらしく、満開を過ぎた花びらが鈴を鳴らす拝殿にも
吹き込む。そのような情景を詠んだのが次の2句である。

　　石磴(とう)や曇る肥前の春の山
　　拝殿に花吹き込むや鈴の音 (212-3)

　漱石の山越えの道は大体現在の耳納スカイラインと重なる。高良
山の森を抜けて尾根筋に出ると急に視界が開ける。当時の尾根筋に
はスギやヒノキの樹林はなく、いくらかの立木や潅木が混じるスス
キやカヤの原野が広がっていた。そこは麓の住民が柴や草を刈り取
る共有の採草地であった。尾根筋まで植林が行われたのは戦後のこ
とである。[2]　明治35年から明治37年にかけて調査が実施された山
麓の村落の『山本村是』や『草野町是』を見ても、林業のなかで群
を抜いて生産高が高いのが柴である。このことからも、このような
共有の原野がいかに広かったかが分かる。

　更に、ここで改めて既に引用した昭和9年刊行の『高良山物語』
を見れば、「察する所其れは東の峯続きなる水縄山の頂上の様に一
本の大木とてもない一面の草山か」の文言を見出す。昭和初期の段

階でも、水縄山ともつくる耳納山[3]の頂上は一面の草山であったと述べられている。

　漱石が歩いた尾根路からは右も左も見事な展望を楽しむことができた。『草枕』は描写する。

　　　立ち上がる時に向ふを見ると、路から左の方にバケツを伏せた様な峯が聳えて居る。杉か檜か分からないが根元から頂き迄悉く蒼黒い中に、山桜が薄赤くだんだらに棚引いて、続ぎ目が確と見えぬ位靄が濃い。少し手前に禿山が一つ、群をぬきんでゝ眉に逼る。禿げた側面は巨人の斧で削り去つたか、鋭どき平面をやけに谷の底に埋めて居る。天辺に一本見えるのは赤松だらう。枝の間の空さへ判然して居る。（389）

　これは現在の森林つつじ公園辺りから兜山とその周辺を見たものと思われる。兜山は別名ケシケシ山とも言い、花が終って花頭部が肥大してできたケシケシ坊主とそっくりの禿山であった。山頂にアカマツが一本あり、それが大きく枝分かれして兜の前立てに似ているところから兜山の名前が付いたと聞く。禿山のてっぺんに赤松が一本見えるという漱石の描写は、明らかに兜山を描いたものである。「薄赤くだんだらに棚引いて」いる山桜は、麓の千光寺の裏山の懐良親王陵の桜だろうか。現在将軍山公園となっている陵のまわりには桜の樹林があり、そのなかには漱石の頃の次の世代と思われる桜の古木がある。

　左手の景観について『草枕』の描写は続く。

　　　巌角を鋭どく廻つて、按摩なら真逆様に落つる所を、際どく右へ切れて、横に見下すと、菜の花が一面に見える。（390）

IV-2 漱石の見た耳納連山

耳納連山はまた屏風山とも言われ、北面は屏風のように切り立っている。南面はゆるやかに傾斜し、山また山が連なる。屏風の背に当たる所が尾根路である。尾根路をたどる『草枕』は更に述べる。

> しばらくは路が平で、右は雑木山、左は菜の花の見つゞけである。足の下に時々蒲公英を踏みつける。鋸の様な葉が遠慮なく四方へのして真中に黄色な珠を擁護して居る。菜の花に気をとられて、踏みつけたあとで、気の毒な事をしたと、振り向いて見ると、黄色な珠は依然として鋸のなかに鎮座して居る。(391)

四方へのびのびと葉を広げるこのしたたかなタンポポは、その辺りが日当たりの良い草地であることを示す。そしてこれらの引用からも分かるように、漱石は菜の花に強く引き付けられている。

漱石の菜の花について更に話を進めるためには、これまでたどって来た山路を少し引き返す必要がある。高良山の森を抜け出た所は小高い台地になっていて、昔から飛雲台という名の展望台であった。今も久留米の市街地や筑後平野を見渡す景勝の地として賑わっている。漱石の10句のうち最も有名な菜の花の句は、ここに据えられた自然石に刻まれている。

　　菜の花の遥かに黄なり筑後川 (212)

この句を読んだ時われわれの目にまず浮かぶのは、筑後川河畔を彩る菜の花の風景ではないだろうか。しかし既に見たように、『草枕』には「一面の菜の花」とあり、「菜の花の見つゞけ」とある。

菜の花の句は明らかにこの句碑が建っている辺りからの眺望を詠んだものである。しかし漱石が眺めた風景は今のわれわれが見る風

景とは全く違っていた。漱石が句碑の位置から筑後平野を見渡したと仮定した場合、そこから見渡すことのできるほぼ全域は当時三井郡の農村であった。戦後になって久留米市と合併した市の東部の農村は言うまでもなく、市街地の東半分もまだ三井郡に属していた。明治37年刊行の『三井郡是』の統計に基づいて算出すれば、郡内に点在する村落のすべてを合わせても、宅地部分の平野部に占める割合は7％弱に過ぎず、平野の殆んどすべてが田圃と畑であった。そして、稲の裏作として麦に次ぐ主要な作物であった菜種の麦に対する割合は、麦10に対して菜種4であった。また『福岡県史』によれば、明治後期の筑後平野は全国一の菜種の生産高を誇っていた。菜種は作付面積としては麦に劣っていても、色彩効果としてははるかに麦より目立つ。このことを考慮すれば、江戸育ちの漱石が見た筑後平野は一面の菜の花であった。

　『草枕』によれば、菜の花と共に漱石はヒバリに強く引き付けられた。『草枕』を読む。

　　　　忽ち足の下で雲雀(ひばり)の声がし出した。谷を見下ろしたが、どこで鳴いているか影も形も見えぬ。只声だけが明らかに聞こえる。せつせと忙(せ)しく、絶間なく鳴いて居る。方幾里の空気が一面に蚤に刺されて居た、まれない様な気がする。あの鳥の鳴く音には瞬時の余裕もない。のどかな春の日を鳴き尽くし、鳴きあかし、又鳴き暮らさなければ気が済まんと見える。其上どこ迄も登つて行く、いつ迄も登つて行く。雲雀は屹度(きっと)雲の中で死ぬに相違ない。登り詰めた揚句(あげく)は、流れて雲に入つて、漂ふて居るうちに形は消えてなくなつて、只声丈が空の裡に残るのかも知れない。

　　　　……菜の花が一面に見える。雲雀はあすこへ落ちるのかと思つた。いゝや、あの黄金の原から飛び上がつて来るのかと思つた。次には落ちる雲雀と、上がる雲雀が十文字にすれ違ふのかと思つた。最後に、

落ちる時も、上がる時も、また十文字に擦れ違ふときにも元気よく鳴きつゞけるだらうと思つた。(389-90)

　この菜の花とヒバリの情景は、山越えの翌年の明治31年に漱石が詠んだ漢詩「菜花黄」[4]にも活写されている。既に述べたように、当時の尾根筋はススキやカヤの原野であった。そのことはまたヒバリの好む草地に恵まれていたことを意味する。漱石がヒバリの鳴き声に包まれたのは極めて自然なことであった。

　森林つつじ公園から少し東へ進んだ所に、「人に逢はず雨ふる山の花盛」(213)の句碑がある。立木らしい立木が殆んど無かった当時の尾根筋に桜の樹林があったとは思われない。それから仮に一本の桜がたまたまあったとしても、「人に逢はず」という出だしは花見の人を予期するものであって、山の中の一本桜には相応しくない。更に、この「雨ふる山」の雨は気紛れな春の天気の時雨とは思われない。しとしとと降る雨である。その雨の句碑が既に述べた「菜の花」と次に述べる「丸い山吹く春の風」の二つの晴天の句の句碑の間に、余り距離を置かないで位置していることには違和感がある。この句はあいにくの雨となった花の名所、発心の桜を詠んだものと解釈する方が自然であろう。

　「人に逢はず」の句から更に東へ進むとほどなく次の句碑に出合う。

　　　筑後路や丸い山吹く春の風 (213)

この句碑の所からは、密生した立木に邪魔されなかった漱石の頃には、兜山などの丸い山が見えた筈である。しかし先に見たように、明らかに兜山と思われる丸い禿山は「群をぬきんでて眉に逼る」と

形容されていて、「丸い山吹く春の風」といった穏やかさが無い。
　高良山から発心公園に至る耳納スカイラインは陸上自衛隊の全面的な協力により、昭和37年5月に着工し昭和43年末に完成した。建設当時の『市政くるめ』の縮刷版の頁を繰ると、殆んど毎号に工事の進み具合を知らせる報道がある。「すばらしい眺望」「みごとな景観」など、左右に展開する雄大な風景をたたえる記事が写真と共に頁を飾っている。戦後の植林で尾根筋にまで達していたスギやヒノキの苗木もまだ背が低く、眺望の妨げにはなっていない。第2期工事の完成を報じた昭和38年8月20日号の『市政くるめ』には、現在の紫雲台と思われる高台から兜山、耳納山、高良山などの丸い山を眼下に展望した写真がある。「丸い山」の句碑からは更に東へ3キロほど山路を歩いた地点からの眺めである。山越えで疲れた漱石は、やれやれとこの辺りの岩に腰を下ろして体を休め、春風に吹かれながら眼下の山々を眺めたのではないだろうか。漱石の「丸い山吹く春の風」にはまさにぴったりの景観である。
　春の天気は変り易い。漱石が発心へ近付いたとき雲行きが妖しくなる。その妖しい雲行きを詠んだのが次の2句である。

　　　山高し動（やや）ともすれば春曇る
　　　濃（こま）かに弥生の雲の流れけり　（213）

「山高し」の山は恐らく発心山であろう。「濃かに」の句は発心城址の西に句碑がある。漱石の山越えは発心の桜を見るためであった。しかし発心に着く前に山路は雨になる。その情景を『草枕』から引用する。

　　　　……空があやしくなつて来た。煮え切れない雲が、頭の上へ靠垂（もた）

れ懸つて居たと思つたが、いつのまにか、崩れ出して、四方は只雲の海かと怪しまれる中から、しとしとと春の雨が降り出した。菜の花は疾(と)くに通り過(すご)して、今は山と山の間を行くのだが、雨の糸が濃かで殆(ほと)んど霧を欺(あざむ)く位だから、隔たりはどれ程かわからぬ。時々風が来て、高い雲を吹き払ふとき、薄黒い山の背が右手に見える事がある。何でも谷一つ隔(へだ)てゝ向ふが脈(みゃく)の走つて居る所らしい。左はすぐ山の裾と見える。深く罩(こ)める雨の奥から松らしいものが、ちよくちよく顔を出す。(396–7)

　当時春の発心山は全山桜であった。先ほど参照した『三井郡是』は付録として三井郡の名勝旧蹟を列挙し、発心山について次の如く述べている。

　　　三井郡草野町大字草野ニアリ　箕尾(みのう)山連峰ノ一ナリ　桜樹山ニ満チ春時香雲爛漫タリ（乙54）

箕尾山は勿論耳納山のことであり、香雲とは咲き乱れた桜花の眺めを雲にたとえたものである。当時発心の桜がどれ位全国に喧伝されていたかは分らないが、発心の桜の歴史は古い。
　中世以来筑後に君臨した草野氏は16世紀後半、草野の吉木地区にあった竹井城から発心山に居城を移した。発心山は山頂から山麓まですべて城として固められた。江戸時代中期に描かれた二幅の若宮八幡宮絵縁起がある。その発心城幅には、山頂の発心城をはじめ、山腹の上の城・下の城・発心権現社などが桜や松に囲まれて描かれ、山麓には草野氏の館を中心とする諸家の屋敷や城下町が、賑やかな往来や花見で浮かれた人々の様子と共に、生々と描かれている。注目すべきは山頂から山麓まで桜樹山に満ちている有様である。更に江戸時代には「1738年1月25日藩主〔7代頼徸公〕、発心山の桜花

を見る。──以後代々の慣例行事となる」との記録があり、1828年の記録には「藩主〔9代頼徳公〕、発心山に桜樹の植え継ぎを命じる」とある。(『久留米市史』年表)

　漱石が発心の桜についてどれ位予備知識を持っていたかははっきりしないが、発心の桜に大きな期待を寄せていたことは間違いあるまい。漱石の期待は雨のために裏切られた。明治33年測図の陸地測量部の地図によれば、当時発心の登山道はひとつしかない。発心公園から山頂へ登る道は、現在尾根ルートと横岩ルートの二つに分かれるが、漱石の頃は谷筋を登る横岩ルートだけであった。そして高良山からの縦走路からこのルートに入るには、発心山頂の手前から左へ折れなければならなかった。この道を漱石は発心の桜を探勝しながら下ったに違いない。しかしあいにくの雨であった。雨に濡れた桜の山路を下りながら、漱石はその時の感慨を次の3句に託したと思われる。

　　　　人に逢はず雨ふる山の花盛
　　　　雨に雲に桜濡れたり山の陰
　　　　花に濡るゝ傘なき人の雨を寒み（212-3）

「人に逢はず」の句については既に述べた。「雨に雲に」の句は明らかに下山途中の場面と思われる。「花に濡るゝ」の句は山麓の発心公園の情景かとも思われ、確かなことは分からない。雨のなかで漱石が見た、かって「桜樹山に満ち」とうたわれた桜は、現在はどうなっているのか。観光案内や登山ガイドなどで見る限り、発心公園のほかに桜の名所は見当たらない。

　地勢から見ても、明らかに発心公園の桜を詠んだのが次の句である。発心公園に句碑がある。

松をもて囲ひし谷の桜かな（212）

　発心公園は草野氏の館跡であった。草野氏の館が桜の季節にいかに華やかな賑わいを呈していたかは、先ほど述べた「若宮八幡宮絵縁起」からも明らかである。そして江戸時代の歴代藩主の観桜が、この草野氏の館跡を中心として行われたであろうことも容易に想像がつく。明治になってからは、市民の花見の公園として整備された。久留米市制施行120周年記念の写真集『ふるさと久留米』には、明治45年に撮影された「草野町の発心公園」がある。咲き乱れる山桜の樹林が鮮明に写し出されていて、漱石の見た桜をほうふつさせる。漱石が公園に着いたとき、雨はまだ降っていたのだろうか。それとも小雨になっていたのだろうか。「松をもて」の句には松と桜の対照が奏でる美しさがある。

　発心公園の桜は当時の山桜に代って今はソメイヨシノである。終戦直後、占領軍兵士の花見を避けるためにすべてが伐採され、今はそのあとに植えられた苗木が大樹となって市民の目を楽しませている。

　「松をもて囲ひし」と漱石が詠んだ松は今は無い。戦前までは、公園のまわりの山は見事なアカマツの林であった。戦中戦後の乱伐のあとスギやヒノキの植林に代えられ、残っていた松も松くい虫のために枯死したという。このような松は、引用した『草枕』にも「松らしいものが、ちよくちよく顔を出す」とあったように、耳納連山には各所にあった。しかしそれらの松も発心の松と同じ運命をたどった。今は、竹林が多い山麓を除けば、どこを向いても植林されたスギとヒノキである。それも放置され、雑木のからみ合ったジャングルになっている。漱石の頃は山麓の住民が先祖以来多年の歳月

を重ねて育て上げた里山であった。

　耳納連山も漱石が山越えをした頃とはすっかり変ってしまった。しかし漱石の頃と昭和10年代のわれわれの子供の頃とは、余り変っていないような気がする。今の時代よりもむしろ漱石の時代に親近感を覚えるのは歳を取ったせいかも知れないが、それだけではなさそうだ。人間社会の「進歩」によって、皮肉なことに、人と自然との共生の象徴ともいうべき里山が破壊されてしまったのである。漱石が見たのは最も美しい頃の耳納連山であった。

　発心公園の桜見物のあとの漱石について、原武　哲の『夏目漱石と菅虎雄』は次のように述べる。

　　もし菅虎雄が妹・順(ジュン)の嫁ぎ先、[5] 善導寺村木塚の一富家で養生していたならば、発心の桜見物の後、一富家に立ち寄ったであろう。(149)

　更に「もし」を続ける。もしその時、雨が既に上がっていたら、漱石は一面の菜の花の彼方に沈む真赤な夕日に向って木塚への道を急いだに違いない。漱石が山越えの句稿と共に子規へ送った句稿のなかに次の句がある。

　　菜の花の中へ大きな入日かな [6]（210）

　このような推測が正しく、またこの句がその時の情景を詠んだ句であるとすれば、この句は山越えの句の最後を飾る11句目となる。[7]
　終りに、これまで述べた漱石の山越えの道の略図を添え、結びに代える。数字は漱石の句に付した番号で、[8] その句が詠まれたと思われる地点を示す。

IV-2 漱石の見た耳納連山

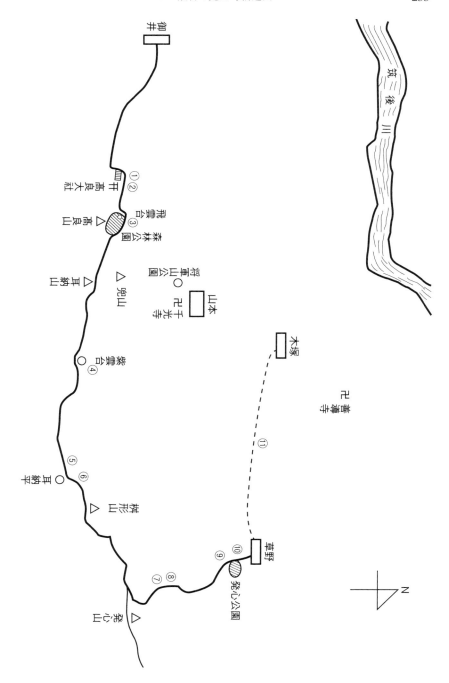

注
1. 執筆に際しては多くの方のご教示に与った。特に、「漱石の句碑をめぐるツアー」のガイドを務めて頂いた原武　哲氏には既発表分を読んで頂き、懇切なご指摘を賜った。また福留久大氏には「村是」のことで教えて頂いた。心からお礼を申し上げたい。
2. 例えば、兜山山麓の柳坂に建てられた「造林記念碑」によれば、植林が開始されたのは昭和23年であり、完成したのは昭和43年であった。そして碑文には「柳坂部落共有原野は約百町歩と伝えられ古より其の大半は薪炭採草地として利用し来り……」とある。
3. この耳納山が耳納山脈の一つの峰、すなわち標高367.9メートルの耳納山を指しているのか。それとも耳納山脈全体をさしているのかは明らかでない。現在「耳納山」には両義があり、そのどちらを指すのかは文脈で使い分けられているが、古来、一般には耳納山脈全体を指して用いられる場合が多い。

　　江戸時代中期に刊行された『筑後志』には耳納山について次の記述がある。

　　　　高良山より、御井・山本・竹野・生葉の四郡に聯（つら）なり、其山勢恰（あたか）も長蛇の宛転（えんてん）するが如く、一山脈の連峯にして、遠くこれを望めば、其状恰も列屏の如し、故に俚俗これを屏風山といふ。山下の村里薪秣（しんまつ）を爰（ここ）に採り、渓水混々として田畝（でんぽ）に灌漑し、良材薬草を産して、其益尤も大なり。（『校訂筑後志』27）

既に江戸時代に、耳納連山が里山として山麓の住民の生計を支えていた有様が如実に描かれていて興味深い。耳納山地一帯の旧四郡は、その後明治29年に三井、浮羽の二つの郡に統合され、その際生葉郡の星野村は八女郡に編入された。

4.　　菜花黄　明治31年3月　　　　菜花黄（さいかこう）　一海知義訳

　　菜花黄朝暾　　　　　菜花　朝暾（ちょうとん）に黄に
　　菜花黄夕陽　　　　　菜花　夕陽（せきよう）に黄なり

菜花黄裏人	菜花　黄裏の人
晨昏喜欲狂	晨昏　喜びて狂わんと欲す
曠懐随雲雀	曠懐　雲雀に随い
沖融入彼蒼	沖融　彼の蒼に入る
縹緲近天都	縹緲として　天都に近く
迢遥凌塵郷	迢遥として　塵郷を凌ぐ
斯心不可道	斯の心　道う可からず
厥楽自潢洋	厥の楽しみ　自ら潢洋たり
恨未化為鳥	恨むらくは　未だ化して鳥と為り
啼尽菜花黄	菜花の黄を啼き尽くさざるを（205）

5. 正確には順はまだ一冨家に嫁いでいない。この時嫁いでいたのは虎雄の直ぐ下の妹の松代である。順が嫁いだのは、戸籍では明治32年となっているが、実際には明治31年の早春の頃であった。（江下博彦29-33）しかし、虎雄が順と共に一冨家で養生していた可能性は大きい。（小城左昌17-20）

6. 坪内稔典の脚注に『「大きな」の右脇に自ら「真赤な」と代案を記す』とある。（210）

7. 小城左昌の『夏目漱石と祖母「一冨順」』はこの句を、「菜の花の遙かに黄なり筑後川」と共に、漱石が高良山から菜の花を詠んだ句として挙げる。同書によれば、漱石が高良山から菜の花を見たのは夕方であり、その日は漱石は追分付近で山を下りて木塚の一冨家に泊り、翌日山麓の道を通って発心公園の桜見物にでかけたという推定である。（20-1）

8. 俳句の番号は次の通り。
    ①　石磴や曇る肥前の春の山
    ②　拝殿に花吹き込むや鈴の音
    ③　菜の花の遙かに黄なり筑後川
    ④　筑後路や丸い山吹く春の風
    ⑤　山高し動ともすれば春曇る
    ⑥　濃かに弥生の雲の流れけり
    ⑦　人に逢はず雨ふる山の花盛り

⑧　雨に雲に桜濡れたり山の陰
⑨　花に濡るゝ傘なき人の雨を寒み
⑩　松をもて囲ひし谷の桜かな
⑪　菜の花の中へ大きな入日かな

参照文献

夏目漱石「草枕」『漱石全集　第二巻』岩波書店、昭和41年。

夏目漱石「書簡集」『漱石全集　第十四巻』岩波書店、昭和41年。

夏目漱石「俳句」『漱石全集　第十七巻』岩波書店、1996年。

夏目漱石「漢詩」『漱石全集　第十八巻』岩波書店、1995年。

『三井郡是』　明治36年調査着手、明治37年完結。

『山本村是』　明治35年調査着手、明治36年中止、明治37年結了。

『草野町是』　明治35年調査着手、明治36年結了。

「若宮八幡宮絵縁起　発心城幅」江戸時代中期、若宮八幡宮蔵。

杉山正仲・小川正格共著『筑後志』1777年。『校訂筑後志』黒岩万次郎校訂、本荘知新堂、1907年。久留米郷土研究会復刻、1974年。

『ふるさと久留米』久留米市制施行120周年記念写真集、郷土出版社、平成21年。

『市政くるめ　縮刷版Ⅰ』久留米市、平成元年。

「二万分一地形図　久留米」大日本帝国陸地測量部、明治33年測図。

「二万分一地形図　草野」大日本帝国陸地測量部、明治33年測図。

『改訂版　自然歩道ガイド――耳納連山――』久留米市観光協会、昭和62年。

『久留米市史　第四巻』現代の久留米、久留米市、平成元年。

『久留米市史　第五巻』民俗、久留米市、昭和61年。

『久留米市史　第六巻』年表、久留米市、平成2年。

『福岡県史　通史編近代産業経済（二）』福岡県、平成12年。

『福岡県の地名』平凡社、2004年。

荒　正人「夏目漱石（金之助）と九州」『ちくご』第11号、福岡県高校国漢部会筑後地区部会、昭和53年。

江下博彦『漱石余情 -- おジュンさま』西日本新聞社、昭和 62 年。
小城左昌『夏目漱石と祖母「一冨順」』(再版) 私家版、平成 22 年。
倉富了一『高良山物語』菊竹金文堂、昭和 9 年。
小宮豊隆『夏目漱石』岩波書店、昭和 13 年。
高山精二『みのうふるさと散歩』創研出版、平成 13 年。
原武　哲『夏目漱石と菅虎雄――布衣禅情を楽しむ心友――』教育センター、昭和 58 年。
原武　哲『喪章を着けた千円札の漱石――伝記と考証』笠間書院、2003 年。
松岡　譲『漱石の漢詩』朝日新聞社、昭和 41 年。

初出一覧

まえがき 「私のアメリカ文学研究」
　　　　田島松二編『ことばの楽しみ』南雲堂, 2006, 361–65.
I-1 「アメリカの小説と『私』」
　　　　九州大学公開講座 8『現代の文学』九州大学出版会, 1983, 203–24.
I-2 "The Cask of Amontillado" を読む— Montresor は復讐に成功したのか
　　　　『九州アメリカ文学』51 号, 九州アメリカ文学会, 2010, 49–59.
I-3 Margaret Drabble の *The Millstone* について
　　　　『英語英文学論叢』26 集, 九州大学, 1976, 51–58.

II-1 An Essay on Herman Melville's *Moby-Dick*—What Is Moby Dick?—
　　　　『大阪府立大学紀要』(人文・社会科学) 9 巻, 1961, 31–44.
II-2 The Resurrection of Ishmael
　　　　『英米文学研究と鑑賞』9 号, 大阪府立大学, 1962, 8–21.
II-3 The Ambiguity of *Pierre* in Relation to *Moby-Dick*
　　　　『英語英文学論叢』30 集, 九州大学, 1980, 46–56.
II-4 "Benito Cereno" における「恐怖」
　　　　『英語英文学論叢』17 集, 九州大学, 1967, 53–62.
III-1 「エドワード・オールビー」
　　　　尾形敏彦編『アメリカ文学の新展開—詩・劇・批評等』(アメリカ文学研究双書 5) 山口書店, 1984, 219–46.
III-2 Vonnegut's Desperado Humor in *Slaughterhouse-Five*
　　　　『英語英文学論叢』45 集, 九州大学, 1995, 1–15.
III-3 Vonnegut の *Cat's Cradle* について

　　　　　　『言語文化論究』6 号，九州大学，1995，111–18.
III-4　Raymond Carver について
　　　　　　『北九州アメリカ文学』No. 2，北九州アメリカ文学研究会，
　　　　　　2015，7–27.
III-5　Raymond Carver の *Beginners* を読む
　　　　　　『*The Kyushu Review*』No. 15，「九州レヴュー」の会，
　　　　　　2014，1–14.
IV-1　An Approach to Yasunari Kawabata's *Snow Country*
　　　　　　Kyushu American Literature No. 9，Kyushu American
　　　　　　Literature Society，1966，41–48.
IV-2　漱石の見た耳納連山
　　　　　　『The Kyushu Review』No. 14，「九州レヴュー」の会，
　　　　　　2012，1–9.

（本書に収録するにあたり加筆修正し、一部題名を変更した）

あとがき

　此の度の出版に際しては、昔書いたものを整理し、読み直す必要があった。読み直すにつれ、学生の頃お世話になった先生方のことがしきりに思い出された。思い出すままに若干の思い出を誌し、恩師のご遺徳を偲ぶと共に、心からなる謝意を捧げたい。

　指導教授であった中西信太郎先生のことは既に述べた。ただ一つ補足すれば、先生は考え考えとつとつと講義を進められた。誠実なお人柄そのままという趣で、ご著書に見る流麗な文章とは対照的であった。
　助教授には、菅泰男先生と御興員三先生がおられた。菅先生には慈母の如き優しさがあり、御興先生には厳父の如き厳しさがあった。
　御興先生の演習では、発表者の発表が終ると、先生から一言「であろうか」との問い掛けがあり、それに対する如何なる発言もないまま、沈黙の時間が流れるのが常であった。その時間は実際には二・三分のことであったかも知れないが、発表者には無限に続く地獄の時間であった。また試験も厳しかった。シェイクスピアのソネットの演習では、穴埋め形式で原詩を復元させる問題が出題され、ソネットの意味を読み取るだけで精一杯だった受講生の殆どが不合格となった。私もその「殆ど」の一人であった。「愛のムチ」に応える術のない怠惰な学生であったことを恥じ入るばかりである。
　学究肌の御興先生に対し、菅先生は古今東西の演劇に通じた文人肌の学者であった。朗々たる美声の持主で、コンパの折など、歌舞伎の声色やシェイクスピア劇の独白などで学生を魅了された。先生

のご専門はシェイクスピアであったが、講義ではアメリカ文学を担当された。文学部三年のとき菅先生の演習で『白鯨』を読んだ。朗々たる「菅ぶし」の名講義に魅せられたのか、メルヴィルに魅せられたのか、それが機縁となって、白鯨を追跡することが、私に課せられた宿命的課題となった。

　最後になるが、九州大学時代の同僚である田島松二氏の叱咤激励が無ければ、本書が日の目を見ることは無かった。田島氏には原稿のパソコン入力を含め全面的な支援と協力を賜った。有難い限りである。また、本書の出版を快く引き受けて頂いた開文社の安居洋一社長のご好意とご尽力に対し、心から御礼を申し上げる。

2016 年 8 月
野口健司

著者略歴

野口　健司（のぐち　けんじ）
1931年生まれ、福岡県久留米市出身。
京都大学文学部卒業（1957）、同大学院修士課程修了（1960）。
大阪府立大学助手（1960-64）を経て、九州大学（1964-95）、
都留文科大学（1995-97）、福岡国際大学（1998-2002）に勤務、
英語・米文学を担当。文部省在外研究員として、イェール大
学およびロンドン大学において調査研究（1971-72）。現在、
九州大学名誉教授。

著書（共著）
『現代の文学』（九州大学出版会、1983）
『アメリカ文学の新展開―詩・劇・批評等』（山口書店、
1984）

アメリカ文学と「語り」
　―白鯨からポストモダン文学へ―　　　（検印廃止）

2016年10月20日　初版発行

著　　者　　野　口　健　司
発　行　者　　安　居　洋　一
印刷・製本　　モ　リ　モ　ト　印　刷

162-0065　東京都新宿区住吉町8-9
発行所　開文社出版株式会社
TEL 03-3358-6288 FAX 03-3358-6287
www.kaibunsha.co.jp

ISBN 978-4-87571-086-8　C3098